MURDER
in an
ENGLISH
CASTLE

BOOKS BY MERRYN ALLINGHAM

FLORA STEELE MYSTERY SERIES

The Bookshop Murder

Murder on the Pier

Murder at Primrose Cottage

Murder at the Priory Hotel

Murder at St Saviour's

Murder at Abbeymead Farm

Murder in a French Village

The Library Murders

Murder at Cleve College

SUMMERHAYES HOUSE SERIES

The Girl from Summerhayes

The Secrets of Summerhayes

THE TREMAYNE MYSTERIES SERIES

The Dangerous Promise

Venetian Vendetta

Caribbean Evil

Cornish Requiem

Rio Revenge

The London Reckoning

MURDER
in an
ENGLISH
CASTLE

Merryn Allingham

bookouture

Published by Bookouture in 2024

An imprint of Storyfire Ltd.
Carmelite House
50 Victoria Embankment
London EC4Y 0DZ

www.bookouture.com

Storyfire Ltd's authorised representative in the EEA is Hachette Ireland
8 Castlecourt Centre
Castleknock Road
Castleknock
Dublin 15, D15 YF6A
Ireland

ISBN: 978-1-83618-181-1
eBook ISBN: 978-1-83618-180-4

PROLOGUE

SUSSEX, APRIL 1959

A pale blue sky, the sharp coolness of early spring and the majesty of a once great castle – what a brilliant setting for this, their final rehearsal of the Battle of Lewes!

He felt alive, invigorated, his limbs programmed to fight. Hector, his best friend, was alongside, and together they'd scaled the broken staircases to arrive on the top wall of the castle, hammering the King's troops for every inch of territory. Now, from his vantage point, he could see their fellow soldiers following them, gaining ground despite fierce opposition, while ahead the royalist women huddled in the entrance to the keep.

Victory was close – he could breathe it, taste it, touch it almost. In the joy of the moment, troubles faded and quarrels were forgotten.

Suddenly, though, an awareness that the wall, broad though it was, had become congested – too many men, too many soldiers, each fighting for their space. He was hemmed in now, trapped. For an instant, he allowed his guard to falter. Only an instant, but sufficient for a hefty thud to his left shoulder have him lose his footing.

Desperately, he sought to regain his balance, find an anchor. But his sword arm seemed no longer to belong to him, flailing wildly as though it hoped to seize hold of the air itself. For support. For strength. But there was none to be had, the stone crumbling beneath his feet and slowly, slowly...

1

TEN MINUTES EARLIER

'Which one is Hector, do you think?' Frowning, Flora turned to her companions for enlightenment. 'I can't make out a single face. Not with those square saucepans on their heads.'

'Or medieval helmets if you're being picky.' Jack Carrington wore an amused smile.

The battle raging in the ruins of Lewes Castle had become confusing – a riot of wrestling men, swords and shields and the occasional axe lost in their midst.

'Hector is playing Gilbert de Clare,' Rose Lawson offered.

Rose was Flora's part-time helper in the bookshop she owned in Abbeymead, a village some fifteen miles to the west of the town.

'He told me he'll be wearing a white cross.'

'And who is Gilbert de Clare?' Flora's gaze was on Jack, standing by her side. Her new husband could usually be depended on to know these things – her very own encyclopaedia, she often teased him.

'Gilbert was one of the Earl of Leicester's men,' Jack obliged. 'He was put in charge of a large section of de Montfort's army.'

'And the white cross?'

'The earl ordered his men to wear white crosses as a distinguishing emblem, though I'm not sure they're the uniforms we're looking at right now. They've been lost to history, I guess. Hardly surprising – the battle was seven hundred years ago.'

'And they're still fighting it,' Flora said, a trifle wearily.

Today, on an early April morning, the Knights of Mercia, a local historical re-enactment society, were in a final rehearsal for next month's grand event when they would stage the Battle of Lewes for a much larger audience. Today's crowd was a motley gathering: some friends, a few relatives, but for the most part made up of people who had stopped by on their daily round to see what was happening on the castle green.

'It *was* a significant battle,' Jack said mildly. 'And certainly worth remembering. You could say it paved the way for democracy.'

Whatever else he had to impart was drowned by the sound of drums in the high street. The musicians had followed the battle down from the surrounding hills to the north of the town, today a popular racecourse, and through the streets of Lewes to the castle where Henry III, his son, Prince Edward, and their royalist army, though twice the size of de Montfort's rebel barons, had been forced to retreat.

'I still can't see Hector,' Flora complained.

Hector Lansdale, apart from being an immensely keen member of the Knights, was the sous chef at the Priory, a luxury hotel on the outskirts of their home village.

'He's there! I can see him!' Rose stood on tiptoe to look over the crowd, pointing towards a tall knight who had appeared at the base of the lower wall. He was chain-mailed and wore a red surcoat with a large white cross emblazoned on his chest.

'He looks handsome, don't you think?' There was a flush on Rose's cheek and Flora and Jack exchanged a knowing look.

'But so does his friend,' Rose continued quickly, her coil of dark hair coming adrift in her excitement. 'And that's Alex – the chap who's fighting at Hector's side. Alex Vicary. I met him when Hector came to the All's Well after Christmas to look through some of the books I'd unearthed on the Battle of Lewes.'

'I can see him now. A tall chap, taller than Hector.' Flora looked out over the circle of greensward that filled the centre of the castle ruins, her gaze travelling over what was left of the stone walls and main staircase and upwards to the keep at the very top. 'Ooh, and there's Sally with another woman, crouching close to the top wall. I really like what I can see of her costume.'

Sally Jenner, the proprietor of the Priory Hotel, had joined the society only recently but taken to it with great enthusiasm. Amazingly so, in Flora's view. Sally had been asked to play one of the royalist wives who had taken shelter in the castle keep, as their menfolk retreated from the surrounding Downs to a town already set ablaze. Sally's enthusiasm, Flora reckoned, was most likely for her sous chef, Hector, rather than for the Knights of Mercia, but this was a topic on which she'd vowed to stay silent. It had caused endless squabbles between Sally and her aunt, Alice Jenner, who was also head chef at the hotel.

De Montfort's forces, having invaded the green, were gradually fighting their way upwards, step by broken step, making for the top wall of the castle, or what remained of it, and then on to the keep where the King and his entourage had joined the women in taking shelter. As they watched, a grey-bearded man, a chain-mail helmet half covering his grizzled face, gained a foothold on a ruined wall, swinging the axe he held between both hands and sending one of the King's men tumbling down the stairs.

Flora flinched. Normally, on a Saturday morning she would be in her bookshop, the weekend being a busy time for customers, but since Hector had made a special plea for as many of his friends as possible to come to what was in effect the dress rehearsal, Flora had decided to close the All's Well. Jack had driven them over in his ancient Austin, collecting Rose on the way. He had offered a lift to Alice, too, but only the three of them had made it to the castle. Alice had refused to attend, declaring it ridiculous. She had better things to do, she'd said, than watching grown men dress up and have play fights with pretend weapons.

'The fight's hotting up.' Jack pointed to the row of 'dead' bodies laid out on the greensward a few yards away. Already, a line of men, all wearing white crosses, had fought their way to the very top wall of the castle. 'De Montfort and his men are about to win, I think.'

Flora looked up to a pair of smiling eyes. Jack was relaxed and it was good to see. His teaching commitments at Cleve College, a local arts establishment, were over for the week and last night he'd taken an enthusiastic call from Arthur Bellaby, his agent. The crime novel Jack had recently submitted – the one he'd been struggling to write last summer while trying to run a crime conference in Abbeymead – was, in Arthur's opinion, a winner.

Jack was right, Flora decided, glancing upwards to the cluster of men engaged in what was a furious fight. Hector and his compatriots looked to be in the final stages of the battle. The King's men in their chequered surcoats were gradually being beaten back from the upper wall and pushed down the staircases on either side of the main turret, more and more of them forced onto the circle of grass that filled the centre of the ruins, where men in white crosses waited to take them prisoner.

'Is the King about to be captured?' Rose asked.

'Doesn't he retreat to the Priory and seek shelter there?' Flora pulled her red wool coat more tightly around her. It was spring, but there was still a chill in the air, the onset of cloud having swallowed any sign of the sun and, by now, they had been watching the display for nearly two hours.

'He does. The King and what's left of his army retreat to the Priory to sign the surrender.'

Jack pushed back a flop of hair – a gesture of relief, Flora thought wryly. They could soon retreat themselves, to the comfort of a hot cup of tea in a Lewes café.

'And what then?' Rose was genuinely interested.

'Henry is made to cede many of his powers to de Montfort – *he* goes on to govern as the uncrowned king of England – but only when Henry's son, that's him, I think' – he nodded towards a weary-looking man fighting somewhat listlessly to their right – 'persuades his father that the town is ablaze, huge numbers of their supporters have disappeared, and the day is lost.'

'Let's hope he starts persuading soon.' Flora stamped her feet. Her shoes, a pair of strappy black patents, had been a stupid choice. 'My toes have grown icicles.'

'Not long—' Jack began.

'Something's going wrong,' Rose burst out suddenly.

'If you're one of the King's men, for sure,' he joked.

'No, with Alex. That woman, the one next to Sally...' Obediently, they scanned the group of royalist women who had taken shelter in the keep and were being corralled by those of de Montfort's army who'd already made it to the top wall. 'She's so angry with him.'

'She will be,' Flora said laughingly. 'She's just about to be taken prisoner.'

'No, it's not that. They're quarrelling badly – for real. It's distracting Alex.'

'Not any more,' Jack muttered. Almost at the same moment that he and Flora had looked where Rose was pointing, the woman had disappeared. 'If there was a row, she's taken off, though goodness knows where.'

'And Alex is back to his swashbuckling, still trying to fight his way into the keep. To get to the King, I imagine. It's difficult to picture, though, isn't it?' Flora screwed up her nose. 'All we have now are broken walls, a ruined turret, a crumbling staircase. It's hard to recapture how it must have been.'

'Just as well, I'd say.' Jack gave her hand a squeeze. 'Even in a pretend battle, Alex has a fight on his hands. He's scrapping his way along that top wall.'

All three of them watched as Alex Vicary, sword in one hand and shield in the other, swung at his enemy right and left and, inch by inch, moved towards his goal. Hector, they saw, was matching him, the two friends thrusting and parrying in unison.

Suddenly, Alex, his back now to the keep entrance, appeared to lose his foothold, his arms windmilling in a desperate attempt to right himself. Hector had half turned, aware of trouble, it seemed, but unable to do anything to save his friend. Alex was plummeting forward. Falling, falling, from the topmost wall to crash onto the ruins of the wall beneath and, from there, down again into what was left of the main part of the castle, his body appearing to bounce from stone to stone as it fell. With a sickening thump, he landed on the paved floor, his head smashing into unforgiving limestone and flint. A thick stream of blood pooled slowly across the grey stone.

There was a collective intake of breath as the audience slowly realised what had happened, and then Jack was running towards the fallen man with Flora close behind. In a few seconds, he was on his knees at the soldier's side, his fingers feeling for a pulse in the man's neck. Rose had joined Flora and together they stood speechless, their eyes riveted on the prone figure, their faces a matching white.

Looking up at them, Jack shook his head. Alex Vicary was dead.

2

Amid the general panic, one of the audience, a man who only a minute ago had stepped in from the street to watch proceedings, had the presence of mind to run to the castle's ticket booth and use their telephone to call for help. Alex Vicary was beyond medical aid, Jack knew, but the arrival of an ambulance crew would start the necessary wheels turning.

Hector had gone from standing stock-still, rigid with horror, his weaponry forgotten, to clambering down from the wall as quickly as he was able, ignoring any stairs and jumping dangerously from rock to rock, to arrive breathless as Jack got to his feet. Now, he stood rooted to the spot, his gaze incredulous and fixed on his dead friend, as though by looking intently he could bring Alex back to life.

'Someone is calling an ambulance,' Rose said softly, reaching out to touch him on the arm. 'But...'

She left the sentence unfinished. Hector had turned ashen, the bones of his face seeming clamped together. When he found his voice, it grated. 'Someone needs to call the police, not an ambulance.'

'I don't think we should do that.' In Flora's voice there was deep sympathy. 'I'm afraid... your friend... it was a dreadful accident, Hector. The police won't think it necessary to attend.'

At this, he shook his head from side to side, a rough movement that sent his helmet askew. 'It was no accident,' he said, his voice harsh but determined. 'I saw. Alex was pushed.'

Jack was startled, but when he spoke it was to ask calmly, 'How could you have seen? You were embroiled in the fighting.'

'I saw,' Hector reaffirmed. 'Out of the corner of my eye. A movement that didn't seem right. Alex was fighting Ferdie – he was playing one of the King's men – and he'd trapped Ferdie on the wall, blocking his escape. It meant that Alex had his back to the keep, but I was still facing it. And I saw,' he repeated yet again. 'Alex lurched sideways. Suddenly. And lost his balance. Someone must have pushed him from behind. Maybe someone hiding in the keep.'

'But who?'

'That's the point. They were hiding and I couldn't see and there were too many people in a small space. But it was a definite push. That top wall is uneven, but it's flat and fairly wide. He couldn't have fallen by accident. I saw Ferdie's face when Alex toppled – he didn't understand what was happening – suddenly his opponent wasn't where he should have been. You ask him.'

'I don't think we'll be doing that,' Jack said quietly. 'We'll need to get back to Abbeymead – as soon as the ambulance crew arrive. Can we give you a lift?'

'I'm staying. I'll not run out on my friend.'

'There's nothing you can do, Hector, if you stay. They'll take Alex directly to the morgue and you won't be welcome there.' It was brutal but there was little point in shilly-shallying. 'There'll be a post-mortem and, if nothing out of the way is discovered, the coroner will almost certainly rule it was an accident.'

When the young man continued to look mulish, Jack said

diffidently, 'If I can offer a small piece of advice? You're deeply upset at the moment – why wouldn't you be? – but take time to let your mind settle. I think when you've had a while to mull things over, you'll come to the conclusion that whatever you think you saw was a trick of the mind and nothing more.'

Hector was silent, his mouth tight with frustration. And anger, Jack could see. He felt sorry for the chap, but from where he'd been standing there was no doubt in his mind that Alex's death had been purely accidental. A tragic fact but true.

'Is he... is he...?' It was Sally Jenner who had emerged from the sanctuary of the keep and run down the stairs to join them on the green. 'Oh, Hector, I'm so sorry.' She must have seen the look on his face and realised the very worst had happened.

He turned away from her, tears in his eyes, but when Rose once more reached out to stroke his arm, she won a wobbly smile from him. 'It's OK,' he told her. 'I'll get through this. But his mother...'

Hector's response had Jack exchange a glance with his wife – Rose was obviously more of a confidante than they'd realised – but it had left Sally looking stricken.

'I'd better rejoin the other wives,' she said sharply. 'It's clear I can't be of any help here.'

And swishing her long kirtle to one side, she stomped towards the lower staircase on her way back to the keep.

It was a silent drive home, a murmured goodbye to Rose as they dropped her off at Larkspur Cottage where she rented a room, and then back to their own. Jack walked into the kitchen and immediately put the kettle on to boil.

'Tea is what we need,' he announced. 'Good strong tea. The panacea for all troubles.'

Leaving him to set out cups and saucers, Flora made for the

sitting room. Tired and bewildered, she slumped down on the sofa, but the minute he appeared in the doorway carrying the tray, burst out with what was uppermost in her mind.

'That was the most awful day. I wish we hadn't gone. I wish I'd stayed working at the All's Well.'

'We went and it happened, my love. We can't turn the clock back, much as we'd like to.'

'I suppose. Here, let me help.' She cleared a space for the tray on the occasional table, while Jack joined her on the sofa.

'I hope at least that Hector felt there was some good in us being there.'

'I'm not sure he did – he seemed quite frantic – but he'll need to calm down once he's back in the Priory kitchen.' Flora swirled the pot to strengthen the brew and poured two cups of tea. 'Alice won't be best pleased to have a distracted sous chef.'

'He's obviously got a bee in his bonnet about Vicary's fall, but thank the Lord we're not involved. On this occasion we were simple bystanders.'

'You don't think there's any truth in what Hector said?'

'No, I don't.' Jack was firm. 'I know what he thinks he saw, but he'll have to come to terms with what actually happened.'

'To be honest, we can't really know for certain. It was so sudden and we were yards away. Hector, on the other hand, was in the middle of it all and I can see why in the fray he's so sure he saw something bad. Whatever the truth of it, the next few days will be tough for him – his mind is likely to be everywhere.'

'I doubt he'll get much sympathy. This morning's tragedy will just confirm for Alice what she's always maintained, that Hector should get what she calls a "sensible" hobby.'

'And she'll be even more upset to see Sally unhappy again,' Flora added, settling back into the sofa cushions.

'What *is* going on between Sally and Hector? I thought they were going out together but today he seemed quite distant with her.'

'They've been to the cinema a few times,' Flora confirmed, 'but I've a hunch the attraction is mostly on Sally's side, and you know how Alice feels about her niece getting hurt. After the Dominic affair.'

Dominic Lister had been Sally Jenner's erstwhile partner at the Priory Hotel, but had proved deceitful and totally untrustworthy in both his business and personal dealings. Alice had been delighted when Dominic had decided to sell his half of the hotel to her niece and disappear; she had her fingers tightly crossed, she said, that he would never return.

'What do you think?' Flora asked. 'About Hector and Rose? The two of them surprised me today.'

'He likes her,' he said cautiously, pouring them both a second cup.

'He likes her a lot, Jack. Remember our housewarming at the college flat, back in October? Sally was pretty miffed then that they got on so well with each other.'

The flat at Cleve College was where the Carringtons lived for half of each week, meaning that Jack was spared too many journeys between village and town, a difficult drive in inclement weather. The college apartment had so far defied all Flora's attempts to make it a home but at least, she thought, she had only to live in it for a few days at a time. Thursday evenings were a delight, when she climbed into the Austin and Jack drove them back to the cottage. The cottage and the bookshop left to her by her dear Aunt Violet.

'Tomorrow is Sunday,' she said, piling the empty cups back on the tray. 'Hopefully, a day of calm. *You'll* spend the time writing, I'm sure, but I've promised myself that I'll tackle the garden – whatever the weather. It desperately needs weeding. I might even sow a few seeds.'

'Is it warm enough?'

'For some of them, I think, but maybe I should ask Charlie first.' She pulled a small face. 'When he's not busy preparing vegetables under Alice's supervision.'

'I miss him, you know, now he's working. Or training, I should say. He was a pain to feed, constantly hungry, and the lemonade he drank... but he was good company and together we made a brilliant job of the Overlay garden.'

Charlie Teague, now almost sixteen, had been Jack's gardening mentor for the past four years, and a very successful one.

'Oh, that reminds me.' Flora paused at the door on her way to the kitchen. 'Overlay House has a new tenant moving in next month. I heard it from our postmistress so it must be true. Dilys rarely gets gossip wrong. I'm just amazed the landlord has managed to find anyone to take it on. It was bad enough when you lived there, but now...'

Overlay had been Jack's abode until he and Flora had married last autumn. Scruffy and under-furnished it may have been, but it had proved a sanctuary when he needed one, shielding him from the village's gaze at a time in his life when all he'd wanted was to hide away. To live the life of a recluse.

'Dilys did say the landlord has lowered the rent,' she added.

'What! You mean he'd been overcharging me – for years?'

'Of course he was.' She was smiling. 'And you know it, and don't really mind.' Her husband never said as much, but she knew he missed the place. Not for its comfort, certainly, but for its peace, she guessed, its silence. 'You loved that house even if it was falling to pieces. Like you love the Austin.'

'My car is not falling to pieces,' he protested. 'She's a classic! The same as Betty. You'll never say goodbye to *her*, will you?'

Flora's bicycle was only a little less precious to her than the cottage and the cottage only a little less than the All's Well.

'That's because Betty *is* a classic,' she retorted.

. . .

It was late the following Friday afternoon and Flora had begun to think of closing for the day – unusually for a Friday, business at the All's Well had been slow and supper was very much on her mind: lamb chops from Mr Preece, the butcher, and some beautiful spring greens put to one side for her by Mr Houseman.

She had collected her jacket from the cupboard, otherwise known as the kitchenette, and was shuffling under the desk for her handbag when Hector Lansdale walked through the door.

'Shouldn't you be whipping up soufflés?' Flora asked, giving him a gentle smile. She'd not seen Hector since that dreadful Saturday and his face, she noticed, was still drawn and very white.

'I invented a doctor's appointment to get away,' he confessed, 'but don't tell Alice. I had to see you, before you and Jack trot off to Lewes next week.'

'Alice is all right?'

The cook was someone else that Flora hadn't seen for days. She wouldn't be seeing her this evening either, despite this being the night that she and Alice met their mutual friend, Kate, for supper and a catch-up of all the Abbeymead news. Kate and Tony Farraday were the owners of the village café, the Nook, and though they had wanted to be at Lewes Castle for the rehearsal, if only to show solidarity, they'd had to dip out. Their baby girl was only a few weeks old and most days Tony was battling to run the café single-handedly. When the Nook landed a special order for the weekend, the Friday evening supper had become another casualty. Both the Farradays were up to their eyes in cooking, when they weren't looking after baby Sarah.

'Alice is fine,' Hector said glumly. 'More than fine, issuing orders right, left and centre. It's me that's not.'

Gingerly, he perched on the edge of the small table where

Flora displayed the newest publications and those most likely to be popular.

'Alex?' she asked, knowing the answer already.

'I'm not happy, Flora. In fact, I'm very unhappy at the way Alex's death has been treated. I know that Jack is convinced it was an accident – you, too, probably. But I'm not.'

She waited for more.

'I rang the police,' he announced. That wasn't what she'd expected to hear.

'When?'

'Lunchtime yesterday. I used my break to walk to the nearest phone box and call Brighton police station. I asked to speak to Alan Ridley. He's Jack's tame inspector, isn't he?'

'I wouldn't call Inspector Ridley exactly tame,' she cautioned. Flora had enjoyed plenty of battles with the inspector over the last few years. 'But he has helped Jack – with details for some of his books. Stuff around police procedures.'

'And he's helped you in the past? The two of you?' Hector pursued.

'Yes,' she agreed, though more cautiously. 'He's come to our rescue on occasion. Did you manage to speak to him?'

Hector nodded.

'And what did he say?'

'That the post-mortem had been completed and hadn't shown anything untoward. Alex's fall would be treated by the police as an accident.'

Hector got up from his perch and walked over to one of the latticed windows. 'But it wasn't, Flora.' He turned to face her. 'I'm absolutely convinced that someone deliberately set out to hurt Alex Vicary. I know what I saw. And don't say it was what I *think* I saw in the heat of the moment. It was for real. The more I look back on that morning, the more I'm sure.'

'I won't say you're mistaken but Jack was right, you know. It's been a huge upset and your mind must still be all over the place. Maybe you need to let go for a while and then think again.'

'No!' He almost shouted the word. 'While I'm letting go, someone is getting away with murder. The police aren't interested – a ruined castle, lots of weapons, a big crowd, accidents are bound to happen. That's their excuse. Alex deserves better. He was a thoroughly decent man; he'd do anything to help anyone.'

He walked back to her and fixed her with a pleading expression. 'You and Jack have been successful investigators. In the past, you've unearthed murderers, sometimes even before the police. You could find this one if you tried.'

He reached out to clasp her hands tightly in his. 'Help me, Flora. Alex needs justice and you two are the only hope I have.'

Without another word, he turned on his heel, walking swiftly to the door and out into the high street, leaving Flora a prey to uncertainty.

3

Flora cycled home slowly, her mind fixed on Hector's request. It was fortunate that Betty was in similarly meditative mood, her wheels turning in time with Flora's thoughts. Alex Vicary's fall should never have happened – she'd thought that at the time. The battle was only pretend, though it looked realistic enough, and Alex had already fought his way up several precarious staircases to reach what looked to be the much safer top wall. Maybe, after all, Hector *had* seen something, but should she mention his visit to Jack? Suggest they begin another investigation?

There were plenty of reasons not to. After last autumn's fracas at Cleve, Jack was feeling a good deal more settled – the murderous caretaker he'd grappled with was dead and an art teacher who'd proved a serial liar had left. His life at the college had resumed a comfortable rhythm. In addition, talk in the staffroom that the current principal, Maurice Dalloway, might be leaving had put a smile on Jack's face – he had little time for the man – and, once his probationary period had passed, the rumour had been sufficient for him to sign a contract for a further six months.

And being married suited Jack, Flora thought. Suited her, too, a fact she still found surprising. Their first Christmas as a married couple had been the best she'd ever spent. They had seen their friends for a celebratory drink or two but passed most of the holiday alone. It had been a treat! Sometimes, it seemed to Flora, they spent less time together now they were married than they had when single. Jack's job for three days a week as mentor to the college's student authors meant that when he was at home he was writing, with little time to do much else. As for herself, she was still adjusting to spending half of every week in Lewes, a town she'd only recently begun to know and, though she tried to stop herself from wanting to be back in Abbeymead – in her cottage or her garden or most of all her bookshop – she couldn't lose the longing.

Jack was still hard at work when she walked through the front door; from the spare bedroom, she could hear the tap-tapping of the Remington's keys. One novel finished, a new plot to hatch. She'd not disturb him, she decided, but make a start on the evening meal so that the smell of lamb chops and roasting potatoes would greet him when the typewriter was put to bed.

In the event, Flora had only just begun to prepare the vegetables when he walked into the kitchen.

'Sneaking in and not telling me!' he teased.

'Dinner was supposed to be a surprise. This is the first Friday evening we've spent together for an age.'

'I guess it is. But I'm sorry you won't be meeting your friends tonight. I know you enjoy those evenings.'

'Not this one,' Flora said stoutly. 'Alice will talk about nothing but Hector and his misdeeds and Kate will be distracted because she's had to leave Sarah in Tony's charge.'

'I'm glad they decided on Sarah as a name.' He bent to kiss her on the back of her neck. 'You must be, too – it was your mother's, wasn't it?'

'It was, and it's Alice's middle name as well,' she reminded him.

'Talking of the best cook in Sussex, what news of her niece? Has Sally's affair with Hector petered out for good?' Jack began to chop the just washed carrots.

'I'm fairly sure it has.'

Hector hadn't talked of Sally in their conversation this afternoon, she reflected, not one mention of the girl – romance had been the last thing on his mind. It was an obvious moment now for her to mention his visit to the bookshop, but should she?

'Dare I ask how the very new book is going?' The decision had been made. Hector had been put aside.

'Not bad. A bit sticky. I'm still at the ideas stage, sketching out a possible plot. Several of them, in fact, but going back to it after a break, I tend to lose the thread.'

'That's working at the college. I always thought it might be a problem.'

'It hasn't helped,' he agreed, 'though I've grown to like the job and I'd be sorry to leave. Shall I put the carrots on?'

'A low heat, I think. The chops are just about to go in the oven.'

'I've come to really enjoy working with the students,' Jack went on, 'but I have to admit it's made a difference to my writing. It's not just the time I've lost, but the focus. It takes that much longer to pick up where I left off, after we come back to Abbeymead each week.'

She closed the oven door. 'You know, Jack, you don't have to stay at the college, even if you do enjoy the work. We have enough money – my inheritance is still in the bank.'

Last year, out of the blue, Flora had been contacted by a firm of solicitors who had worked for her family when she was a child and unexpectedly presented her with the proceeds of the house her dead parents had owned. Carefully invested, it had grown into a considerable sum.

'I have a contract with Cleve,' he reminded her. 'I can't break that.'

'Maybe they'd understand. It's your writing that's most important – it's why the college has hired you – but if the job has become a hindrance...'

She left the sentence unfinished, a secret hope that Flora wasn't proud of, that he would say goodbye to the college and they could move back to Abbeymead for good.

'I'll see it through,' he said decisively. 'After all, I've only just passed my probation and signed a new contract. Though I might not renew next time. And you must admit the salary is helpful – we'll have the most amazing holiday in Venice.'

'Talking about Venice—'

'Before we do, we should leave the meal to cook and open the last bottle of Arthur's wine.' Arthur Bellaby wasn't only Jack's agent but a good friend too, keeping them regularly supplied with fresh coffee and the very best wine. 'We can't talk about a honeymoon – particularly a delayed honeymoon – without a glass of wine.'

In a few minutes, two of the mismatched glasses that Jack had brought from Overlay House were filled with bubbles.

'So...' he began, sitting down opposite Flora at the kitchen table, 'about Venice...'

'Yes, Venice. It's the hotel. Can we stay in the hotel I've found? I think it might be a little expensive but I so want to stay there. It's called the Cipriani.'

Jack's eyebrows reached for his hairline. 'Expensive? You could say that. It's only the best hotel in town.'

'I don't mind if we have to travel to Venice by coach, it's the hotel that matters. I've seen photographs in a magazine that Kate passed on – there was a two-page article as well. Apparently, the hotel is on an island, just across the water from Venice itself, quiet and secluded, and it has a beautiful garden and an amazing swimming pool and—'

Jack held up his hand, laughing. 'We can stay at the Cipri-ani, but we are not travelling by coach! It would take most of the week to get there and back. We can go by train. Or how about going really wild and taking a plane?'

'That would be massively expensive as well.'

'Perhaps, but... it would mean we'd have more time in the city. A Comet from London Airport would take only a couple of hours to get there.'

Flora was unsure. Flying to Venice would take a large chunk of the money she'd inherited, money they would need for the future. And she wasn't at all certain that she wanted to take to the air. She knew no one in Abbeymead who'd done so, and it felt just a little risky.

'But the Cipriani – it's a promise?'

'Have I ever failed you?'

Jumping up from her chair, she walked round the table to wrap her arms around him, spilling the last of her wine down his shirt.

'No, Jack, you haven't.'

Saturday morning was Flora's time in the week to catch up with the routine chores of running her bookshop, since other days were spent despatching orders or arranging books for delivery in the village, and simply serving customers. The worst job on a Saturday was the accounts, but they were a task she knew wouldn't wait – not keeping the books up to date, she'd learned to her cost, meant a lot more work later in the year.

She couldn't resist, however, first taking a look at the new books that had arrived while she'd been away – she'd tripped over a couple of empty boxes in the kitchenette. It was impor-tant she made sure they'd been shelved correctly, she told herself, and, in the case of the most popular items, displayed prominently. After a rocky start last year, Rose was doing well as her assistant, but there was a streak in Flora, and she acknowledged it honestly, that no matter how good the help, she couldn't entirely relinquish control.

She was tempted, too, to check on the shelves that lined the back of the shop. Had they been properly dusted? Were the books displayed to their best effect? It was easy to forget them, tucked away as they were. The All's Well's building was old – parts of it from the fifteenth century, her aunt had told her – and its angled bookshelves had been fitted to walls that twisted and turned in dizzying fashion, often ending in a dead end. Relatively few customers walked this far into the shop, but the bookcases there contained some of the most expensive volumes Flora held.

She had only just opened her accounts ledger and begun to enter figures for the past week when the doorbell clanged and Rose Lawson walked through the door.

'Rose! Good morning. Can't you keep away?' she greeted her laughingly.

Rose, however, wasn't laughing. She was paler than usual, the bright red cotton jacket she wore only serving to emphasise her lack of colour.

'I'm sorry to bother you when you're working, Flora, but I really need to talk to you.' Her eyes were troubled. 'Before you leave for Lewes again.'

The words were an uncanny echo of Hector's, and it was Hector, it turned out, that Rose needed to talk about.

'He's feeling desperate,' she said, plunging straight in, 'and I want to help him. He's quite sure that Alex Vicary didn't die from an accident and so angry that the police are doing nothing.'

'I know.' Flora was calm. 'He was here yesterday, telling me much the same. I understand he's badly upset by his friend's death, but we think he must be wrong.' In truth, Flora was still unsure how she felt. 'No one else,' she pointed out, 'from either of the "armies" who were fighting that day has raised an alarm.'

'Well, *I* don't think him wrong. I believe him,' Rose said stubbornly. 'Losing his friend has been a dreadful blow, I grant you, but Hector was only a few yards from Alex when he fell. He was facing his friend and if Hector says he saw him pushed, then he did.'

Flora wasn't sure how to respond. Rose was so obviously sincere, but Jack's warning words were in her ear.

'Alice, you know, calls it play-fighting and I'm inclined to agree. No one gets hurt at these re-enactments, at least not seriously.'

'Usually not, but it doesn't mean that no one ever gets hurt. And think what a perfect opportunity a battle provides in masking a fight that *is* serious.'

'But who would want to hurt Alex?' This seemed to Flora the most important question.

'He had enemies, did you know? Hector wouldn't speak of it, I think, but there are people who wanted to do Alex and his mother harm. Stuff going on with the house they rent. The landlord, Larry Morton, has been trying to evict them, even though the Vicarys have a signed tenancy. Hector felt that something was wrong when he called at the house one day. The landlord was there and Mrs Vicary was really upset, but when the man saw Hector arrive, he disappeared. Hector asked his friend about it but Alex said he was dealing with the problem.'

'But the landlord – you're suggesting he might have some-thing to do with Alex's fall? – how would he be involved in the re-enactment?'

'He wouldn't, but his nephew was there. David Morton – I saw him. Hector pointed him out to me one evening at the Lewes Odeon. He was in the queue for *Carry on Nurse* and I thought then that he looked a brute.'

'You were in Lewes with Hector?' The news temporarily distracted Flora.

'It's not important.' Rose sounded impatient. 'What is important is that I saw the man who's been threatening the Vicarys, at the rehearsal. He was in the audience, watching Alex, and then he disappeared.'

'But Alex was on the top wall, near the keep. How...' Flora trailed off.

'The castle is a rabbit warren. There are all kinds of passages that no one uses. What if there are stairs that aren't obvious? A back staircase, say, from where you can climb to the keep and the top wall without being seen from the castle entrance or the green.'

'That seems a little... far-fetched?'

Rose's lips compressed. 'Why was David Morton there? It wasn't for any love of history, I'm sure. From what I've learned, the landlord and his nephew are too busy making money to have any other interests. Certainly not re-enactments. So... why was the man at the rehearsal if it wasn't to use the battle for his own ends? To rid his uncle of a stubborn tenant? A family he didn't want around and was determined to get rid of.'

4

Cycling along Greenway Lane several hours later, Flora was brought to a halt by a small red van. Barry Tubbs, the postman, wound down his window.

'Just left you a parcel,' he said. 'A right big'un, too. All the way from Cornwall, by the looks of it.'

It would be from Jessie Bolitho, the friend that she and Jack had made when they'd taken a cottage in Jessie's home village of Treleggan, primarily for Jack to gain background for a novel. In reality, they'd spent most of their stay searching for a killer, their landlord having been brutally murdered within hours of their arrival.

'Thanks, Barry. I didn't recognise you. Not in a van – what's happened to the bike?'

'Pensioned off. I got this now!' he said proudly, slapping the steering wheel with his palm. 'Gone up in the world!'

Pressing his foot hard on the accelerator, he shot forward in a noisy cloud of dust, leaving Flora looking after him.

· · ·

'A parcel from Jessie,' Jack announced from the doorway as she wheeled Betty up the front path.

'So I've heard. It must be the recipes she promised Alice.'

Jessie was now Alice Jenner's friend, as well, the two of them having done Jack and Flora proud the previous October with a wedding breakfast that was still the talk of the village.

'It's way too big for just recipes. Come and look. I've put the kettle on – there could be saffron buns lurking inside.'

Flora made straight for the kitchen and, breaking open the box, was quick to unearth a delicious-smelling packet. Saffron buns, indeed!

'You're being thoroughly spoiled,' she said. 'Jessie's actually sent two batches. I'll take the second up to Alice this afternoon, along with the recipes. Oh, and a large heavy cake, too. We can snaffle half of that – Alice won't mind.'

'But she'll be working this afternoon, won't she?'

'She'll have time for a brief chat, I'm sure.'

It was said airily to cover the guilt Flora felt. Hector, rather than Alice, was the person she needed to speak to, and that wouldn't make Jack happy. He had been clear that he'd no intention of involving himself in another investigation and he wouldn't want her to either. It was only six months since they'd survived the dangers of their last adventure together.

Flora couldn't dismiss Alex's death as easily. There were doubts lingering in her mind and it had been she to whom Hector had appealed. She who'd been the one Rose had spoken to. Jack hadn't seen their faces or heard the desperation in their voices when they'd asked for help, but she had.

If she asked only a few questions, it might be sufficient to convince herself that both Hector and Rose had it wrong. That Alex Vicary's deadly fall had been an accident. She would take Jessie's presents to the hotel this afternoon and hope to be granted a few minutes alone with Hector.

· · ·

'She's a splendid lass, that Jessie,' Alice said, unpacking her saffron buns and her share of the heavy cake. 'And she's remembered the exact recipes I wanted.' Alice waved a bundle of handwritten pages at Flora. 'A splendid lass,' she repeated. 'I'll tuck these cakes away, so they don't get eaten by mistake.' She sent a baleful glance shooting around the Priory kitchen, which included the figure of Hector, busy at the far counter.

He was bent over a chopping board, intent, it seemed, on his task. The kitchen was a bright and airy space with whitewashed plaster and tall windows set high in the wall, but even so Flora couldn't see his face very well. His body, though, hunched and tense, told her all she needed to know.

'I dunno, I can't get a word out of him,' Alice muttered, following Flora's gaze. 'Since that friend of his died, he's proper clammed up.'

'You always said that he talked too much!'

'Well, he did. It was all this battle and that battle, this sword and t'other, but now he's like one of them Trappists. You know, the monks who don't speak. And his work's gone downhill, that's for sure. No concentration. Made hollandaise sauce yesterday instead of Béarnaise, when I'd told him clearly what was needed. I had a rush to make the right sauce and in the meantime the customer's steak was going cold.'

'He's bound to be upset. Alex was a very close friend, and dying so suddenly... Give Hector time and he'll come about.'

'Hmm. He's not too upset to be hanging round that Rose Lawson.' Flora had wondered when Rose might appear in the conversation. 'It's caused no end of trouble – I've a mind, you know, to ask Sally to turn him off!'

'Surely you wouldn't do that.'

'Not for his cookin'. Likely he'll buck up soon and know the sauces he's makin'. But for Sally's sake. When she's not short-tempered, she's mopin'. And all because of him.' Hector received another fierce glare.

'He and Sally?'

Alice shook her head. 'He should never have asked her out. He's her employee, not her boyfriend. And she should have had more sense than to go. I tell you, Flora, I've given up with that girl. She couldn't pick a decent man if he came beggin' on his knees. Anyways, I best get back to this risotto. I don't want another disaster on my hands, but thanks for bringin' the parcel, my love.'

'Of course, you must get on. I'll just say hello to Hector before I cycle home.'

Alice nodded absently, her attention already on the risotto before Flora had walked to the other side of the room and laid a gentle hand on Hector's shoulder.

'About yesterday, Hector,' she began quietly. 'I'd like to help, but I don't think I can involve Jack.'

He turned quickly to look at her. 'But *you'll* help? Help me convince the police they need to investigate?'

'I can't promise but I can try. I need a clearer picture, though, of what happened. I know it's painful to think back to last Saturday, but can you go through the details with me – where you were fighting, where Alex was, who was fighting alongside both of you? I think I remember you saying that Alex was fighting with his back to the keep.'

He nodded. 'He was a yard or so in front of me. We'd fought our way up to the top of the staircase and just reached the wall which leads into the keep and the tower. All the time we were pushing the royalists back. Back into the keep, we hoped. That's when we'd take them prisoners. Ferdie was fighting Alex—'

'Who is Ferdie?'

'Ferdie Luxton. He's a publican, or used to be. Mine host at the Masons Arms.' Hector gave the glimmer of a smile.

'And there was just Alex ahead of you when you reached the wall?'

Hector put down the knife with which he'd been chopping

and screwed up his eyes, trying, it seemed, to capture the scene. 'I think so. No. There was someone on the other side of Alex, slightly ahead. Bruce. He's a teacher.'

'Not Bruce Sullivan?'

'Yeah, that's right. Why? Do you know him?'

'He teaches at the school where I volunteer – when Jack's working at Cleve College.'

Hector's face cleared. 'You read with the children, is that right?'

'Yes. I started this spring term. It's fun and I'm enjoying it.' But not enjoying Bruce Sullivan, she thought to herself.

'Why are you so interested in where everyone was fighting?'

Flora didn't answer him directly. 'If you were fighting up the staircase and onto the wall, you must have been facing the keep, so how did Alex have his back to it?'

'It happens. You dance around, trying to get an advantage. Ferdie is a big chap. He was flinging a mace around, so I guess Alex must have dodged under his arm and ended up facing me.'

'Did anyone else dance around?'

'I saw the fronts of several helmets, but I'm not sure whose.'

'You didn't see who was nearest to the keep entrance?'

Hector gave her a long look, his eyes clouding. 'It wasn't one of the Knights who pushed Alex, if that's what you're suggesting,' he said hotly. 'They're good blokes.'

'I'm not suggesting they aren't.' She would need patience, Flora could see. 'But anyone who was ahead of you might have seen someone dart out of the tower and push Alex, as you believe.'

'Right. Maybe Ferdie saw something.' Her companion had adopted a more conciliatory tone. 'It could be worth talking to him.'

'It could, though again I'm not promising. But if I do, is there anyone else I should speak to? Did Alex have any close friends in the society, other than yourself?'

Hector thought for a while. 'Not really. Diane was a girl-friend, sort of. Diane Croft.'

'Sort of?'

'It wasn't serious between them. A bit on and off.'

An image floated into Flora's mind of an angry young woman erupting from the keep entrance to berate Alex Vicary furiously. Had that been Diane Croft? Nothing serious between them? Or maybe there had been and Diane was part of the puzzle – but she kept the thought to herself.

5

Flora was halfway down the drive on her way to the Priory's elaborately ornamented gates when she spotted Sally Jenner deep in conversation with one of the hotel gardeners. She would have been happy enough to wave a greeting and carry on – Sally might only be short-tempered with her aunt, the two of them prone to regular spats, but Flora was not in the mood to risk it. Her friend, however, had other ideas and stepped onto the gravelled drive, bringing Flora to an inevitable halt.

'I'd no idea you were here. Why the visit? And why did nobody tell me?' There was a smile on Sally's face and it seemed a good omen.

'I had a parcel from Jessie Bolitho today – recipes for Alice and some wonderful Cornish cakes,' Flora explained. 'Take a trip to the kitchen and you could win yourself a bun, but make it soon or they'll all have been snaffled.'

The minute she'd mentioned the kitchen, Flora wished she hadn't. In an instant, Sally's smile had disappeared.

'I tend to stay clear of the place these days, but perhaps Dottie will bring me a treat with my tea.'

'Make sure she does – the saffron buns are truly delicious.

You could ask for two!' Flora made to pedal away, keen that Hector's name remained unspoken.

'I'd better not indulge. I've an evening at the Cross Keys tonight and there's bound to be food.'

Had Hector come good after all? Flora tried a hazy smile, hoping she might not have to ask.

'I'm meeting Diane,' Sally offered. 'Diane Croft. Do you know her? I suppose you might – she's in the same business as you. Works in a bookshop in Lewes.'

Flora shook her head. When they'd first moved to the college flat, she had expected to spend time browsing the town's many bookshops, but volunteering at Riverdale school had put an end to the idea. From an initial two classes, she now had half a dozen groups reading to her several times a week.

'She's a member of the Knights of Mercia,' Sally went on. 'We've become good pals since I joined the society.'

Was it pure coincidence that Diane's name had been on Flora's mind as she'd cycled along the drive? A girl she'd known nothing of until minutes ago.

'I've never met her,' Flora said, 'but have fun at the Cross Keys. I've heard the pub is buzzing in the evening.'

'Not too sure about the fun! Diane is very upset at the moment – she's asked me out this evening to talk. I think it's about last Saturday and it could be heavy going.'

'She was Alex's girlfriend, wasn't she?' It was always better to pretend ignorance.

'She was, sort of, but they had a really bad quarrel the day he died.'

'Oh,' was all Flora said and waited to hear more. The phrase 'sort of' had reappeared, but what did it actually mean?

'Diane was alongside me at the rehearsal – we were both playing royalist women – but before the performance started I saw her and Alex having a pretty heated conversation and then later during the fight, she really went for him. When she asked me to meet her this evening, she said that she'd been horrible to Alex and felt dreadful now.'

'Do you know why they quarrelled?'

'Not for certain, but it was probably for the same reason they'd quarrelled before.'

Flora's face wore a hopeful expression.

'Diane felt hemmed in,' Sally said quietly. 'Coerced I suppose you'd say, and they often had tiffs about it. She mentioned it several times. It was really getting to her.'

Flora leaned on Betty's handlebars, her mind busy. 'If their disagreements were that frequent, she shouldn't feel too bad about this particular argument, surely.'

'Except the row on Saturday was much worse than usual and she feels wretched.'

'In what way worse?'

'I don't know for certain, but Alex always wanted more from her. No matter what Diane said or did, it was never enough. He was pressuring her to get engaged, I do know that.'

'And Diane didn't want an engagement?'

'She liked him, liked him a lot, but she was happy with things as they were. Nothing too serious.' Sally paused. 'Diane's very pretty,' she said wistfully. 'You could say she likes to play the field. She always has plenty of offers, so why not?'

'Presumably Alex didn't see it that way?'

'He was becoming a serious problem, I think, but she said that at the rehearsal she told him something she was sure would put an end to his badgering.'

'What was that?' Flora was completely engaged in the story by now.

To her disappointment, Sally shook her head. 'Maybe I'll find out this evening,' she said brightly. 'And thanks for bringing the cakes.'

'Make sure you enjoy them!' And waving her friend good-bye, Flora rode on to the gates.

Sally was telling an entirely different story from the one Hector had suggested, so what was the truth? Was Diane a casual girlfriend or the woman Alex had wanted to marry? If it was the latter, why hadn't he told his best friend that he intended to propose? And what bombshell had Diane dropped on him that day?

If the bombshell hadn't worked, Flora continued to speculate, freewheeling down Fern Hill, a favourite treat of hers... if Alex had kept pushing her into something she didn't want, would that have been enough to seal his fate? Along with Sally, Diane had retreated to the keep with the other royalist womenfolk as de Montfort's army advanced. After her furious outburst, had she stayed angry enough to reach out and push a man whose concentration would be entirely on the fight? Maybe she'd not meant to kill, maybe it had been a spurt of temper that had gone tragically wrong.

She needed to talk to Diane, discover just what kind of relationship she'd had with Alex. Or perhaps... should she first speak to Alex's mother? Susan Vicary should know the true situation between her son and the girl he loved. The poor woman would be wrapped in grief and any talk of her son would be difficult, but if she called to pay her respects – it would, in any case, be a decent thing to do – she could judge better whether or not to ask any questions.

That night, a storm swept in from the English Channel, wailing down the cottage chimney and seeping through every small crack in its windows. By morning, the squalls of rain had turned much of the garden into a quagmire and the Sunday Flora had planned was ruined. She felt herself restless and irritated and, for once, was eager to return to the college. Even the prospect of spending tomorrow at her treasured All's Well failed to quell her impatience. She was ready – that was the problem – to begin a new adventure.

Jack's entire weekend was taken up with writing and, since he was squirrelled away in the spare bedroom and appeared only for meals, Flora was spared the temptation of confessing what she intended to do. She had doubts – could she really strike out on her own without telling him? – but she purposefully pushed them away. Tuesday afternoon was earmarked as the time to call on Mrs Vicary. She would read with the children in the morning but, rather than returning to an emptily bleak flat at Cleve, she would have lunch in the Lewes tearoom that a certain Roberta Raffles had shown her, then take the bus to Newhaven. The café held unhappy memories, but did a wonderfully tasty cheese on toast.

It was a quiet drive to Lewes on the Tuesday morning, both of them lost in thought: Flora busy reviewing the plans she'd made once she finished at school that day and Jack, no doubt, mulling over the students he was due to meet. He had a long list of appointments, morning and afternoon, and was beginning, she could see, to build a reputation in the college. Whereas the first few months of his tenure had been quiet – his sole customers a young man keen on retelling the story of the Battle of Hastings in blank verse, and another unsure whether to write a ghost story or a romance – he was now in far greater demand both for consultations and for the occasional talks and workshops he ran.

By lunchtime, Flora had read with three separate classes, the school allowing her to use their small library for much of the time, and was packing away the last set of books when the head teacher appeared in the doorway, her manner flustered and the usually immaculate hair, Flora noticed, looking decidedly awry.

'Good morning, Mrs Carrington. Another splendid class, I see. It's so very good to have you here.' The head rarely sought her out and compliments had been few. Flora wondered what was coming next. She learned almost immediately.

'I wonder, Mrs Carrington, Flora, could you do me the most immense favour? Mr Sullivan called in sick today and there's no teacher available to take his class this afternoon. If you could stay on, maybe read with his pupils the book he's chosen this term, I'd be immensely grateful.'

'Yes, of course.'

Flora felt unable to refuse such a pointed request, but it threw her plans to visit the Vicary house into disarray. She had been expecting an entirely free afternoon to allow sufficient time for the journey to Newhaven and back.

Frustrated, she stacked the reading books into a cupboard, collected her handbag, and walked over to the cafeteria on the other side of the playground – no delicious cheese on toast, she mourned – while questions over Bruce Sullivan's absence began to gather strength. She'd noticed when she'd arrived this morning that his usual parking space was empty, but had thought he was simply late for school. Was it suspicious that he'd called in sick? Apart from Ferdie Luxton, he had been the soldier nearest Alex. Nearest, as well, to the entrance to the keep from where Hector imagined the attack had come.

She tried to think through the men's exact positions at that moment in the battle. According to Hector, Bruce Sullivan had been slightly ahead of both Alex and himself, and it might not have been difficult for the man to step back, collide into Alex and, with a hand or an arm, help him over the edge of the top wall. Why he would do so, Flora had no idea. But if Alex's death had not been accidental, there had to be a motive behind his fall. And someone behind that motive. Hector refused to hear ill of the man, or of any of the Knights, but no one, in her opinion, should be ruled out. The fact that she disliked Sullivan, she tried to put to one side. Be objective, she told herself.

The setback to her plans had given Flora time to reconsider.

Saying goodbye to Bruce's class later that afternoon, she decided she'd keep to her plan to visit Mrs Vicary – she would go tomorrow now – but think again whether she should be doing it without telling Jack. Before their wedding in October, she'd been guilty of keeping secrets from him and had sworn she would never do so again but, here she was, once more preparing to keep silent. Today's delay had happened for a reason, she argued to herself. She must be honest. She would tell Jack what she intended.

'Jack,' she said over baked potatoes at the kitchen table that evening – the cooking had to be simple, the oven in the flat a relic from a bygone age – 'I have a confession to make.'

'Another one?' he asked, jokingly.

'It's about Hector and his friend.'

He gave a loud groan. 'You've not started to believe his mad theory, have you?'

'Not entirely, but I don't disbelieve him either. I think it would be right to ask around.'

'Ask what and who? The post-mortem was conclusive. Alan Ridley told me – I spoke to him a few days ago.'

'You didn't tell me you'd be in touch with the inspector.' Was Jack being secretive, too? If so, she deserved it.

'I had a question for him – about prisoners on remand – and Alex Vicary's name came up in the conversation.'

'And what did the pathologist say?'

'That Alex had injuries consistent with falling on to flag-stones from a considerable height.'

'That's not conclusive,' she countered. 'It doesn't prove *how* he came to fall, only that he fell.'

Jack looked at her across the table, his expression pained. He had no wish to hear any contrary argument, she thought, but she was afraid he was going to have to.

'It isn't only Hector who's convinced his friend was pushed,' she went on. 'Rose Lawson believes it, too.'

'But she would, wouldn't she? Hector and Rose... she'd have to support him.'

'She says the Vicarys were in trouble. Their landlord was trying to push them out of the house they rent and Rose is sure that she saw the landlord's nephew at the rehearsal.'

'He was one of the audience? But a lot of people stopped by to watch the display, so why not him?'

'From what she said of the man, it would be unusual. But there's Diane to consider, too.' She would recount all the 'evidence' she had and hope that Jack would at least wish her well.

'Diane?' He pushed his empty plate to one side. 'Diane?'

'Diane Croft. A girlfriend. Apparently, she had a bad quarrel with Alex before the performance and then really went for him during it. We saw it... you must remember... Rose pointed out the woman, a very angry woman on the top wall. Sally says Alex was pressuring Diane to get married. What if—'

'Whoa! Too many people with too many opinions. Can't we just accept it was an accident? Alan Ridley does.'

'Because an accident makes life easier for him. I admit I thought initially that Hector was too upset to be thinking straight, seeing things that weren't true, but now, I'm not sure. And I've promised to help.'

'Flora!'

'I know you won't be happy that I have, but you don't have to get involved, and I'd like to put Hector's mind at rest.'

'How does looking for a murderer put his mind at rest?'

'If there isn't one, he'll have to accept it really was an accident. All I'm saying is that I want to help him, but I'm on my own, I understand that. Tomorrow, I thought I'd speak to Alex's mother. I was going to do it today but then something intervened.'

Bruce Sullivan intervened, she muttered to herself.

Jack said nothing for a moment. 'I'd rather we didn't get mixed up in this,' he said at last. 'Life is humming along nicely – Arthur likes the new book, I'm working on ideas for the sequel and work at the college has settled down, but...'

'But?'

'You're not on your own, Flora. You never are, and if you're determined to ask questions, I'll be with you.'

'But tomorrow you'll be busy, seeing students.'

'Not tomorrow afternoon. I was due to give a talk but the hall roof is leaking – the deluge we had over the weekend made sure of it – and there's nowhere else in the college large enough to cater for the numbers who have signed up.'

'So, you've the afternoon off?' Her heart considerably lighter, she began clearing their plates, at the same time wondering whether there was enough plum tart left to make a decent pudding.

'I did have,' he said, getting up to help her. 'But not any longer, it seems.'

6

Jack had taken the precaution of asking a fellow teacher who lived in Newhaven the directions to Mantell Street, the address Hector had supplied when Flora telephoned him that morning at the Priory. The house proved easy enough to find, tucked into a small terrace that ran parallel to the sea, and to one side of the busy port. The road, a cul-de-sac with a leafy copse to its rear, appeared a peaceful haven despite being only a few paces from the bustle of working docks.

It was Mrs Vicary who answered a front door that badly needed repainting. A tall woman – almost as tall as Jack – and dressed in a drab wrap-around apron that made her look years older than was likely; she had a kind face, he thought, though at the moment, it was wearing an anxious expression. A noise from the hall beyond signalled that she was not alone in the house.

'My name is Jack Carrington,' he began, 'and this is my wife, Flora. I hope you'll excuse us calling but we're friends of Hector Lansdale and we wondered if we might talk to you for a short while.'

'But not if we're disturbing you, Mrs Vicary.' Flora, too, had realised the woman had company. 'We can always come back later.'

'No, please.' She went to stand back, though she sounded uneasy. 'I'm sure it will be—'

'Mrs Vicary isn't seeing people at the moment.'

A man had stepped out of the hall's shadow and, half pushing Susan Vicary aside, filled the doorway.

'And you are?' Jack asked, noticing the thick fist clenched at the man's side.

'David Morton, if it's any business of yours.'

'Perhaps, Mr Morton, it's Mrs Vicary who decides on her guests?' Unsurprisingly, he had taken an instant dislike to the man.

David Morton's face would be plain at the best of times, but the heavy scowl and flattened lips made him downright ugly. And dangerous, Jack surmised.

'I'm her landlord,' he spat out. 'Or my uncle is. This is *our* house.'

'But not, I think, when Mrs Vicary is paying you rent. In fact, I don't believe that legally you have the right to enter the house without her permission.'

'Fancy yourself as a lawyer, do you?'

The man walked forward and stood face to face with Jack, barely inches away. Beside him, he could feel Flora tense herself and prayed she wouldn't decide he needed protecting.

'No lawyer,' he responded, 'just someone who knows a little about renting property. I think perhaps you had better leave? Or I could always walk to the telephone box at the end of the street and ask the police to persuade you. I have a friend at the Brighton station, an Inspector Ridley, who might be interested in your activities.'

Jack excused himself for taking Alan Ridley's name in vain, but the situation had taken on a menacing air and he was profoundly thankful that he'd accompanied Flora today. Morton seemed a man for whom women were fair game.

The man's eyes bulged but, seeming to decide that the fight wasn't worth having – perhaps the mention of his 'activities' had been key – he barged past them and sloped off down the street.

'I'll be back,' were his last words to Mrs Vicary. 'When your friends have gone.'

'Rose wasn't wrong,' Flora whispered as Susan gestured them inside. 'There *is* something bad going on.'

Jack was beginning to think so, too. The fact that David Morton so obviously didn't want them talking to Alex's mother had stirred his interest in a way that Flora's account had not. There was definitely something amiss, and an accidental death had begun to look a good deal less certain.

Refusing the offer of tea, they followed their hostess into a sitting room which, though small, was charming. It was evident that over the years Mrs Vicary had worked hard to make a humble dwelling into a beautiful home. Comfortable, high-backed armchairs, covered in a deep red chintz, warmed the whitewashed walls, while scattered across slate tiles that had been polished to a high shine was a collection of brightly coloured rugs. Decorative plates in floral designs – bought from local markets, Jack imagined – shared wall space with numerous family photographs. Most of them featuring Alex. This poor woman had not yet buried her son was his immediate thought.

'We wanted to say how sorry we are, Mrs Vicary,' he began. 'We were at the castle rehearsal and witnessed the accident.' At this stage, safer not to raise doubts. 'It was a dreadful thing to happen but, I wonder, would you mind talking to us about Alex?'

'Hector was keen we did,' Flora put in quietly.

'I don't know why that is.' Mrs Vicary smoothed out the

creases in her apron, her hand trembling slightly. 'But he's a nice lad, Hector. Such a good friend to my Alex.'

'Hector is a little uncomfortable about the circumstances of your son's death,' Jack said tentatively. How else could he put it?

'I don't know why that is,' she repeated. 'It was an accident, like you say.' Her hands were clasping each other tightly now and the trembling had stopped. 'The police lady came to tell me what had happened, then a very nice man, an inspector, I think, called later to say that the post-mortem had confirmed what they believed. I didn't want Alex to have a post-mortem, you know. It's dreadful what they do, cutting up the body like that.' There was an audible swallow of tears.

'When a person dies unexpectedly, I don't think they have a choice.' Flora's voice was gentle.

'Well, it's not that unexpected, is it, if you go fighting in ruins? I always said to Alex it was dangerous, but he was so keen on that society. He enjoyed his job – he worked for the council in Lewes, you know, at their visitor information desk – but it was the historical stuff that was his real passion.' She gave a sudden smile. 'He was the Knights' armourer and very good at it.'

'Really?' That was an item to store away, Jack decided.

'Oh, yes. He built a shed in the back garden. All his equipment is still there. You can see it from the window. Take a look!' Obediently, they peered through the sitting room window at a square of garden and the large wooden structure that occupied a good half of it.

'If I have to leave...' their hostess murmured. There was another swallowing of tears.

'Why was Mr Morton here today?' Flora asked directly. 'Was he... threatening you?'

There was a long silence before Mrs Vicary answered and, when she did, it was with reluctance. 'He wants the house back, or his uncle does. Larry Morton wants to sell. He's had an offer for the house – big money – there's someone trying to buy up the whole terrace, I've heard.'

'But you have a signed tenancy?'

'For what it's worth.' Her face was filled with misery.

'So... what's been happening, exactly?'

Flora was right to try a direct approach or they would learn nothing. Susan Vicary appeared scared to talk.

'There have been things... things going wrong,' their hostess said vaguely, glancing helplessly from one to the other.

'What things precisely?' he asked, trying to pin her down.

The woman took a deep breath. 'It was the rubbish first. Our dustbin upended every few days, rubbish everywhere – in the road, across the front garden. When it rained...'

'And?' Flora prompted.

'The chickens were stolen. I kept hens in the back garden,' she explained, 'just behind the shed. Alex always liked an egg for breakfast.'

'Did you ever get them back?' It was hardly likely, but worth asking, he thought.

Susan shook her head. 'They were like family,' she said sadly. 'I had names for them all. I haven't had the heart to get more – not that I could afford them now.'

'Your rent has gone up?' Flora was guessing.

'I can barely pay it,' the woman said forlornly. 'What with that and the garden fence being knocked down – the Mortons said it was rotten and needed replacing – then someone throwing a brick through that window.' She gestured to the street beyond. 'The repairs took what little I'd saved.'

'You never discovered who took the chickens or broke your window.' It was a statement not a question, since Jack already knew the answer.

'And the Mortons?' Flora asked. 'What role did they play in this mayhem – apart from putting up your rent?'

That was the crux of the matter and, as he'd expected, Mrs Vicary balked at laying blame.

'I've not accused them of anything,' she said quickly. 'It was probably a young hooligan that threw the brick and the fence was likely rotten. Alex's dad put it up years ago.'

'Did Alex accuse the Mortons of causing trouble?'

Flora had hit the nail on the head. That's exactly what he had done.

'I told him not to tangle with them. Larry Morton – he's got a name in the area, if you know what I mean. A hard man. What he wants, he usually gets.'

'But Alex was determined that this time he wouldn't?'

'He said we'd fight the Mortons in court if necessary, but I couldn't see how. That would cost money and we don't have any.'

'Perhaps Alex was hoping to borrow?' Flora suggested.

'That wouldn't be like him, not at all. Alex was a saver. I don't earn much, just enough to keep food on the table, but he's been the one to pay the rent and the bills since Bertie died – such a good son. I knew he had money put by but it would never have been enough. He promised he could get more if we needed it but, when I asked him how, all he'd say was that he was keeping that little secret to himself for the moment. I don't think he had any idea, really. He was just trying to cheer me up.'

'He'd be determined to defeat the Mortons however he could,' Flora said thoughtfully. 'He wouldn't want you to lose your home.'

'I know that, bless him. But he would never have won. Larry Morton will do anything to make money and when he inherited this house from his father – last year, it was – he was going to sell no matter what we did. But I've lived here since I was married. Bertie, that's my late husband, he found the house just before the wedding and I loved it when he brought me to see it.

Alex was born in the bedroom up there.' She pointed at the ceiling.

'It must have wonderful memories for you. But tell me, did Alex bring Diane to see you here?' That was quite some turn of conversation, Jack thought wryly, but Flora never lost sight of her goal.

'Diane? Yes, she's a nice lass. She'd come to tea sometimes.'

'Were they thinking of getting married maybe?'

Susan looked blankly at the wall. 'They may have been. I don't rightly know. Alex didn't talk about his feelings a lot, and I didn't like to ask.'

'You would have been happy to have Diane as a daughter-in-law, though?'

'If that's what Alex had wanted, but it was never mentioned. I did hear that her folks might be moving – at the last WI meeting – Mrs Croft is a member. So, I'm not sure it would have worked out.'

'The Crofts live in Newhaven?'

'Kingston, that's where they live. Lewes Women's Institute is nearest to Mrs Croft, but she didn't like it much there. A bit cliquey, she said. And we're a friendly bunch at Newhaven.'

'Is Diane planning to leave with her parents, do you know?'

'She could be, I suppose. If it *was* serious between them and, with Alex gone, maybe she won't have anything to keep her here. But she has a lot of friends in the area and she's in the society.'

'The Knights of Mercia is where your son met her?'

'That's right.' Susan became animated whenever she talked of her son. 'They struck up a friendship straight away. Diane thought him very skilful – she'd help him in the shed sometimes, painting the shields he'd made, or polishing the helmets. All of it's still out there in his workshop. I don't know what I'm going to do with the stuff now.'

'You could donate it to the Knights of Mercia,' Jack suggested.

'Or maybe sell it?' Flora said.

The woman's face brightened slightly. 'I don't want to lose that little bit of Alex but... I could do with the money.'

Walking back to the main road where Jack had parked the Austin, Flora asked, 'What do you think of David Morton?'

'He's a thug.'

'I can see that, but what about his being at the rehearsal? Rose said she saw him at the castle and I know now that I did, too. I recognised him as soon as he stepped out of the door. Did he just drop by that Saturday morning to watch the fighting, or did he go there deliberately to torment? It would be another way to make Alex's life a misery. Or perhaps a way to kill him?'

'Killing a man in order to reclaim property seems extreme, even for a thuggish character like Morton,' Jack objected. 'You may have seen him in the audience and Rose, too, but how did he get from the green to the top of the castle without being seen? To push Alex to his death, he would have had to be on the wall itself or at least lurking in the keep entrance.'

'Rose mentioned there could be a hidden staircase.'

Jack's eyebrows shot skywards. 'Clutching at straws comes to mind.'

'We're not far from Lewes – why don't we take a look? The castle will still be open to visitors. And while we drive there, we can talk about Diane Croft.'

'There's not much to talk about. Mrs Vicary knows almost nothing – Alex didn't confide in his mother.'

'Except she believes the Crofts are planning to leave the district. I'm wondering if Diane decided that she'd go with them, either because her relationship with Alex really was as casual as Hector seems to think or because she felt bullied by him and moving away with her family meant an escape.'

'Does it matter?'

'Well, yes, it does – if it was why they quarrelled so badly. Diane told Sally she had something to say to Alex that would put an end to his badgering. Did she say it and provoke a row that was so bitter it continued into the actual fighting? Was it perhaps that she was leaving Sussex for good and Alex along with it?'

'So... after the castle, we talk to Diane Croft?' Jack was slowly resigning himself to an investigation he hadn't wanted.

'Absolutely.' She slipped her hand in his. 'You know what this means, Jack? We're on another adventure!'

7

They parked at the bottom of School Hill, from where it took only minutes to reach the castle that stood at the very centre of the town. Turning off the high street, they walked uphill along the cobbled lane that led to an enormous barbican, a defensive barrier still even without its portcullis and thick doors.

Jack tipped back his head to glance upwards, then pointed to a run of large openings. 'See those gaps in the floor of the barbican? I've never noticed them before, but Martin Winter – he's the history buff at the college – told me to look out for them on my next visit. Apparently, they're unusual for a motte and bailey castle.'

Flora was unimpressed. 'They're just holes.'

'But not any old holes,' he said. 'If you were defending the castle, you could drop rocks, stones, anything you had to hand, on those below. Maybe if the barbican had been built before the Barons' War, King Henry might have won.'

'The barbican wasn't here when Simon de Montfort attacked?'

'When Simon was around, you got into the castle through a

simple gatehouse – unless you were storming the walls, which we aren't. Not today. So, we'd better buy tickets!'

The offices of the Sussex Archaeological Society, custodians of the castle for many years, were on their right and Jack walked in to pay the entrance fee. It seemed there were few customers this afternoon and they would have the castle ruins more or less to themselves.

Flora promptly forgot about barbicans and holes in the floor to ask the question that was bothering her. Two, in fact. 'What's a motte and what's a bailey?'

'That's a motte. The very steep hill the tower and the keep are sitting on. They were designed to see – you can spot what's advancing on you from miles away – but also to *be* seen. To remind the Anglo-Saxons that the Normans were in control and resistance was futile.'

'And the bailey?'

'Just a flat piece of land adjacent to the castle, normally bounded by a low wall. I think it's where the bowling green is now. At the time, it would have been a hive of activity: people had their houses there and there'd be traders of all kinds. Blacksmiths, bakers, candlestick makers, the lot. Come on, let's attack the tower for ourselves.'

They walked across the grass to the first staircase. It proved a relatively easy climb, but from there a second flight of steps leading to the infamous wall from which Alex had fallen was a great deal longer and steeper. Panting slightly, they arrived at the top, the entrance to the keep yawning ahead of them.

'So far, so good.' Jack looked down on the staircases they'd climbed. 'Alex and Hector fought their way up those stairs and had reached about here.'

'Bruce Sullivan, too,' she added. 'He was just ahead. The three of them were fighting uphill and Ferdie Luxton and the rest of the King's men were gradually being pushed back along the wall and into the keep.'

'There would be a host of others, too, but trying to discover who else was on the stairs or the wall that day will be difficult, if not impossible.'

'We have enough names to be getting on with. It's only if we find nothing interesting that we'll have to look further. But what a wonderful view!'

Together, their gaze swung around to follow the river, the Ouse meandering its way through acres of pasture – cows munching, sheep huddling – to meet the rolling downland in the distance.

'It was a wealthy town when William the Conqueror invaded,' Jack remarked, 'and you can see why. A hugely fertile area. No wonder William de Warenne became one of the richest men in England when given the rape of Lewes.'

'And all he had to do was defend the castle and its surroundings. Money for old rope, I'd say!'

Jack looked doubtful. 'He had a lot to control. Not just military affairs but local trade and agriculture as well. Power radiated from this castle, that's for sure.'

'The question is, did de Warenne need a hidden staircase? One he could use if, heaven forbid, someone actually dared to attack *him*?'

'If there is one, it should lead to the keep, the safest hideout. We can walk along this wall to it, but take care. It might be better not to look down.'

That was enough, of course, to make Flora look. 'That is one very big fall,' she said, quickly averting her eyes.

The staircases they had recently climbed were formed of sharp flints and jagged rocks, the building material for every wall that surrounded them – an overwhelming mass of stonework for a fragile body to hit. Alex Vicary was vivid in their thoughts, that moment of impact haunting them both: the thud of soft flesh, the pool of blood, the lifeless eyes.

With bowed heads, they walked along the remainder of the

wall and through the gaping entrance of the keep. Inside, it was dark and for a short while they were forced to stand still while their gaze adjusted to the different light. Then two pairs of eyes began to search the empty space.

'If I'd known we were coming on this expedition, I would have brought a torch.'

Flora glanced slowly around. 'I can't see any obvious opening that might lead to a staircase.'

'Probably because there isn't one.'

Jack began a stroll around the circle of the keep, his hands feeling for any slight break in the thick walls, but they appeared a continuous run with no suggestion there had ever been an exit other than the opening they'd just walked through.

'Is this a Famous Five moment, do you think?' Flora couldn't quite repress a giggle. 'A hidden door will suddenly spring open and reveal a spiral staircase leading to no one knows where.'

When Jack looked slightly pained, she gave him a consolatory hug. 'Don't let's give up,' she urged. 'We could try searching the tower at ground level.'

His expression suggested that this could be as much of a fool's errand but, with a small shrug, he followed her out of the keep and onto the wall, ready to clamber down the staircase they'd climbed earlier. For a moment, his eyes fell on a chunk that jutted slightly from the other side of the wall. Most of this far side was covered in ivy with just this one flat ledge of stone protruding. Jack stopped and looked again.

'Don't look down, remember!' Flora said, a laugh in her voice.

He continued to stare until she retraced her steps to stand beside him. 'What is it?'

'I'm not sure. Let's do what you said. Go down to ground level and walk around the tower.'

She was uncertain how that would help but, when they had

circled the base of the tower and were standing at its far side, she could see they were immediately beneath the entrance to the keep. She looked up, and her hand went to her mouth.

'A hidden staircase,' she whispered.

'Not much of a staircase, but definitely a way to climb to the keep.'

A series of large, flat stones, just visible through the ivy, jutted from the wall, the regular spacing and precise angle forming them into rudimentary stairs.

'They could be difficult for a woman to climb – the spaces between are for longer legs – but let's see...'

Jack reached up to grab the second step some feet above and pulled himself onto the first ledge, then hand over hand, climbed steadily, rock by rock, to emerge on the top wall again, inches from the keep entrance.

He gave a wave. 'I'll use the regular staircase to get down. We'll meet on the grass!'

Flora retraced her steps around the tower and Jack arrived a minute later. 'It would need someone who knew the castle well to find those steps,' he said, a little out of breath from navigating what seemed a hundred stairs. 'The ivy makes it almost invisible. I had to be looking down at a particular angle even to realise they were there. I wonder how many visitors have stood at that particular spot and worked it out.'

'Not many, I imagine. But, even though she didn't know it, Rose was right. There *is* another way into the keep.'

'But would David Morton know it? And if he did, could he have walked across open grass, around the tower, and climbed those steps unseen?'

Flora thought for a while. 'I reckon he could. He could have slipped away from the crowd while everyone's attention was on the fight. Remember how confusing it was – flags waving, a melee of swords and shields, a tangle of bodies. Would anyone have noticed a man sneaking to the rear of the tower?'

'He wouldn't be wearing a costume,' Jack said. 'Once he left the safety of the crowd, he would have stood out as an intruder.'

'There were others who weren't in costume. I saw them. They were at different points in the ruins, directing the rehearsal. Maybe in the hubbub anyone who saw Morton wouldn't register that he wasn't part of the society. Wouldn't realise he shouldn't be there.'

'The only fault with that theory is that it could apply to anybody, not just Morton. Someone else in the audience could have slipped away and climbed that rear staircase.'

Flora sighed. 'I don't want to give up on Morton – he's so clearly a violent man – but you're right, there are others who are more likely suspects. People who were on the wall or in the keep. Ferdie Luxton, for instance. He was fighting Alex, but he could have stopped pretending and started to fight for real. And Diane was in the tower with the other royalist women. We know there was a massive row with Alex. What if he didn't believe her when she told him she was leaving Sussex with her parents? What if he simply refused to listen? It would infuriate her, wouldn't it? In a temper, she might have pushed Alex off that wall. It's even possible she could have done it deliberately – as a last resort.'

'It's unlikely but I guess it's a possibility. We definitely need to talk to her.'

And talk to David Morton, Flora thought, though they'd need to be careful. And Ferdie Luxton – they would have to run him to ground. *And* Bruce Sullivan.

That was one conversation she wouldn't relish, but as soon as Sullivan was back in school, she would tackle him. Almost from her first day there, she'd found him unpleasant. He'd refused her offer to hear his pupils read, muttering loudly about volunteers who knew nothing of school but got in the way of real teachers. Whenever she met him in the corridor, he ignored her, and would make a point of regularly pushing past her in the queue for lunch. On one occasion when the only seat available in the cafeteria had been at her table, he'd turned tail and stomped out.

She wouldn't enjoy pressing him for information, but when she next walked into school, Bruce Sullivan would be in her sights. Flora wasn't a girl to be defeated.

8

The opportunity to talk to Diane Croft came sooner than either Flora or Jack expected. Thursday evening saw them driving back to Abbeymead, Jack's work at Cleve College over for the week and, as they turned off the Brighton Road, it was Flora who let out an involuntary exclamation.

'What is it?' Jack glanced across at her. She'd sounded frustrated.

'I forgot to ask Rose to check the dusters before she left the All's Well today.'

'Dusters?' Flora's passion for her bookshop could sometimes go too far, he felt.

'I think we need new ones, and some polish, and maybe soap for the kitchenette. I could bring it all from home tomorrow if I knew exactly what.'

'Is this a way of saying you want to call at the All's Well before we go home?'

He subdued the inevitable sigh. Flora calling at the bookshop could prove a lengthy business and he'd been looking forward to a cup of tea and a slice of Jessie's heavy cake.

'If we can,' she said hopefully. 'I'll only be a few minutes.'

'I'll be timing you.'

In the event, Jack had no need of his watch. He'd parked the Austin outside the shop – there was virtually no traffic at this time of day – and Flora was climbing out of the car when she literally bumped into Sally Jenner, on foot and with a woman neither of them knew.

'Flora, the very girl I was hoping to see,' Sally exclaimed. 'We were making for the All's Well but then I remembered you're not there until tomorrow and, in any case, we're too late. The shop will have closed an hour ago.'

Flora looked enquiringly at the unknown woman and then back at Sally. 'This is Diane,' Sally explained. 'We came by so I could introduce you.'

Flora shook hands, followed by another round of hand-shaking when Jack, having locked the Austin, walked over to join them.

Flora took a long, though she hoped surreptitious, look at Sally's friend. Diane Croft was indeed pretty. More than pretty. Slim, petite, a peach-like complexion with shining shoulder-length curls and eyes that in the early evening light appeared green. Quite a combination, she decided, and watched Jack's reaction.

He seemed unfazed by this vision of loveliness, after the greetings asking cheerfully where they were off to. There weren't many places in Abbeymead that you could be off to at six o'clock on an April evening, and sure enough it was the Cross Keys they were making for.

'Didn't you go the other night?' Flora asked.

'Oh, we did,' Diane said, an appealing smile on her face, 'and it was such fun that we decided to do it again.'

'You said the pub would be buzzing, Flora, and it was,' Sally added. 'It perked both of us up.'

'And tonight I don't even need perking,' Diane put in.

For a girl who less than two weeks ago had seen her

boyfriend die in front of her eyes, Flora felt this a tad insensitive. But who was she to judge? She had no idea of the real state of their friendship.

'Why don't you come along with us?' Sally was asking. 'You could stay for a quick drink.'

'Oh, we—' Jack began to say when Flora was there before him.

'What a good idea!'

It was inevitable that Flora would grab the opportunity to talk to Diane, he thought wearily, particularly when the girl was likely to be at her most relaxed.

'We could have a single drink, Jack, then go home for supper.' Flora's tone was persuasive.

'Much the best idea,' Sally concurred. 'We did try the pub food but...'

'Say no more.' Jack had had too many disgusting meals at the Cross Keys to disagree, but resigned himself to spending at least an hour on an uncomfortable seat in a noisy pub.

Taking that as agreement to accompany the two women, Flora moved to walk by Diane's side and was quick to draw her into conversation. 'Sally tells me you work in a bookshop.'

'Play It Again. Do you know it?'

Flora did. It had been the shop she'd visited the day she'd met Roberta Raffles, or rather the day that Roberta had engineered the meeting.

'I called in there once,' she said cautiously.

'We sell a little fiction but it's biography we're really big on. We have a huge selection and a large travel department, too.'

'I'll make sure to visit when I'm next in Lewes,' Jack heard her say. 'We're off to Venice very soon and an up-to-date guide would be helpful.' It was as good a way as any to start a conversation in which Flora, he knew, would be mentally listing the questions she wanted answers to.

'You must look Bianca up for me,' Sally put in from behind. 'I keep meaning to mention it.'

'Bianca?' Flora swivelled around.

'The Italian girl that Dominic hired because she was pretty – even though she'd never worked as a chambermaid in her life. You must remember, Flora! I was so cross, but we ended up good friends, having a laugh at him together.'

'I do remember now. She kept talking in Italian and then giggled when we didn't understand. I didn't know you were still in touch.'

'On and off. We phone occasionally. Her English is much better these days.'

'And she comes from Venice? I didn't know that either.'

'I didn't until she left. After the Priory, she was at the Old Ship for a year or so and then went home – she's working in a hotel there. I'll give you her number before you leave. Don't let me forget.'

In the saloon bar, they were lucky to find an empty table – not easy, even this early in the evening – and Jack, armed with their orders, made for the bar, Sally following him to help carry glasses. Flora caught his look as he turned to go and understood his message. A waggle of eyebrows had signalled that he'd take his time while she got busy.

~

'Diane' – Flora leaned forward and patted the girl on the arm – 'we won't speak of this again, but I do want you to know how sorry both Jack and I are about Alex. We know he was a special friend of yours.'

Diane's face crumpled slightly. 'He was.' She paused. 'That Saturday was truly dreadful. We saw... I saw...'

Flora leaned further, her hand covering the girl's. 'Jack and I were in the audience. We saw it, too.' Did she dare ask Diane about her quarrel with Alex or would it appear insensitive when they'd only just been introduced?

'Sally tells us it's been particularly difficult for you.' Flora decided to risk it.

Diane nodded. 'We had a quarrel before the performance,' she confirmed. 'I said some bad things to Alex and I'll never forgive myself.'

'You must forgive yourself.' And Flora meant it. 'We all say things we don't mean.'

'But I did mean them.'

She was startled and her eyes flashed to Diane's face. The girl looked back at her, her expression frank. 'I know that sounds dreadful but really Alex was becoming impossible.'

Flora gave an understanding nod, hoping Diane would continue but, disappointingly, the girl seemed lost in thought.

'Are all men the same?' she asked eventually.

'All men? Alex wasn't your only problem?'

'He was the worst, but Kenny's not much better.'

'Kenny?'

'Kenneth Buckley.'

'Does Kenny belong to the Knights of Mercia, too?'

Diane nodded. 'He joined about six months ago. It was after he came into Play It Again last summer. It was a book on the Tudors that he wanted, for his girlfriend he said, and I told him about the society. He seemed very keen on the idea and the next time I saw him was at the Knights' summer party – we have one every year. He's a nice man, don't get me wrong. Very generous and easy enough to get on with...'

'You seem to like him.'

Diane sighed. 'I did, until he started to get as possessive as Alex. They were awful together, acting like children – picking fights with each other over stupid things, trying to outdo one another. Alex bought me flowers so Kenny had to buy me earrings. Alex invited me to a New Year's party, so Kenny had to throw a bigger one. It got embarrassing.'

'Unsettling, too, I imagine. Is that why you wanted to leave Sussex? You're moving soon, I hear.' Flora was careful not to specify how exactly she'd come by the information.

'It's my parents who are moving.' Diane was quick to correct. 'I've decided to stay put, though I did threaten Alex I'd be going – I hoped it would stop him harassing me. But it made absolutely no difference.'

'Where are your parents moving to?'

'My father has a new job in Scotland, in Edinburgh, which I'm told is a beautiful city. I *was* tempted, but in the end I couldn't face leaving my friends. Or the Knights, for that matter. I'll have to find somewhere to live once the family house is sold – that's the downside.'

'You told Alex you were moving to Scotland?' Flora needed to get back to the quarrel.

Diane nodded again. 'It was why we had such a tremendous row. I told him I was going and he said I needn't worry – that he'd move to Scotland, too!'

'And you said you didn't want that?'

Out of the corner of her eye, Flora had glimpsed Jack with a tray of drinks and Sally carrying snacks. She needed to finish this particular conversation quickly.

'Of course I did. It was ridiculous for Alex to say he'd uproot himself to follow me. Give up a job he enjoyed, leave his mother on her own.'

'Perhaps he wasn't serious, Diane. Just testing you.'

'He was serious all right. He said he'd follow me wherever I went: Scotland, Italy, China.'

Flora was taken aback 'That's... that's pretty suffocating.'

'Exactly. That's just what it was. I felt smothered. I couldn't bear it. We were called for the performance then and never really finished the row. At least, I hadn't said what I really wanted to. But later, when I saw him again, I told him he had to stop pestering me or I'd call the police! I wouldn't have, of course, but when he said he'd keep following me, it was the last straw.'

'You saw him again during the battle?'

'He'd fought his way up the stairs and made it to the top wall. He'd just killed the man he'd been battling, one of Henry's men, and there was a kind of pause in the fighting before that publican took him on. That's when I told him he was over-bearing and a bully. I told him I... I hated him.'

'Gosh!'

'I know. I feel so bad. The next thing I knew, Alex was fighting again but had somehow lost his balance and was falling.'

Falling from the push you gave him? Flora wondered. 'Jack' – she turned to greet her husband – 'that was quite a queue.'

'It was, but we have drinks and we have crisps.'

'Brilliant.' Diane blew her nose loudly. 'I think I'll just pop to the Ladies, if you don't mind, before we get stuck in. I won't be long.'

When she was out of earshot, Flora turned to Sally. 'I can see what you mean about Diane. She's quite beautiful.'

'The rest of us don't stand a chance when she's around.' Sally pulled a face.

'Who else thinks she's beautiful?' Jack asked. It was a sneaky way, Flora thought, of discovering what other boyfriends might be lurking.

'Quite a few.' Sally was amused. 'Most men, in fact. Kenneth Buckley seems to be in the lead at the moment. He's a local solicitor, smooth, charming, a bit...'

'Smarmy?'

'I knew you'd say that, Flora. He's nice enough, I guess, just not for me. He's been *very* nice to Diane. Taken her to all the best restaurants, bought tickets for this, tickets for that. Even offered to buy her a second-hand car. A run-around, he called it. Poor Alex was never going to compete. His mum's cakes were the best he could offer.'

'He must have been jealous.'

'Furiously. That was the problem. Diane didn't see why she shouldn't go out with them both but Alex wanted her for himself.'

'Is Kenneth Buckley a member of the Knights of Mercia by any chance?' Jack took a draught of his beer. He'd not been privy to Diane's account.

'He is.' Sally wrinkled her nose. 'Myself, I think he only joined because of Diane. He seems to be that kind of man. Sets his mind on a goal and goes for it. Mostly it's winning over other men's girlfriends. He's well-known for it.'

'And when he reaches his goal?' Flora asked, though she foresaw the answer.

'That's another matter.'

'Was Buckley at the rehearsal?' Jack had thrown in the question as casually as he could, Flora could see.

'He was in the audience, I think. He doesn't get involved in the fighting – not since the accident.'

'The accident?' Flora's eyes widened. Was this something else to explore?

'It happened at the display we did at Laughton. The head came off the mace Kenneth was fighting with and he was lucky to escape with just a broken finger.'

'If he doesn't take part in the action, what does he do?'

'Don't sound so suspicious, Jack,' Sally chided. 'He undertakes research for the Knights. Consults historical accounts so the society can produce a re-enactment that's as authentic as possible.'

'With Lewes Castle, he'd have hundreds of accounts to trawl through.'

Sally nodded, absently sipping from her glass of shandy. 'I

suppose. I know he drew an amazing map of the castle – and the whole area – as it would have been in the thirteenth century.'

'He'd know the building inside out, presumably?' Jack pursued. And know of the back staircase, Flora finished in her mind.

'Are you two sleuthing again?' Their questions had suddenly begun to make sense to Sally.

'Not at all,' Flora was quick to say. 'We're just... interested.'

Their friend's face was dark with suspicion but at that moment Diane appeared at the table and slid into her seat. 'Well, this *is* nice,' she said. 'How about a toast to start the evening? "To better days", maybe.'

'To better days,' they echoed.

9

Walking into the bookshop the following morning, Flora realised that, annoyingly, she'd forgotten to bring the cleaning materials she'd set aside – the excitement of questioning Diane Croft the previous evening had blotted it from her mind. She would have to soldier on with what she had and was burrowing in the kitchenette cupboard, trying to find a duster that was more material than holes, when she heard her name called.

Rose was standing by the front desk, a packet in one hand and a broom in the other. 'Dusters,' she said quietly. 'I thought we needed them. And I'm afraid I caught the broom in the door yesterday and broke it. This is one of Mrs Waterford's. It's a spare and she doesn't want it back.' Mrs Waterford was Rose's landlady.

'That's kind of you, but you shouldn't have come in on your day off.'

'It's only a day off from the All's Well. I'm due at the post office at ten – Dilys has asked me back for a while and needs me to stay late tonight to help her with stocktaking.'

Flora pulled a face. 'That should be fun! But tell me, how did the All's Well do this week?'

'We had good sales. *Ordeal by Innocence* is still flying off the shelves – you must have reordered that book a dozen times.' Rose sounded flat, her voice hardly matching her words.

'An Agatha Christie is always a winner. But... is something troubling you?' It was plain to Flora that her assistant's usual enthusiasm was in retreat.

Rose paused. 'It's my problem, not yours, Flora. And the same old one, I'm afraid.'

'Your ex-husband?' The woman nodded. 'But you'd worked things out. He'd agreed, hadn't he, that he'd treated you badly and was making amends?'

'He's gone back on his word,' she said simply. 'Not that I should be surprised. It's the kind of person he is.'

'He's stopped the allowance he was paying you?'

She nodded, the faint lines on her forehead becoming more pronounced. 'Naturally, it's made my life more difficult. I can scrape by, now that I'm here three days a week. And I'll be doing extra for Dilys soon, working alongside Maggie. But I'd come to rely on the extra money – for emergencies. And an occasional treat.'

Flora plumped heavily down on her stool, troubled to hear Rose's news. 'Is there nothing you can do about it?'

'It was a verbal agreement, there's nothing in writing, so no, except...' She paused again, seeming unsure whether to go on. 'This chap,' she said at last, 'he came into the All's Well this week, Wednesday I think it was – he couldn't get the book he wanted at his local bookshop, but had forgotten to bring the title with him. It was a book on Sussex landscapes and he said he'd recognise it if we had it on the shelf.'

That wasn't unusual, Flora thought. People came in with vague requests all the time and it was up to the bookshop staff to find a likely contender.

'He was a solicitor, he told me,' Rose went on, 'from Lewes, and seemed really pleasant. It took me a while to find what he wanted – I knew I'd seen a volume on landscapes but couldn't remember exactly where. I found it eventually in one of the bookcases at the back of the shop. On the highest shelf!'

Rose fidgeted with the broom she was still holding. 'Anyway, while we were searching, we started talking. He was in Abbeymead, he said, because he'd been to see a client, not in the village, but not far away. It was a divorce case. He didn't say much about it, he couldn't as a professional, and I didn't want to know, but when I mentioned my divorce and how bad it's been for me, he said I should think of getting the original settlement renegotiated.'

'Can that be done, once it's been agreed by a judge?' Divorce was so rare that Flora was hazy on the details.

'He seemed to think so – if it was grossly unfair on the wife. Which, in my case, it was. He offered to help. Promised he'd do the work for me cut price – even so, it would be difficult to afford.'

Did solicitors discount their fees, and for women they didn't know? Flora suffered a premonition and it wasn't at all comfortable.

'What was his name?'

'Hang on, I've got his card here. I'm still mulling over what he said.' A few seconds of digging through her shoulder bag and she handed Flora a slightly crumpled business card.

Kenneth Buckley, it read. *Buckley and Moss, Solicitors*, followed by a Lewes telephone number.

Silently, Flora handed it back. She had been right to be uneasy.

After closing the All's Well that day, she cycled as quickly along Greenway Lane as Betty permitted, arriving back at the cottage with only a short time to change for the evening ahead. There'd be no chance to talk to Jack about Kenneth Buckley, though there seemed plenty to say.

According to Sally, Buckley was a smoothie, a charmer who liked women – more women, apparently, than just Diane Croft – and found it easy to get them to like him. Flora was certain now that his visit to the All's Well had been a sham. Any self-respecting local bookshop would hold a selection on Sussex, including at least one book on landscapes, and his tale of not finding what he wanted elsewhere was suspicious. He remembered absolutely nothing of the title? She found that difficult to believe. Difficult to believe there had been a title.

Had Buckley's appearance in Abbeymead been purely to make up to Rose? Perhaps he'd seen her at a Knights of Mercia get-together, or out with Hector, and liked what he'd seen. Perhaps with Alex dead and no longer a rival for Diane, the challenge had gone cold and he needed a new one. That would accord with what Sally had said of him: winning over other men's girlfriends was what he did and once he was successful...

Or maybe, there was something more significant.

At the re-enactment, the solicitor had played no part in the fighting, but he was a man with a detailed knowledge of the castle. Had he used that knowledge to infiltrate the fight? To creep unseen by the audience into the keep and from there launch an attack? As part of an organising team who wore 'plain clothes', his presence in the tower was likely to go unquestioned.

Why, though? What had been Buckley's true relationship with Alex Vicary? There had been evident jealousy over Diane Croft, but would he have killed for that? Surely, there would have to be something else. Something more serious. Buckley was a professional man, but his offer of a personal discount to Rose if she used his services suggested that he was willing to bend the rules if necessary. Had he done so in the past, perhaps, and Alex had discovered something to his discredit?

Hadn't Mrs Vicary mentioned – at the time, it had struck

Flora as a strange thing to say – that Alex had promised he'd get the money to fight the Mortons in court, but how he'd do it would stay a secret? Susan Vicary had dismissed her son's words as just talk to keep her happy, but what if they hadn't been? What if there'd been an actual secret? A secret, maybe, about a fellow Knight. If Alex had possessed harmful knowledge about Buckley's personal life, or about his work as a solicitor, might he have been prepared to use it? It was a very long shot, but nevertheless still a possible explanation of why Alex had died.

And again, if the young man had been privy to damaging information, had he passed it on before he was killed? Talked about it to his best friend, say. Talked about it to Hector, who was still very much alive. It would be important for Kenneth Buckley to discover just how much Hector knew, but without giving himself away. Cosying up to Rose might be a first step. Rose Lawson was a likely recipient of any worries Hector might have and gaining her confidence would seem a sensible move.

Too much speculation, she thought. Too many possibilities. Talking to Jack should bring the clarity she needed, but not until the evening was over. As last Friday's supper had been cancelled, the friends had been determined to meet tonight, and Alice determined to cook. Flora couldn't let them down.

'I've had to bring Sarah,' Kate said apologetically, as Alice helped her manoeuvre the carrycot through the front door. 'She's sleeping at the moment and cross fingers she'll keep sleeping. I couldn't leave her with Tony. He's been battling a cold all day and once we'd closed the Nook, he gave in, finally, and crawled into bed.'

Alice gave a sniff. 'That's a man for you.'

'It's a very bad cold.' Kate was quick to defend her husband.

Their friend gave a small humph and no more was said of the hapless Tony. The Nook, though, was another matter.

'How are you goin' to manage the café tomorrow if he's no better? With Sarah an' all.'

'Knowing Tony, he'll drag himself up. We'll have to cope as best we can. And Ivy comes in on a Saturday – she can't cook but she can serve.'

Alice pondered. 'I suppose I could lend you Charlie for the day.'

Charlie Teague was training as a chef, a day or so at the Nook every week but most of his time spent at the Priory, and always at the weekend.

'Could you do without him?' Kate, usually so calm, was looking harassed.

Flora felt sorry there was nothing *she* could do to help. Except, perhaps... try to look after Sarah while running the bookshop? It wasn't ideal, not least because she hadn't the slightest idea how to care for a tiny baby.

'I can do without Charlie tomorrow,' Alice decided. 'It's goin' to be a quiet Saturday – no big parties in for dinner. And he can be a real help to you. Just stop him eatin' as much as he cooks.'

'That would be wonderful! You're a treasure!' Beaming, Alice bustled into the kitchen to check the various pots she had cooking.

They sat down to eat almost immediately, Kate worried that Sarah would wake before the meal was over, but the baby continued to sleep deeply and her mother gradually relaxed. Until Alice's banana cream pie appeared on the table, conversation centred on village events: Evelyn Barnes had broken her ankle on the golf course and her husband had the unenviable task of caring for her while she was in plaster – an awed silence followed this snippet as they thought of poor Harry's forthcoming tribulations; Dilys Fuller had badly upset Mr Houseman, generally an easy-going chap, by telling him his cauliflowers were too small and too expensive; and Elsie

Flowers had scandalised almost everyone by returning from a trip to Steyning with hair a delicate shade of blue.

Flora was relieved there had been no mention of Hector. She'd been careful to skirt round any comment that might have involved him, and Alice had remained remarkably silent on her sous chef. Perhaps Hector's cooking had recovered since Flora's visit to the Priory. Now that she and Jack had offered to help uncover the truth of Alex's death, Hector might be feeling a good deal happier. That was something else she wouldn't be mentioning to Alice. Her friend had always been severe in her disapproval of 'that sleuthin' nonsense'.

As though she'd been able to dip into Flora's thoughts, their hostess suddenly announced over the banana pie, 'It's Alex Vicary's funeral next weekend. I've asked Sally to give Hector the day off, hoping the lad will feel better once it's over.'

'The funeral is in Newhaven?' Flora asked.

Alice shook her head. 'No. Up country, Horsham way. His dad's family came from there and his dad is buried in the churchyard at St Cuthman's. Hector's gettin' a lift, he said. From one of them Knights. The chap who used to run the Cross Keys way back. You girls won't remember.'

'Before our time?' Flora asked, amused.

'You'd have been around, the two of you, but hopefully not in the pub. Now who wants seconds?'

'Please,' they chorused, offering two empty bowls.

'He was the chap who went on to run a pub in Lewes.' Alice was reminiscing.

'Really?' Flora's mind stirred. 'Was he called Ferdie Luxton, by any chance?'

'That's right. You do remember him.'

She didn't, but she had no intention of divulging how she'd guessed the name.

'That's him. Luxton,' Alice continued. 'He's drivin' over from Lewes and pickin' Hector up on the way.'

'We seem to have had an awful lot of landlords at the Cross Keys,' Kate said.

'And none of them too special. Think of that Daniel Vaisey.'

For a short while, they thought, but Flora wanted to know more of Ferdie. 'Did you know Mr Luxton well, Alice?'

'I never went near the pub when he was the landlord,' she said a trifle indignantly. 'It had a bad reputation – took a good few years after he left to shake it off. Not that it ever did completely.'

'Why was it so bad?'

'Allowin' drinkin' after hours, settin' up a gamblin' den at the back of the pub. That kind of thing. If I remember rightly, Luxton lost his licence and got a criminal conviction, though he never went to prison. Paid a fine instead.'

'If he was convicted, how could he have gone on to run a pub in Lewes?' Kate asked. It was the question burning a path through Flora's mind, too.

'Search me. He probably lied,' Alice said. 'Perhaps the brewery didn't do much diggin'. Or mebbe Luxton bribed anyone who knew about his past to keep quiet. He got a second chance, however he did it, and by all accounts it went well.'

Flora's brain was still working at full speed. 'How many people might know about his past?'

Alice frowned at the question. 'Anyone who's lived in the village all these years.'

'I didn't know,' Kate said, 'and Tony wouldn't either.'

And neither had Flora. Had Alex Vicary?

Flora had already gone down this road in suspecting Kenneth Buckley, but the secret she'd envisaged had been hazy... nebulous... pure speculation. *This* was something definite. Luxton had a shady past and one he wouldn't want re-examined.

Ferdie Luxton had actually been fighting Alex when the boy fell. How easy it would have been to push harder than Alex was expecting, in what was a pretend battle. But was having his past revealed a big enough threat for Luxton to commit such a dreadful deed? According to Alice, he might have bribed people in the past to keep his secret – presumably he could bribe again. But he'd been retired for years, hadn't he? No matter what was revealed, it would no longer affect his job, so it wasn't that much of a threat.

Yet... he must be drawing a pension from the brewery. Would that be put in jeopardy if his earlier conviction came to light, particularly after he'd lied to them to get the job? What if Alex had demanded money to keep quiet, but this time Ferdie had decided he wasn't going to pay? This time maybe didn't have the funds to pay.

Flora's imagination had broken free and roamed wildly.

'Why are you so interested in Ferdie Luxton anyways?' Alice was staring across the table, her eyes sharp with suspicion.

'It's a scrap of local history, that's all – they're always fun to collect.' Flora dismissed her curiosity with a laugh.

Her imagination might be too vivid, she thought, finishing her second helping of pudding, but either she or Jack needed to find Ferdie Luxton, and swiftly.

10

On Monday morning, Jack had waved goodbye to Flora and Betty on their way to the All's Well and was halfway up the stairs to the spare room – he still thought of it as the spare room rather than his study – when the telephone rang in the hall below. A problem at the All's Well? It couldn't be. Flora would have to be an Olympic cyclist to be at the bookshop already and Betty would certainly have had something to say about that. A dignified trundle was her preferred style.

It was Alan Ridley on the line, Jack hoping very much that it wasn't with an invitation to eat lunch at the Cross Keys. A batch of new ideas for the current novel had been gathering pace in the last day or so and were now hurting his head in their effort to burst out and find themselves a place on the page.

He needn't have worried, however.

'Jack,' the inspector began. 'I need a bit of help.'

'Yes?' It was always good to be cautious.

'This chap, Hector Lansdale, is a friend of yours?'

'Yes,' he said, feeling even more cautious. What had Hector been up to?

'The bloke's making a bit of a nuisance of himself,' Ridley said. 'There was another complaint before I'd even sat down at my desk this morning. He's been kicking up a fuss over in Newhaven. First, at the police station there, yelling at the desk sergeant to complain we weren't doing our job – that was after he'd rung me to say the same. The sergeant told him to go home. Next, there's a chap doing the complaining – about Lansdale! He's called us several times.'

'What kind of nuisance are we talking about?'

'Abusive language, preventing the rightful owner from entering his property, all minor stuff but I don't want an escalation. I was wondering if you could have a quiet word? Tell Lansdale to knock it off or we'll be forced to intervene.'

'Can I ask who made the complaint?' He probably didn't need to ask, Jack reflected, but it was always good to be certain.

'I'm not at liberty to say.'

'Come on, Alan. If you want my help, I have to know the situation. I'm not exactly going to blab the news around the neighbourhood.'

Down the line, Jack could hear the inspector fidgeting at his desk, pens rattling, papers being shuffled. At length, he said, 'It's a chap called Morton. David Morton. I know his uncle, or rather the police do. A real piece of work, but the nephew – as far as I know there's nothing against him.'

'And nothing against Hector. He's a chef at the Priory and as far as I know has led a blameless life.'

'That's it – a storm in a teacup. So, if you could have a quiet word? I know his friend died, tragic for such a young man, and it could be knocking Lansdale a bit out of kilter, but he's got to stop.'

After Jack replaced the receiver, he walked slowly up the stairs to his desk, sat down and uncovered his typewriter. But instead of inserting paper into the roller, he sat staring at the keys for a good few minutes. Then deliberately got to his feet, re-covered the Remington, and walked down the stairs to the hall, collecting his coat and fedora on the way. Mornings and evenings were still chilly enough for him to be wearing his favourite hat.

He was in luck. Mrs Vicary was at home and recognised him straight away, inviting him in and offering him tea before he had a foot on the threshold. It wasn't tea he wanted; it was information that Jack wasn't sure he'd get. Susan Vicary had been wary on their last visit of saying anything that would point the finger at the Mortons. Would she be as wary this time?

'I hear Hector has been to see you recently,' he began.

She looked nervous, sinking deeper into her chair. There was evidently substance to whatever complaints Ridley had received.

'He's a good lad,' she said.

'I'm sure he is. But... Mrs Vicary, what's been going on?'

She sat with her hands gripped tightly in her lap, seeming unable to speak.

'You wouldn't want Hector to get into trouble, would you?' he prompted.

'He's not in trouble, is he?' When Jack didn't answer, she looked down again at her clasped hands, saying quietly, 'He's been to see me – several times. He was here yesterday.'

'And?'

'A few days ago, David Morton turned up just as Hector arrived.'

'Threatening you as he did when Flora and I were here?'

'Not threatening, not exactly,' she said, sounding a little desperate. 'He wanted to come in and check the back boiler, he said, but Hector told him to go away and when he tried to push past, Hector got hold of him and, well I suppose you'd say he threw him onto the ground.'

Good for Hector, Jack thought, but aloud he said, 'That must have taken some muscle. Morton is a hulk and probably tough. But then, as a member of the Knights of Mercia, Hector would have to be pretty strong, I guess.'

'I imagine so. Alex certainly was. It's all that historical stuff, isn't it? They pretend to fight, but they have to be fit to pretend. Those shields are some heavy, not to mention the swords and the helmets.'

'So, Morton ended up on the ground that time, but yester-day, when Hector came, was that different?'

'Morton brought a dog with him. A big dog. An Alsatian, I think.'

Jack's mouth tightened. David Morton was intent, it seemed, on escalating his threats to a whole different level. If he was using a vicious dog to intimidate his tenant, that was a police matter.

'And what happened?'

'Hector emptied a full watering can over him.'

'Over Morton?'

There was a shadow of a smile on Susan Vicary's face. 'Over the dog and he didn't like it. Not one bit. He broke free of his lead and ran off. Morton had to chase after him down the street.'

It would be comic, Jack thought, if it weren't so serious.

'I'm moving out,' she said suddenly. 'You can tell Hector – it should put his mind at rest.'

'You're leaving your home?' Jack was stunned.

'I can't cope with all this, not after losing Alex. I know my son would tell me to stay, battle it out, and I feel a coward giving up. But I'm at the end of my tether and now that Hector has taken on Alex's role – facing up to the Mortons the way he has – it makes me sick with worry what they'll do to him.'

'Do you have anywhere to go?'

'I've been looking and Diane's been helping me. She's a lovely girl and she's been asking around – friends and neighbours and shop customers. Asking if they know of any flats. Ones I can afford. That's the problem. There's plenty to rent, but mostly they're way too expensive.'

'I'm sorry you feel you have to leave.' Looking around the attractive home that over the years Susan had made for herself and her family, Jack felt genuine sadness. 'I hope that Diane can find you something suitable very soon.' He paused. 'How about Alex's workshop? Have you made plans for it?'

Briefly, her face cleared. 'I had a word with the president of the society. The Knights of Mercia will take Alex's equipment in exchange for giving me a donation. Quite a big one, too. But what's most important is that it's going to a good home. To people who'll value Alex's skill.'

Jack wasn't sure what to say. It looked as though the Mortons had won. He would have liked to urge Susan Vicary to stay, to fight her corner, tell her he'd ask the inspector to look into the Mortons' shady business methods, but it was unfair to this poor woman to prolong her distress. Perhaps, if she made a new start... but looking around at the comfortable chairs, the ornaments, the photographs, the fire burning cosily in the grate, he thought how wrong that was.

'Don't make a decision just yet,' he said suddenly. 'Things could change.'

Susan Vicary looked lost. 'What things?'

'I'm not sure, but don't make a final decision – not for a few weeks.'

His hostess shook her head and Jack was left unsure of what she would decide. He'd got to his feet, ready to leave, when she said, 'There is one thing you could do, Mr Carrington. I forgot to give it to Hector but you could do it for me.'

Puzzled, Jack remained standing by the front door, aware of

her footsteps in the bedroom above. In a short while she returned with a small box in her hand.

'I found this when I was tidying Alex's room. I think he must have meant it for Diane, but I can't be sure. I wondered whether I should offer it to her. I thought that maybe Hector would know.'

She passed the box over.

'May I open it?' he asked.

'Yes, of course. You can guess what it is.'

Jack had guessed and it seemed only to complicate matters, but he flicked open the box anyway.

A large ruby in a circle of gold winked back at him.

He had driven along Mantell Street and was travelling eastwards, with the docks on one side and a packed terrace of housing on the other, when a saloon car pulled out of a side street. Its engine revved and for a split second, Jack saw a heap of black metal powering towards the Austin. Yanking the steering wheel violently to the left, he managed to avoid a direct hit, the saloon instead grazing the car's rear bumper.

He was congratulating himself on his quick reflexes, when he realised that in slewing the car so viciously to one side, he had breached the red-and-white chain that provided a safety barrier to the docks. One of his front wheels teetered perilously over what was very deep water.

The engine had stalled in the manoeuvre and Jack had no intention of pressing the ignition. He needed to get help as quickly as he could but, moving to climb out of the vehicle, the car lurched even further to the left and through the passenger window he caught sight of a sheet of grey water coming up to meet him. He was only feet from a sea that was fathoms deep at this point.

Taking a long breath, he schooled himself to keep calm. He bent his head sideways to glance into the driving mirror, now sitting at an odd angle. The road behind him was empty, the road ahead empty, too, and the doors of the houses opposite firmly shut. He would have to rely on himself for rescue.

Over the next few minutes, he tried again and again to wriggle himself out of the car, but every time he opened the door even slightly, the Austin lurched a few inches further left, the ever present risk of drowning becoming more certain. He was making things worse and he felt his heart beating too loudly. It seemed that he was trapped.

In a state of panic, a knock at his window made him jump, causing the car to slip further still. 'Got yourself in a bit of pickle, mate?' A large, hairy man, bending his head to speak, looked in at the window.

'It appears so.' Jack gave an embarrassed smile. It was pointless recounting what had actually happened. His assailant had reversed immediately he'd done the damage and, in a squeal of tyres and thrashing of engine, he'd roared away, taking the road out of town.

'Wait there,' the man told him, 'and I'll be back.' As though he had any option, Jack thought.

Five minutes later, his rescuer had returned with three companions, all as large though not as hairy.

'Keep still,' the chap advised, 'and we'll get you and this rattletrap back on the road.'

Jack felt immediate indignation at the description of his beloved car, but this was not a moment to quibble. Two of the men took the front bumper and two the rear of the vehicle, between them lifting the Austin to safety within seconds. Jack felt a heavy thump as all four wheels landed back on the road.

He almost fell out of the driver's door, his body weak from the tension of near drowning. Diving into his wallet, he produced a ten shilling note. 'I owe you chaps a decent lunch,' he said. 'Thank you for your help.'

'Thank *you*, squire! You can come back and do it again if you like.' There were guffaws of laughter from his mates.

Jack gave them a sickly smile and watched as they trooped back to their work on the docks.

11

He wouldn't drive directly back to the cottage, he decided, when once more he was behind the wheel and leaving Newhaven. First, he would call at the All's Well; after what had been a deliberate attempt to harm him, he must speak to Flora. If the attack he'd suffered was a result of calling on Susan Vicary, Flora could be a target, too. She'd been with him when they'd tangled with David Morton on Susan's doorstep and he needed to warn her – to take care, to be extra vigilant, and *not* to go to Newhaven on her own.

In less than an hour, he was parked outside the All's Well. Flora was alone in the shop and looked up with a smile as he walked in. The smile, though, was short-lived.

'Something's the matter. What's happened?'

'Do I look that bad?'

'Yes,' she said frankly. 'Tell me.' And, holding out her hand, she led him to the cushioned seat that ran beneath the latticed windows.

Jack told her, omitting nothing: Ridley's phone call, the visit to Susan Vicary, the deliberate crash, the plight of the Austin.

'It's fortunate the car isn't badly damaged.' He turned his

head to glance through the window at the vehicle parked in front of the shop. 'It still drives, but I'll have to get the bumper fixed.'

'Never mind the car. What about you? You have to tell Alan Ridley what's happened. It was Morton in that saloon and he was out to kill you.'

'We can't know for certain that it was him. It happened too quickly for me to see who was driving.'

'Of course it was Morton. Who else would it be? He must have seen you at Susan Vicary's house and decided you were a threat he needed to get rid of. You have to tell the inspector,' she repeated.

'He didn't succeed, though, did he? Getting rid of me. I'm still here, and not even bruised.'

'If Morton had done what he wanted, hit you broadside before he escaped, the car would have been pushed into the harbour and bruises would be the least of your worries. You would have drowned.'

Jack knew she was right but still felt reluctant to involve the inspector. 'If I go to Ridley, it could distract the police – and us – from following the right trail. It could mean that we'll never discover the truth of how Alex died. And why.'

'How do you make that out? After what happened today, Morton has to be our killer, surely. He should be in prison, and you can help the inspector put him there. Then Mrs Vicary will be safe in her home and no one else will get hurt.'

'You can't be certain it's him, Flora, you're jumping ahead, narrowing the focus when we've only just begun to investigate. You tell me to keep an open mind...'

'But that's why Morton attacked you. He's worried that we're on to him.'

'If it *was* David Morton behind the wheel of that car, it doesn't make him Alex's killer. He could simply have been warning me not to interfere with his uncle's plan for Mantell

Street. And what about the Knights as suspects? You seem to have forgotten them.'

'I haven't, but Morton is the one doing bad things.'

'He's the one we know about,' Jack cautioned, 'but there could be others doing equally bad things. And I'm afraid I've brought home another complication.'

He reached into his pocket and brought out the small box that Mrs Vicary had handed him.

Taking hold of it, Flora pushed open the lid, and stared. 'A ring! Alex was going to propose! No wonder they quarrelled. When I asked Hector about the row, he said it was probably because Alex had forgotten Diane's birthday, but that never sounded right. The truth is far more serious. She was threatening to move to Scotland and here he was with a ring in his bedroom!'

'Does that make Diane our murderer?' He was laughing.

'An open mind, Jack! No, my money is still on Morton, but you have to admit the ring gives her a strong motive. She must have known it was only a matter of time before he'd force an engagement on her.'

'I don't see that. When he proposed, she could have refused him – nicely.'

Flora shook her head. 'There's no nice way to refuse a man, and particularly one who ignores everything you say. I believe Diane when she says that Alex was harassing her. Sally told me that he kept turning up at her house. Telephoning her. Perhaps even following her. Men with an obsession do that.'

'She could always have followed through with her threat to leave for Scotland. That would be pretty final – she didn't need to kill him to break free.'

'She wouldn't want to leave Sussex and really, why should she? She must have felt cornered, and that's why they had that blazing row. Diane was in a fury and could have lashed out, not thinking what she was doing.'

'It would have had to be a very forceful push then. Alex cut a sturdy figure during that fight and I have Mrs Vicary's word that her son was physically very strong.'

'Still... it could have happened. Oh, it's such a muddle!' For a moment, she clasped her hands to her head. 'Morton, Diane, Ferdie maybe, and there's Buckley, too.'

Jack looked questioningly at her.

'Kenneth Buckley. Remember? He was Alex's rival, always trying to win Diane from him. He's been enormously generous to her and must have wondered why he wasn't getting anywhere. He would have blamed Alex for that.'

'Blamed him and decided to remove him from the field – literally?'

'He could have done. He was at the rehearsal, not fighting, but he knows every inch of the castle.'

Jack shook his head. 'If either Diane or Buckley is our villain, it means that love or what passes for love was behind Alex's death. My gut feeling – yes, I do have them' – he'd seen Flora's wry expression – 'is that it's much more likely to be money. Which brings us full circle back to David Morton.'

The following morning they were late leaving the village, Jack having temporarily lost the notes he'd made on a manuscript from his most promising student. A frantic search eventually found them stuffed behind the sofa cushions though how they'd arrived there was a mystery. It was fortunate the traffic was light and the journey to Lewes swift; he was able to open his office door with minutes to spare before his first appointment, having dropped Flora at Riverdale school.

Flora, on the contrary, had felt her first class a trifle rushed, but rather than a leisurely saunter to the staffroom for a mid-morning cup of tea, she made sure she walked quickly and was already ensconced in a corner chair when Bruce Sullivan strolled in. He cut an imposing figure and she eyed him warily. He had been an athlete in his past, she decided, but gradually muscle had turned to fat and now the shirt he wore was straining at the buttons. One of them might pop at any minute. She smiled at the thought and, at that moment caught his eye. His expression was sullen.

Taking her opportunity, she bounced off the chair and crossed the room to the hot-water urn where Bruce was ham-fistedly making himself a mug of tea.

'Mr Sullivan,' she said breezily, 'good morning. I hope you're feeling better?'

A grunt was his only response.

'It's good to see you back,' she persevered, 'and you'll be glad to hear that your class did very well with their reading last week.'

Another muffled grunt was his sole acknowledgement. Really, this encounter gave a whole new meaning to getting blood from a stone.

'I was wondering if I might talk to you for a moment. Not about your class, in this instance.'

At that, he twisted around but, in doing so, managed to spill tea from the overfull mug. Angrily, he shook his hand at her. 'Thanks for that. My hand needed a burn.'

'A little exaggeration perhaps?' She smiled brightly and, ignoring his ill temper, carried on. 'I know that you're a member of the Knights of Mercia—'

'So what?' he interrupted.

'We have acquaintances in common. I'm a friend of Hector Lansdale. You must know Hector, and Alex Vicary, too. They are... were... fellow Knights. Alex was the society's armourer, in fact. I wondered if you knew him well.'

'What's it got to do with you if I did?'

Flora refused to be deterred by his rudeness. 'I think I saw you at the rehearsal at the castle,' she went on. She hadn't, but others had and it was something he couldn't deny.

'Again, so what?'

'Alex Vicary died that day.'

'Are you trying to tell me news? If so, you're a bit late.'

'No, I'm asking if, when you were fighting – you were playing one of de Montfort's men, I believe, and was close to Alex on the wall, just ahead of him – whether you saw anything... odd?'

'Odd?' Bruce snatched up his mug and drank down what was left of the tea.

'Alex fell to his death. I imagine it isn't usual for a Knight to die in that way.'

'Of course it isn't.' He could have added stupid woman, but she was spared the insult. 'Vicary's death was an accident and accidents happen. Anywhere. Any time. And if you've quite finished, I'll get on with what I came to school to do. Work.' Turning his shoulder on her, he marched towards the staffroom door.

Well, that went well, Flora thought, drifting back to her chair.

Once back at the college flat, she telephoned the Priory and asked the receptionist to pass a message to Hector, for him to ring her when he was free. She was keen to discover how much he knew about the ruby ring Mrs Vicary had handed Jack. The ruby itself sat gleaming wickedly at her from the one occasional table the flat possessed – Flora had thought it safer to bring the jewellery to Lewes. For some time, she remained motionless, staring at the circle of gold, trying to puzzle out the truth of Alex's relationship with an apparently reluctant girlfriend.

An engagement ring didn't just involve Alex. If known about, it could have been significant for others: it could have stirred emotions, encouraged rash conduct. She was thinking particularly of Kenneth Buckley and his pursuit of Diane. The money he'd spent, the presents he'd lavished on the girl, the plans he'd been making, all brushed aside by a ruby ring? Diane hadn't wanted an engagement, but how thoroughly would Kenneth believe a denial? If he'd known of the ring, feared he was about to lose the battle to Alex, what might have been his response? Here was a man who clearly didn't like losing – he was the one who took other men's girlfriends, not the other way round. When earlier she'd spoken to Hector about the society, he'd been adamant that his fellow members were all good blokes who could have had nothing to do with Alex's death. But, though David Morton remained her prime suspect, in Flora's mind there was a good deal more to tell.

'Jack went to see Mrs Vicary yesterday,' she began, when Hector's call came through around four o'clock that afternoon. 'Inspector Ridley asked him to. Apparently, there's been more trouble in Mantell Street.' Hector would know what trouble – he'd caused it – and Flora hoped he would take the hint and keep clear of Newhaven for a while. 'While Jack was there, Mrs Vicary gave him a ring she'd found in Alex's bedroom. A ruby, an engagement ring. She thinks it was meant for Diane but wasn't sure whether or not to give it to her.'

'A ring!'

'You didn't know what Alex planned?' She could sense Hector shaking his head. He'd sounded dumbfounded.

'He never said,' he mumbled at last. 'I didn't realise...'

So, Alex was keeping more than one secret, it seemed. From both his mother and his best friend.

'Of course she shouldn't give it to her,' Hector burst out suddenly. 'Diane never deserved it. She... she was flighty.' Such an old-fashioned word. And an old-fashioned attitude to describe a woman's wish to control her life. 'And now Alex...' he choked, and for a moment was unable to go on. 'His mother should keep it,' he said finally, regaining his calm. 'Sell it. She needs the money.'

'I think so, too. We'll make sure we take it back to her before we leave Lewes. There's no need for you to worry.' Judging Hector to be dangerously wound up, the last thing Flora wanted was for him to rush to Newhaven and land himself in more trouble.

'While you're on the phone, Hector, there was something else I wanted to ask. Kenneth Buckley is a member of the Knights of Mercia?'

'We have all kinds of people joining,' Hector said defensively. 'Even people like Buckley.'

'You don't like him?'

'He's a louse.' Well, that was pretty definite.

'And Alex thought so, too?'

'Ken was jealous of Alex – he wanted Diane for himself. He's that kind of person. Goes after other people's girlfriends then once he's got them, drops them like a hot potato. Diane should have seen that for herself.'

'Perhaps she did. He doesn't appear to have had much luck with her.'

'Good, though it means he'll be after some other woman now.' That tallied, Flora thought. If her guess was right, Buckley was now fixed on attaching Rose.

'Someone told me,' Hector went on, 'I don't remember who, that Ken Buckley was cautioned once for bothering a woman, not leaving her alone when she'd made it clear that she didn't want to know.'

'Were the police involved?' If they were, Alan Ridley could be tapped for the report.

'I dunno, I reckon so. I heard it was pretty serious.'

'Buckley was at the rehearsal that Saturday, even though he didn't fight?' she asked, changing the topic but eager to find out just what role the solicitor had played on the fateful day.

'He's at every rehearsal,' he said glumly. 'As long as there are women around.' There was a loud shuffling and a clank of keys at the other end of the line. 'I'll have to go soon, Flora. Alice is on the warpath and I've still several flans to make.'

'Just a few more minutes, I promise. What do you know of Bruce Sullivan?'

'You seem to have got it in for the society,' he muttered.

'It was members of the society that were there that day,' she reminded him gently. 'Did Alex know Bruce well, that's all I'm asking?' She'd got nothing from Bruce himself, and crossed her fingers that Hector would deliver. She was not disappointed.

'They used to meet at the racecourse.'

'Lewes racecourse?'

'Yeah, Alex loved the horses. He always wanted to own one – part of one, racehorses are very expensive – but he never had the money.'

'Did Alex gamble?' she suggested quietly.

'You're joking! On his salary! Bruce did, though.'

'Excessively?'

'Maybe a little,' Hector muttered.

'How did he do that? He's a teacher, and not on a huge salary either.'

'Sullivan has a wealthy wife, that's the story.'

'You say that Alex met him at the racecourse, but did they meet elsewhere?'

'What is this about Sullivan?' There was an edge of anger to Hector's voice.

'I'm just interested. Jack and I are both interested. In everyone who was at the castle that Saturday. You did ask us to help,' she said reprovingly.

'I suppose. But Bruce is an okay chap. Alex and I used to meet him at the Masons Arms on a Friday evening. He's OK,' he repeated, 'maybe a bit reluctant to get in the rounds and he did like the horses. But then, I like them, too. Bruce was a bit more daring than me, that's all.'

'What do you mean, more daring than you?'

'He'd bet on outsiders. Say he had a sure tip.'

'And did he?'

Hector gave a half laugh. 'I don't think so.'

'Let me get this right. He was confident enough to place extravagant bets, but couldn't pay his round?'

'He paid sometimes.' She could feel Hector shrug.

'And others? He has a wealthy wife, you say.' Flora pounced on the anomaly.

'I don't know his personal circumstances. Maybe the rich wife is just a rumour.'

She sighed inwardly. How could men meet each other, Friday after Friday, and not know the most basic things about each other's lives?

'I wonder...' She was speculating now. 'Did Bruce ever borrow money?'

'Not from me he didn't.' There was a dry chuckle at the other end of the line. 'Not on what the Priory pay me.'

'But from Alex?'

'Not in my hearing.'

'Did they ever meet on a Friday evening when you weren't around?'

'Yes,' he acknowledged gingerly. 'And it's possible they talked of money. I wouldn't know.'

'And if they did, would Alex have lent money, do you think?'

'He had savings. I told him to keep hold of them.'

'But he might not have listened to you,' she pursued. 'He might have lent to Bruce.'

'Perhaps. But why not? Bruce was a pal.'

How much of one? Flora wondered, as she put the phone down.

12

'Can we call at the Masons Arms before we leave on Thursday?' Flora asked that evening, over a supper of sausage and chips.

The oven the college had felt suitable to install had become so unreliable lately that Flora had taken to using only the gas rings to cook. The result was an even more limited menu for their days in Lewes.

'We're going drinking?'

'We're going to look for Ferdie Luxton. I don't know where he lives, but I bet he still haunts the pub that he managed for years.'

'And if he doesn't?'

'Then the barman might know where to find him. I think it's important we talk to Luxton. There are questions, aren't there, over every one of the people who were close to Alex on that awful Saturday? Diane in the keep, Buckley lurking in the wings, Bruce Sullivan just ahead of Alex on the wall and Luxton fighting against both of them.'

Jack said nothing, finishing his last sausage with a sigh of content. 'These are good. Not from Preece, I imagine.'

Mr Preece was the Abbeymead butcher and, while he could still be depended on to supply a decent lamb chop, his sausages had become less tasty of late, rarely hitting the mark.

'I've found a small shop on the way back from school and started buying from them.'

Jack looked at her thoughtfully. 'And how is school?' he asked. 'You rarely mention it. Are you still enjoying the volunteering?'

'I love the children. And I think I'm doing some good. It gives me a real lift when I see how their reading has improved, but... I haven't made many friends at Riverdale.'

'And you miss the village?'

Flora did, badly, but she wasn't going to admit it. 'The teachers are busy and I'm just an extra,' she said airily. 'I can understand they don't have much time for me.'

'But they're not unfriendly?' He sounded worried. 'Because if they are, we can give up this experiment.' He reached across the table to take hold of her hand. 'We can retreat to Abbeymead – permanently.'

It would be a retreat, she thought, and that wasn't in her nature. 'School is OK, more or less, and now that you're enjoying your life at Cleve a lot more, we should stay.'

'Talking of Cleve, I met the new principal today, paying us an advance visit. A Dr Summersby. She takes over next term and seems personable enough, though everyone's holding their breath over the likely changes she'll make.'

'Hopefully, she'll be a better chief than Professor Dalloway. He seems to have little or no interest in your work.'

'As long as I'm bringing money into the college via new students, he's happy. We'll have to wait until next term to discover how Dr Summersby will turn out. But the school, Flora.' He wasn't going to allow her to escape questioning. '*Has* anyone there been unpleasant to you?'

'Bruce Sullivan,' she said immediately. 'I really don't like him, Jack.'

'Another Knight of Mercia! They get everywhere. He was at the rehearsal, you say, fighting just ahead of Alex. So... a de Montfort man?'

She nodded.

'Is he on our rapidly expanding list of suspects?'

'Well, he had the opportunity. He could have pushed Alex from behind.'

'But a motive?' Jack got to his feet to clear the table.

'At the moment, I'm not sure he has one, though the fact that he met Alex regularly – apart from at society meetings – seems important. They appear to have known each other well: both enjoyed a drink, both liked horse racing, though it was Sullivan who did the gambling rather than Alex. Hector says the three of them used to meet at the Masons Arms most Fridays.'

'Sullivan was a mutual friend then, so why the suspicion?'

Flora joined him at the sink. 'I have a hunch he may have borrowed money from Alex. He seems to have been quite wild in his gambling and, according to Hector, hardly ever won. Perhaps he is funded by his wife, but somehow I doubt it. I've been wondering... what if Alex lent him money – Hector almost confirmed it, but then went vague on me – but if Alex lent him money and then asked for it back when the Mortons started their campaign, but Sullivan couldn't repay...'

'Another of your "what ifs",' he teased. 'But I've got one myself. If Luxton *is* a regular at the Masons Arms, he might have seen the men on a Friday evening and maybe can tell us more. We'll call at the pub on our way home.'

'Thank you, Jack. There's just one more thing...'

Jack stopped stacking plates for a moment, staring at the kitchen tiles and waiting to hear his fate.

'Hector mentioned that Kenneth Buckley had been

cautioned by the police for harassing a woman. Could you ask Ridley about it? I'd like to know more.'

'When don't you?' He gave a sigh but followed it with a kiss. 'I'll ask.'

The Masons Arms was already bustling at six on Thursday evening. They had walked from the bottom of the town – Jack had had trouble finding a place to leave the Austin – and the cheerful buzz of chatter and clinked glasses travelled towards them as they turned into Mount Place. Several musicians passed them carrying heavy instruments and pushed their way through a door with 'Masons Arms' etched on its glass panel. It seemed a live band was due to play later that evening.

Neither of them had ever visited the pub before and, walking along the passageway towards the larger room at the rear – the front snug was ignored – Flora took time to look around. It was an old building, constructed around two hundred years earlier and situated within an arrow's shot of the Norman castle. And as with any old building, it had its quirks. The larger saloon was panelled in wood, as though the pub had shaken hands with a stately home, but a Victorian cast-iron fireplace, this evening sporting a modest fire despite the time of year, suggested the industrial heritage of the town. At the polished wood counter, the barman was already busy, his customers three deep.

When the crowd had dissipated somewhat, Jack walked up to the bar, Flora a few steps behind, and waited while the man pulled his umpteenth pint.

'I'm looking for a chap called Ferdie Luxton,' he began, when the last customer had been served. 'I wonder... do you ever see him here?'

The barman's smile spread across his face until it appeared

to take up every inch. 'You could say that,' he agreed. 'Every so often – like every night. Now, what can I get you and your lady to drink?'

'A shandy,' Flora decided instantly.

'And a half pint for me, please.'

The man began to fill the half pint glass. 'Over there,' he said, nodding his head in the direction of a table that had tucked itself away so securely it had become almost part of the panelling.

Jack looked puzzled.

'Ferdie Luxton. You wanted him. He's over there.'

'Oh, thank you.' Taking a drink in each hand, he followed Flora who was already shimmying between tables and chairs to reach the wooden settle at the back of the saloon. Ferdie, his cheeks tinged an unhealthy red, sat staring into space, one hand clutching a pint glass and the other a copy of the local newspaper.

'Mr Luxton?' Flora asked.

The man looked up, slightly startled. 'Yes?'

'May we join you?' She gave him her best smile, Jack saw.

Ferdie looked around the saloon. It was busy but there were plenty of spare seats to be had.

'My name is Carrington,' Jack said quickly. 'I work at Cleve College, and this is my wife, Flora. We're friends of Hector Lansdale.'

'Oh, right.' Ferdie shifted a little along the settle which Jack took as an invitation to sit themselves down.

'You must know Hector,' Flora said, coming straight to the point. 'Alex Vicary, too.'

Luxton frowned. 'That was a bad business.' He took a large gulp of his beer, allowing the newspaper to drop to the wooden floor.

'It was,' she agreed. 'We were at the rehearsal and saw what happened. You were fighting as a royalist that day, I think.'

'True enough.' He took another large gulp from his glass.

'Do you get to choose the roles you play?'

'Some folks are awkward. They have to be this or that. Myself, I don't care. Royalist, rebel, it's all one. Just a bit of fun.'

'Not fun for Alex,' she remarked. 'Not that day. It was a terrible accident. *Are* there many accidents?'

Luxton thought for a while. 'No,' he said at last. He was obviously a man who favoured the monosyllable.

'But there have been others?' she pressed.

Ferdie chewed on a pair of false teeth that looked decidedly unsafe. 'There was that one with Ken,' he decided finally.

'Kenneth Buckley? We heard he'd had an accident at some time.' Had Sally mentioned it? She wasn't sure, but this was a way of learning more. 'What actually happened?'

'Head came off of his mace, didn't it?'

'My goodness, that must have been dangerous.'

'Got a bump on his head.' He chuckled. 'A big bump. And a broken finger.'

'Is that why Buckley doesn't fight any more?' Jack put in.

Ferdie gave another chuckle, deeper this time. 'Said he wouldn't, not while Vicary was the armourer. Didn't trust him, you see. But Alex was OK. Buckley's a bit of a weed. Solicitor,' he said, as though that explained Kenneth's weediness.

'The two of them quarrelled.' Jack remembered he had beer to drink and took a sip.

'Yeah. They were always having a go at each other. Not sure if it was the mace that was the problem or the girl.'

'The girl being Diane Croft,' Flora suggested.

'That's her. Have you met her? Pretty little thing.' He chewed on his teeth again. 'You know a lot about the Knights,' he said, suspicion beginning to colour his voice.

'Only what we've been told.' She spoke soothingly. 'Hector speaks warmly of the society and its members. He used to come here with Alex, I believe, and Bruce Sullivan, as well. You must have seen them occasionally.'

'Saw 'em, but didn't get involved. Just youngsters, you know.'

Jack exchanged a quick glance with Flora and saw her disappointment. If Ferdie spent his evenings alone on this settle, it put paid to any hope that he'd know what might have passed between the trio.

'Pubs are good for everyone, aren't they?' Flora said brightly, pushing her shandy to one side. 'A place to relax. Hector must have enjoyed his evenings here – his life is pretty busy. He's a chef at the Priory Hotel, you know, working with Alice Jenner. Perhaps you remember her from your time in Abbeymead?'

Jack allowed himself a small smile. Flora had tacked successfully and was now sailing in a different direction, though Luxton didn't vouchsafe an answer.

'You ran the pub there, the Cross Keys, for some years, Alice said.' Ferdie was firmly in Flora's sights – he was already looking uncomfortable – and though he didn't know it yet, she wouldn't be giving up. 'According to her, it didn't end well.'

Jack held his breath. This was where, if he was going to, Luxton would stand up and walk out.

'Old busybody, she is. Don't take no notice of her. I ran this pub fine, didn't I? Built it up. Made it the most popular in town.'

'You did, and it's still very popular, I can see. Alice was remembering the old days but I don't suppose many others do.'

Luxton's shoulders lost their stiffness slightly.

'It were a long time ago and it's all done and dusted,' he said with satisfaction. 'A load of old lies, in any case. Someone was out to get me, trying to ruin me, but they didn't succeed. I got through it and made good.'

'Who would want to hurt you?'

'I got my ideas,' he said darkly, 'but it's water under the bridge. It's been over for years. I sorted it.'

'I suppose it's how you sorted it that might prove a problem one day.'

He looked shifty. 'What d'you mean by that? Why come in here raking up stories that aren't true?'

'It's just a thought, Mr Luxton. We wondered if Alex might have heard something about your time at the Cross Keys – you know how gossip sticks around – and threatened to mention it. To the wrong person perhaps? It wouldn't have been nice if you were forced to revisit such a bad time in your life. I can understand if it made you angry.'

'I don't know what you're talking about. There's nothing to know and no one threatened me,' Ferdie said angrily, 'and I'll thank you to finish your drinks and go.'

They finished their drinks and went. 'What was all that about Luxton's past?' Jack asked, when they were walking down the hill to collect the Austin.

At first, he'd been puzzled by Flora's line of questioning, then realised she must have learnt something she thought useful, at one of her Friday suppers perhaps, and forgotten to mention it to him. He was unsure how useful, though. It seemed to him that Flora's questions had achieved nothing but to anger Luxton and put him on his guard.

'What would it matter if Alex knew something of Luxton's history?'

'There was talk in the village that Ferdie lost his licence when he ran the Cross Keys and only narrowly escaped going to prison. Alice reckons that he must have lied to the brewery to have been given the Lewes pub. I wondered if Alex might have heard the gossip, discovered it was true, and used the information to get the money he needed for his fight against the Mortons. If Ferdie couldn't pay... and he doesn't look as if he could.'

'That's quite an accusation. What you're suggesting is blackmail.' Jack was silent for some minutes before he said, 'Why would Alex have done that anyway? He had money of his own. He had savings, his mother said – you've been speculating that he lent some of it to Bruce Sullivan.'

She pursed her lips. 'But did he have enough to fight a court case? I don't think so. He told Susan that he would get all the money they needed to stay in their home, but how he'd do that he refused to say. What if he meant to use what he knew about Luxton, and was ashamed to tell her?'

'That doesn't sound like the man Hector was so fond of.'

'No, it doesn't.' The creases in Flora's forehead deepened. 'That's the problem. But what is certain is that the Vicarys were threatened with eviction and needed money to prevent it. If Alex *had* lent to Sullivan – I know we don't know for sure – but if he had, and Sullivan couldn't pay him back, he might have been desperate enough to try tapping Luxton for the money. Might have suggested to Ferdie that he'd keep damaging information to himself in exchange for cash.'

'If Alex knew something, so did other people,' Jack argued. 'Alice, for instance.'

'She knew of a *rumour* and that would be true of other villagers. It was only hearsay. But if Alex discovered it was true – maybe found the actual proof that Luxton really was stripped of his licence and fined heavily – it could spell danger for Ferdie.'

'Except that he no longer works for the brewery. They can't sack him.'

'He's no longer employed by them but they pay him a pension, I'm sure, and they might take a very dim view of the tale, particularly if Luxton lied to them about his past to get the job – and that seems likely. You heard what he said. *He sorted it.* How else could he have "sorted" what was a criminal conviction other than to lie about having one? If he's being paid a pension under false pretences...'

'That's quite a thought. But I still can't believe that Alex would have behaved so underhandedly, not if he was the chap Hector believed him to be.'

'If you're desperate, Jack... you know the mantra Alan Ridley always spouts. And it was you who suggested it was money rather than love that was behind Alex's death.'

'You're right. I did. I'll bow out right now.'

'Gracefully?'

'Always gracefully!'

13

As soon as Flora left for the All's Well the following morning, Jack rang Brighton police station, though he wasn't at all sure he should. The post-mortem had been clear. Alex Vicary's death had been an accident, and to appear to be digging for evidence of foul play – more than 'appear', Jack thought wryly – was impolite at best. He respected Alan Ridley's judgement. In the past, the inspector had occasionally been wrong, but only occasionally. For the most part, he'd been clear-headed and an excellent policeman. And Jack couldn't forget the number of times Ridley had rescued them from a predicament entirely their fault. But there were questions, he admitted, and Flora, he knew, would continue to ask them even if he didn't.

And who knows, she might be right. Since Alex Vicary's death, they'd become aware of people who had strong motives to be rid of him. A fair number of them, in fact. Either love or money, they'd decided, was behind the murder and after last night's conversation, they could add revenge. Kenneth Buckley held Alex accountable for a faulty mace that had wounded him badly, and from what Jack had learned of Buckley, it would be the embarrassment, the pricking of his vanity, that the man would feel as the greater damage.

Nearly every one of their suspects had secrets, secrets they would fight hard to prevent being revealed. If Hector were right, Buckley's past was chequered, a police caution on the books for his harassment of women – what would that do to a solicitor's business if it was widely known? Though not a secret as such, Diane Croft had been suffering just that kind of harassment and been desperate to free herself of the two men making her life miserable. Ferdie Luxton's criminal record had so far stayed hidden but, if it became widely known, could well affect his brewery pension. And Bruce Sullivan, possibly borrowing money for gambling – hardly fitting conduct for a teacher. Jack wasn't sure how the education authorities would view Bruce's gambling, but it could well be grounds for dismissal. Had Alex known about any or all of this, had one of these secrets been the way he hoped to get sufficient money to protect the home his mother loved? And continue his pursuit of Diane?

Walking from the kitchen into the cottage's small square of a hall, Jack lifted the receiver to call the Brighton station, and was lucky to raise the inspector at his first attempt.

'Alan,' he began cautiously, after small talk on the weather, 'I was hoping' – it was better to name himself than Flora – 'you might know if the police hold anything official on a solicitor called Kenneth Buckley. He has offices in Lewes.'

'Not thinking of getting divorced already, old chap?'

'No, most definitely not. He – Buckley – has come into my life recently and I'm curious.'

In his ears, it sounded incredibly feeble. To the inspector's ears, too, it seemed.

'This bloke came into your life? And you're curious? Pull the other one, Jack... what are you up to?'

Jack thought rapidly. Ridley's tone warned him from confessing his real intention. 'The man has been hanging around Flora's bookshop and I'd like to know more.' That surely would do, he congratulated himself.

'Really? See, we are talking divorce, after all!'

'It's not Flora he's interested in, at least I hope not. It's her assistant. The man's becoming something of a pest. I wondered...'

'Give me an hour and I'll see what I can dig up.'

'Thanks, Alan. Anything that might deter him would be helpful.'

It was less than an hour later that the phone rang.

'Your friend has form,' the inspector announced jovially. 'A litany of complaints from a lady in Brighton, who'll remain anonymous. Kenneth Buckley was harassing her: unwanted phone calls, constant rings on the front door, a torrent of letters through the mail.'

'Buckley was a solicitor at the time?'

'Oh yes, the woman was a client, in fact. We warned him off and advised her to change solicitors.'

'But no further action was taken?'

'What else could we do? It was all pretty vague, the letters were unsigned, the phone calls untraceable. It was one person's word against another.'

And he was a solicitor, Jack factored in silently. The police would tread extremely carefully.

'Then, according to the paperwork, Buckley came back with a complaint of his own.'

'Against the woman?'

'No, against Alex Vicary.' The name acquired a grim emphasis. 'I wondered when Mr Vicary would appear in the conversation.'

'What was the complaint?' he asked as casually as he could, knowing the inspector had found him out.

'Buckley joined the Knights of Mercia – but you'll know that' – the grim intonation was back – 'and came a cropper on his first outing on the battlefield. The end of the mace he was flinging around worked loose and struck him on the hand and the side of the head. He was lucky there wasn't more damage. Vicary was the society's armourer, but you'll know that, too. He was the one who'd produced the mace.'

Jack ignored the comment. 'Buckley was battered, you say, but otherwise unharmed?'

'It seems so. I reckon humiliation was his greatest hurt.' That was very much what Jack had assumed. Embarrassment was a powerful emotion, particularly for a man like Buckley. 'He must have looked a bit of a twerp and if he's one for the ladies... not a great way to impress.'

'What happened to the complaint?'

'We filed it,' Ridley said laconically. 'Not much else we could do. It was clearly an accident. Re-enactments are a dangerous business, Jack.'

'So it seems.'

If Buckley had been the one to push Alex from that wall, he might simply have wanted to make the young man look stupid rather than any desire to eliminate a love rival. A vow to get even on the embarrassment stakes, perhaps, that had consequences he couldn't have foreseen.

'And the Mortons? What's happening on that front? I'm hoping Lansdale has kept away from Newhaven.'

'Whatever you or Mrs Carrington said to him seems to have done the trick. I've heard nothing more from that quarter but, after the nephew made the complaint, I had another look at the Mortons' business. It's supposedly a letting agency but for some years we've suspected Larry Morton of running a sideline, acting as a fence for stolen goods. So far, we've been unable to prove it and without at least some evidence we've no excuse to go rummaging. But when I went back some way into the paperwork, I unearthed something else. A number of historic complaints from tenants over unfair treatment – sudden rent rises, overt bullying, that kind of thing. Nothing in the last few years, however. It seems to have stopped until the Vicarys had trouble. Maybe Morton was trying to keep his nose clean, protect his under-the-counter business, and didn't want us poking around.'

'He no longer feels the need to protect himself?'

'Maybe he's prepared to risk it – if he wants the Vicary house badly. But I'll get Sergeant Norris to call at the Mortons' business premises tomorrow and remind uncle and nephew that Mrs Vicary is protected until her lease runs out. He can have a sniff around while he's there. And I'll get the finance chaps to look into the letting agency a little more thoroughly. The complaints we have on file should give us cover. You never know, the boffins might pick up something new.'

'Thanks again, Alan. You're a pal.'

'You're welcome, my friend. Just remember that young Vicary's death was an accident. The pathologist was quite certain, and raking up an investigation which is going nowhere does nobody any good.'

'I'll remember,' he promised.

Flora's memory, though, would be another matter.

Flora was hungry. She'd had a busy morning – Fridays, when she once more took charge of the bookshop, was a time to tick off the 'to-do's on a list she'd been compiling while in Lewes – but about to unwrap the unappetizing luncheon meat sandwich she'd brought from home, she was surprised to get a telephone call from Sally Jenner.

'Sorry this is such short notice,' Sally began, 'but the meal this evening—'

Flora put a hand to her mouth. 'I'm sorry, too,' she burst out.

'I'd completely forgotten. It's this constant travelling between houses. Who's cooking? It's not me, is it?'

'Relax!' Sally laughed. 'No one is cooking and it's good you've forgotten – I'm afraid it's another cancellation. There won't be a meal tonight.'

'Alice isn't ill, is she?' was Flora's instinctive response.

She felt a moment of panic. The fact that Alice was rarely unwell could be misleading – her dear friend, she should remember, wasn't getting any younger. The thought of her much-loved aunt was never far from Flora's mind and Violet's sudden onset of illness and swift decline had the power to haunt her niece all these years later.

'Alice is fine, but the Priory is offering a gala dinner this evening. I wasn't sure it would go ahead, but it turns out that we're fully booked! Today's is a try-out but if the dinner is successful, I hope to make it a regular event on a Friday or Saturday evening. Twelve courses, Flora! And with specialist wines to accompany. Auntie has been run off her feet for the last few days.'

'She must have been, but have you managed to get extra help?'

'It's been difficult,' Sally admitted. 'I've hired additional waiters, that's not been a problem, but only one of the cooks the agency offered me was at all suitable. And Hector is off work today, so really the hired man just replaces him.'

'Is it Hector that's not well?'

'I don't know what ails him. He doesn't confide in me.' Sally's voice tightened. 'But it's Alex's funeral tomorrow and really, I couldn't risk a disaster this evening with Hector not knowing which way up a casserole dish goes.'

'I *hadn't* forgotten the funeral was tomorrow.'

'Tomorrow morning. I've decided not to go. I wasn't a particular friend and there's bound to be a large contingent from the Knights to show support. Hector is being picked up by

Ferdie Luxton – Auntie must have mentioned it – and they're taking Mrs Vicary with them. Anyway, sorry about this evening being cancelled but if it's any comfort, I don't think Kate would have made it either. Apparently, Sarah has colic.'

After Sally's phone call, Flora had felt concerned for Alice and still felt it when she woke the next morning. Taking on sole responsibility for producing what would need to be a brilliant twelve course meal – customers would expect nothing less, having paid an exorbitant price – was a huge undertaking, even for a younger cook with a fully staffed kitchen. She hoped Sally realised the likely strain on her aunt.

But it was Alice, bustling along the pavement, a basket in each hand, that Flora spied as she cycled along the high street that morning, ready to open the All's Well at nine o'clock.

She pulled into the kerb to arrive beside her friend. 'How are you?' was her immediate question.

Alice slewed round. 'Better for seein' you, my love. I dunno where this week's gone but gone it has and I haven't seen hide nor hair of you or that lovely husband of yours.'

'You've been hugely busy, I hear. Sally rang yesterday and told me of the gala dinner.'

Alice dropped her baskets and propped herself against the vegetable stall that spread across half the pavement, while Mr Houseman buzzed around her, cheerfully arranging a new batch of cabbages.

'That was some evenin'!' she said.

'And?' Flora waited anxiously.

'It went fine, my love. Nothin' to worry about – though I did have a few collywobbles yesterday mornin', what with Hector off and a chef to work with I'd never seen before. But the lad did well.'

The lad, Flora imagined, could be anything up to fifty years old.

'And Sally is pleased?'

'Can't stop smilin'. And I'm pleased for her. It's puttin' the Priory well and truly on the map.'

'How many gala dinners is she planning?'

'One every few months, I think she said. Not too many – she wants to keep it exclusive. And that suits me. By then, Hector may have sorted himself out and be back on song.'

'I hear he's at the funeral today.'

Alice nodded. 'That's why I'm doin' the extra shoppin' the kitchen needs. Ferdie Luxton came over early and picked the boy up. *He* didn't look too grand, I must say. But there, it's a funeral.' She paused. 'The Crofts came to the meal last night, you know.'

'Diane's parents?'

'That's right. And they brought her with them. It was a special birthday for Mrs Croft. Did you know they've sold their house in Kingston and they're ready to up and leave for Edinburgh? The dinner was likely a double celebration.'

'Diane will be at the funeral today, I suppose.' Flora couldn't see how the girl could refuse, though it would be a painful experience for her.

'She's goin' all right. I had it from her ma. Mrs Croft's that worried about her daughter. Came into the kitchen, she did. She's a keen cook, too, and she loved the meal, so since Sally's a friend of Diane's she arsked me if I minded Mrs C comin' to look the kitchen over. Course I didn't. You know me, any excuse to talk food!'

'But she's worried?' Flora prompted.

'About her girl, yes. Has nightmares, she says, most every night. And with this funeral today... well, she's dreadin' the outcome. Still, at least, the girl's finished with some smarmy boyfriend she had who was botherin' her. Mrs Croft was pleased about that.'

That was almost certainly Kenneth Buckley. Now he was on the prowl again, could Rose Lawson look forward to more visits from her friendly solicitor? And Diane – those nightmares. Evidence of guilt? Flora wondered.

'I'd best get on,' she said aloud. 'But you must come over for tea tomorrow. Kate, too, if Sarah is more settled. We'll make up for missing last night.'

Alice looked doubtful. 'What about Jack?'

'Jack can go for a long walk and join us for the cake!' she promised.

14

The long walk never materialised. Jack had happily donned jacket and fedora – a stroll through the woods, he'd decided, would help decide the plot he'd finally go with – when Alice arrived at the cottage well in advance of teatime.

'I had to come as soon as I could,' she panted. 'Had to let you know. Such a to-do at the Priory this morning. And thank goodness we're closin' the dining room tonight – Hector is beside himself and I'm takin' the rest of the day off. I'm fair worn out.'

It was Jack who'd answered the door but Flora, poised on the landing, had heard Alice's breathless arrival and come rushing down the stairs.

'What's happened, Alice? Are you OK? Has something happened to Hector?'

'Not Hector, lass... I must sit down,' she wheezed. 'I've fair scooted up that lane.'

Flora took hold of her hand. The idea of Alice scooting anywhere was comical, but her friend's normally ruddy cheeks had turned ashy and she was quick to lead her into the sitting room. Ditching his jacket and hat, Jack followed, but only after dashing into the kitchen for a glass of water.

Once Alice had taken a few sips, she was ready to unburden herself. 'It was the funeral yesterday,' she said. 'Well, really, after the funeral. Ferdie Luxton was driving...'

Flora nodded. Alice had told her the same thing yesterday.

'And he had Mrs Vicary in the car. Hector insisted they took her home first. Poor lady, she'd been so upset during the service. Inconsolable she was, Hector said. He'd told Ferdie to drive to Newhaven and he'd make her a cup of tea and stay with her a while. Then find his own way back to Abbeymead.'

'So, what happened?' Flora had wriggled to the edge of her seat.

'It was when they went in, you see.'

'In the house?' she asked.

Alice nodded, taking another large gulp of water. 'Ferdie had gone by then, of course. There was just the two of them, but immediately they went through the front door, Hector knew somethin' bad had happened.' Alice paused and looked from one to the other. 'You wouldn't believe the mess, he said. The house was in chaos. Chaos! Food, paper, clothes, strewn everywhere. Drawers open, a cupboard door nearly off its hinges, some china broken.'

'A break-in,' Jack said. 'What was stolen?'

'That's the thing.' Alice lowered her voice. 'It's what makes it so creepy. I mean, what kind of lowlife breaks into a house when they know a grievin' mother is buryin' her son – and all for nothin'?'

'What!' they exclaimed in unison.

'Nothin',' she repeated. 'Hector stayed a few hours. Helped put stuff away, mended the cupboard door, brushed the tiles and the carpet clean. Bless the lad, he did his best to look after the poor woman. But when he asked her what had been taken –

he assumed it was a burglary – she said she couldn't see what.
Nothin' had gone.'

'How odd.' Flora wrinkled her forehead.

'Creepy,' Alice repeated. 'Hector phoned the police straight
away, before he cleared up. He wanted them to see the mess for
themselves, but they didn't have anyone they could send, they
said, and asked him to make a list of the missing items. Except
there weren't any.'

'And Mrs Vicary has stayed in the house?' Jack asked. His
mind, Flora thought, had fixed on the likely perpetrator. The
attack had the marks of the Morton duo all over it.

'Where else can she go? Hector said he would have stayed
but Susan Vicary was adamant he should go. He'd put the place
back to rights, she said, and she'd be OK.'

'And what does Hector think?' Flora had a fairly good idea
and was worried he might once more take the law into his own
hands and land in trouble again.

'He reckons it's them Mortons to blame. Trying to frighten
Susan. He was all for goin' to confront them right then, but she
managed to talk him out of it and when he told me this mornin'
what had happened, I added my voice. It's up to the police, I
said. They need to get movin'. It's not the first time the Vicarys
have been targeted by them no-goods, after all. And what's that
inspector doin' about it, Jack?'

Jack was taken unaware. 'He sent his sergeant to speak to
the Mortons, I believe. To warn them off.'

'Fat lot of good that's done.' Alice huffed. 'They need
lockin' up.'

'They do,' Flora agreed wholeheartedly. 'They're thugs,
pure and simple, both of them. They need to be behind bars.'
She stared at Jack, willing him to remember his own skirmish,
one that could have been deadly, but kept her silence –
supplying more ammunition against the Mortons, that Alice
might pass on to Hector, was unlikely to help.

'How about tea?' Jack asked hopefully, keen to move on. 'I'll put the kettle on before I make for the woods. There's a nice angel cake – Flora baked it this morning.'

Alice smiled for the first time since arriving.

'It's just you and me,' Flora told her friend. 'Kate phoned earlier to say that Sarah is still quite poorly and she's reluctant to leave her.'

'No matter. Tea for two sounds champion.'

And it was. For an hour or so, they put aside the difficulties Mrs Vicary was facing to catch up with what had been happening in both their worlds this last week. Now that Alice had got the shocking news off her chest, she was in expansive mood. Harry Barnes, apparently, had been spotted several evenings in the Cross Keys as well as most lunchtimes at the golf club – it seemed that Evelyn's convalescence was proving more wearing than even he'd imagined. The fish and chip shop, Alice reported, was thinking of opening another business, actually next door, in the premises vacated by Colin Palmer's land agency.

'Since he went bankrupt, I've been waiting to see what would happen to those offices,' Alice said, with a look that made Flora fear the worst. 'And now I know.'

'Another fish and chip shop?' Could the village support a second chippy? Flora wondered. As well as the mobile van that visited every week?

'No! A Chinese restaurant!' Alice announced dramatically. 'I ask you! Brighton, I could understand, but Chinese food in Abbeymead! I'll not be happy having that on my doorstep, I can tell you.' Flora made commiserating noises.

'And Mrs Waterford... you know how her arthritis has played up for years?' Alice was in full stream now and didn't wait for an answer. 'She's found this new cream, or rather her niece has. Sent it over from America. Brilliant stuff, it's been – worked a miracle. I might ask her if she could get me a pot.'

'You're suffering from arthritis now?'

'Well, no,' Alice admitted. 'Not at the moment. But it's good to be prepared.'

Flora wasn't sure if the cream balanced out the Chinese restaurant, but her old friend had regained a sunny smile so perhaps it did.

'I know the dining room is closed tonight, but do you have to go back to the Priory today?' she asked, hoping to stem the flow.

Alice beamed. 'Not on your life. Hector's been in charge of the kitchen. It's just lunch today and occasional snacks – no fancy cookin', but he'll have had the team to manage and that will have done him good. Given him something else to think about.'

'How do you think he's got on?' Flora asked tentatively. 'He's not been exactly...'

'I was worried, but he turned up this morning, on time as well. A bit of a miracle, that.' Alice leaned forward to drop her empty plate onto the tray. 'Perhaps the shock he had yesterday, comin' after the funeral, too, jolted him out of his misery. For a while, at least.'

They were silent for a moment, while Flora finished her tea and offered her guest another cup. Alice shook her head. 'No thanks, my love. I'd best be goin' in a minute. I'm plannin' an early night. That dinner fair wore me out,' she confided, 'and I'm still sufferin' a bit. But I'm glad we did it. Sally's had phone calls all weekend, she told me, congratulating the Priory, saying what a good evening people had. And a reporter from the *Worthing Echo* wants to do a feature. He rang to ask if the paper could cover the next gala dinner!'

'It's sounding good, but you'll need a few weeks to recover from this one!'

'I'll get my breath back in no time, lovey. Don't you worry. And the next dinner will be even better!'

It was as they were washing up that evening that Inspector Ridley called.

'I hear there's been more trouble at the Vicarys' place,' he said without preamble.

'More than trouble, I'd say.' Jack slumped down into the hall chair. 'Someone turned the house over while Mrs Vicary was at her son's funeral.'

'Bad, very bad. I sent Norris over a few days ago to speak to the Mortons. Give them a gentle warning. Though maybe not so gentle.'

'It doesn't seem to have worked.'

'You reckon this was their work?' Did the inspector have doubts? he wondered.

'Who else? It has their fingerprints all over it. General mayhem along with plenty of fear, but nothing stolen that could be traced back to them.'

'Hmm. It's a difficult one. I've a team down there now, trying to unearth some evidence, but we'll be lucky if we find fingerprints we can use. The Mortons are past masters at this kind of thing and I doubt they've left any.'

'Is there nothing more you can do to protect Mrs Vicary?' Jack felt despairing.

'From now on, the local bobby will be pounding her street pretty regularly, but other than that, no. Still, my finance colleagues are having a field day with Morton's business records – I may have news on that very soon.'

'The sooner, the better. Susan Vicary has more than enough to cope with. But thanks for letting me know.'

'Keep in touch, Jack. And watch that lad, Lansdale. I don't want him muddying the waters.'

When he walked back into the kitchen, he found Flora

looking thoughtful, having, it seemed, washed the same plate several times over.

He dropped a kiss on the nape of her neck. 'A penny for them.'

'Were the Mortons responsible, do you think?'

'It seems obvious.'

'That's what I mean. Maybe too obvious. You mentioned Sergeant Norris would be paying them a visit.'

'He did, and issued them a warning.'

'But they still went ahead.' The plate was finally slotted into the draining rack.

'A riposte to the police? You can warn us, but we don't care?'

Flora took up a second plate, dipping it lazily in and out of the washing bowl. 'Maybe, but Larry Morton is a businessman, isn't he? A crooked one, I agree, but still a businessman. His main aim has to be protecting his businesses, including the illegal sideline that the inspector reckons he's running. The last thing he'd want is the police breathing down his neck, and now, that's just what he's got.'

Jack nodded. 'Ridley has sent a forensic team to the Vicarys' house and the local bobby will be keeping an eye out on a daily basis.'

'So, close surveillance of a property Morton is intent on repossessing.'

Jack grabbed a tea towel and began drying the few plates Flora had washed.

'I take your point but if the Mortons aren't responsible, it has to have been a burglary and, if so, why was nothing taken? Because there was nothing of value in the house? It's not a rich home, true, but I can't believe a thief would go to the bother of breaking in and then find nothing he or she could sell.'

'It wasn't a regular burglary,' Flora said decidedly. 'It can't have been. And if the break-in wasn't designed to intimidate –

that would be the Mortons – the only other reason must be that someone was looking for something.'

'Someone? Something? The whole house turned upside down.'

'What if the intruder knew what they wanted but hadn't a clue where it would be? That would necessitate the whole building being searched. And think of the way it was searched – chaos, Alice said. That's not usually the method a professional burglar or even an amateur one would go for. It's too much of a muddle, too time-consuming. A regular burglar would want to get in and out as swiftly as possible, and that means being methodical. This search appears to have been frantic.'

'Frantic or not, Mrs Vicary swears that nothing is missing.'

'Is that because Susan doesn't know?' Flora emptied the bowl of water with a loud sloosh, a small note of triumph in her voice. 'Because she doesn't know there's an item in her house that someone wants very badly. And maybe a someone who isn't a million miles away. The break-in occurred on a day when the burglar must have been aware the house was empty – he or she knew of Alex's death and knew of the funeral.'

'We can discount Ferdie Luxton then. He knew of the funeral, for sure, but he was actually there and ferrying other mourners.'

'He could have had an accomplice.'

'Do you really believe that?'

'We're keeping an open mind. And he has a criminal record. So does Buckley, of course, and I wonder who else?'

'Are we assuming that Alex had something in his possession he thought valuable but never mentioned to his mother?'

'And was going to use for their benefit? Yes, I think so. He had a secret, he said so himself. A secret he could use to gain money. Something he knew could hurt if he broadcast it. I've been thinking it was gossip, rumour, a snippet of information with which he could threaten, if he had to. But what if he had actual physical evidence of whatever wrongdoing he'd discovered? And whoever broke into the Vicarys' house knew of its existence and was determined to get it back.'

'I wonder if they did? Get it back, I mean.'

'We can't know for sure, but judging by Alice's description of the house, the havoc they left behind, I reckon they didn't succeed.'

'So... lovely wife, where do we go from here? Watch and wait, I guess, for their next step. There's bound to be one.'

'I don't think I can wait. Mrs Vicary is in trouble and it's *us* who should be the ones taking the next step.' She twisted round to face him. 'We should talk to Diane again, *and* Kenneth Buckley. And when I'm back in school next week, I'll tackle Bruce Sullivan. I got nowhere with him last time but I'm determined he'll talk to me – about the rehearsal, about Alex, about his gambling.'

'You're still thinking he owed Alex money?'

'I can't be certain, but it's something we should find out, and find out if he ever repaid it. It might take us a little closer to the truth. He brushed me off when I asked questions before, rudely, too, but I won't let him do it again. This time, I'll be a whole lot tougher.'

Jack gave a shout of laughter, holding his arms wide and scooping her into them. 'Poor Bruce Sullivan! I almost feel sorry for him.'

15

That night the weather misbehaved badly, the gales that beat up the English Channel so fierce they travelled many miles inland. April was going out like the proverbial lion. On Monday morning, with the storm still raging, Flora left Betty tucked in her shelter and walked to the bookshop, or tottered more like, she thought, laughing at herself. She could barely keep upright and would certainly not have trusted herself to stay in the saddle.

It proved to be a lonely day at the All's Well. Few customers ventured out to buy and when, at lunchtime, she was blown along the high street to the Nook – one of Kate's mushroom pies seemed a good choice – there was no sign of her friend or the baby.

Tony was behind the counter of an almost empty café, looking haggard and with spectacular bags beneath his eyes. He appeared to have aged several years since Flora last saw him.

'Kate's at the doctor's,' he said wearily. 'Again. To tell the truth, we're a tiny bit worried – we thought the colic would have eased by now but all last week we've been back and forth to the surgery.'

'And Sarah seems no better?'

'One or two nights she's slept reasonably well, but one o'clock this morning she woke up crying again, her little fists clenched, her knees pulled up to her tummy. We've gone through bottles of gripe water.'

'What does the doctor say?'

'That it will pass. We must keep her wrapped and warm, cuddle her, wind her, take her for a walk, and then... just wait.'

'That's tough and I'm so sorry.' Flora thought rapidly, the week ahead reviewed in seconds. 'Would it help if I forgot about going to Lewes this week and worked here for a few days? I'm sure the school would understand if I phoned them today.'

'You're a good friend, Flora.' Tony gave a weak smile. 'But no need for you to worry. I've managed to rustle up some extra help. Ivy is coming in this afternoon and has promised to work the rest of the week.'

'Perhaps next weekend then? I could look after Sarah and let you both get some sleep,' she suggested as a last resort, wanting very much to help but feeling inadequate.

Tony had a kind look on his face. 'It's a lovely offer but Kate is glued to the baby.' And you wouldn't have a clue, Flora translated. 'No, you go off to Lewes and, by the time you're back, things will have sorted themselves out and Sarah will be as right as ninepence.'

Flora, however, didn't go off to Lewes the following day. Halfway through the night, a tremendous crack sounded overhead, causing Jack, who'd been sleeping lightly, to sit bolt upright in bed. Very groggily, Flora followed suit.

'What?' she asked, staring owlishly at the bedside clock.

'The roof – I'd best go and look.'

'In this weather?' Driving rain had now joined the ferocious winds. 'You'll be washed away.'

'Hopefully, not. I'd better check – it sounded bad.'

Flora stumbled downstairs in his wake, holding the front door open for him, as firmly as she could. Jack, his figure hunched into an old Crombie overcoat, battled his way into the garden, torch in hand.

Within minutes, he'd tumbled back into the hall.

'Bad news,' he announced, shaking the rain from a head of very wet hair. 'It's the chimney. A couple of the bricks have been dislodged and are lying loose on the front grass. We'll have to watch for a leak in the sitting room.'

Flora had visions of her sitting room floating out of sight. The storm had reached biblical proportions. 'It will need mending straight away,' she said decidedly.

'We can't do anything until the morning.' He looked at the kitchen clock showing just four o'clock. 'A bowl in the fireplace should catch any water, as long as it doesn't arrive too fast, but tomorrow...'

'I'll telephone Michael. He might be able to help.'

'But is he a roofer?'

'He's an everything man. And if he can borrow a ladder long enough, he'll fix the bricks, I'm sure.'

'Someone needs to be here and I have a workshop in the morning.' Jack ran a hand through an already tangled flop of hair.

'You go to Cleve and I'll stay home. I'll ring the school first thing – my first class isn't until after morning break.' There was a guilty delight that she was almost pleased to have a faulty chimney. Even with her time in school, her days in Lewes could seem long.

Michael, when she phoned a few hours later, had jobs already booked for that day but, as soon as he heard it was an emergency, he set about postponing them and made a call on a friend of a friend who he was certain had a ladder long enough to reach the roof. He'd have those bricks back in place by the afternoon, he promised. Fortunately for them both, the wind had abated somewhat and, for the moment, the rain clouds had disappeared.

She would do her accounts, she decided, as she waved Jack goodbye, do them while she waited for Michael to appear. This last weekend, her Saturday morning had been too busy for her to make up her records as she usually did and, fearing she might fall too far behind, she set off for the All's Well to collect her paperwork soon after breakfast. The wind was blowing more lightly now and she could take Betty with her. The bicycle might not like battling along the lane – she certainly wouldn't – but it didn't do her good to be stationary for too long.

Rose looked up from the desk as the shop bell clanged, an expression on her face that puzzled Flora. Was it relief? A figure moved from behind one of the bookshelves as Flora walked towards the front table. Kenneth Buckley, she was sure!

'Mr Buckley?' she asked brightly.

'It is.' He looked taken aback. 'And you are...'

'How nice to meet you, but what brings you here – in this weather, and so early?'

Flora had a very good idea what, but was hoping she'd make him feel as uncomfortable as Rose looked. Hector's prophecy appeared to be spot-on. Having failed with Diane, Buckley now seemed intent on attaching Rose Lawson.

'I was in the village,' he said awkwardly. 'Just called in for the odd browse.'

'Really? You don't have sufficient bookshops in Lewes?'

'It's always useful to add to the list. I'm a great reader.'

'That's good to know. And what's the book you've chosen today?'

'Well, actually... not quite got round to that yet.'

'Then I mustn't stop you. Please, browse all you like.'

He shot his cuffs forward and looked hurriedly at his watch.

'Running a bit late today,' he muttered. 'I'd better get moving – but I'll be back.' I bet you will, Flora thought, but not if Rose doesn't welcome your company.

Flashing a smile at them both, he walked purposefully to the door and closed it very carefully behind him.

'It's Tuesday,' her assistant began, 'isn't it?' She seemed bemused.

Flora laughed. 'It is, but I've had to stay home. We've a problem at the cottage, with the chimney. I thought I'd collect the accounts and work through them while I wait for Michael Worthington to bring a ladder.'

'It sounds serious, but I hope he can fix it for you.' Her tone verged on the listless and Flora decided to jump in. It seemed the best way.

'What's happening, Rose? With Mr Buckley?'

The girl's face crumpled slightly. 'You know that he's a solicitor? He's been trying to persuade me – a lot – to renegotiate the divorce settlement with Peter. I think I mentioned it? I was attracted by the idea at first but, since then, I've had second thoughts. I think it will stir up more trouble, employing a solicitor, even if I could afford him, and I'd rather try to speak to my ex-husband myself. It probably won't work, but I really can't cope with more upset.'

'You've told Kenneth Buckley that?'

She nodded. 'I keep telling him, but he's insistent.' She began to tidy the pens and pencils lying on the shop desk, her fingers shaking. 'I feel caught, Flora. As if divorce hasn't been enough to cope with.'

It was clear she was very near to tears. Rose was another woman feeling trapped between two men and, in both cases, one of those men was Kenneth Buckley.

'You need to be strong,' Flora urged her. 'Tell him a definite no. Be rude, if you have to.'

'I've tried, but he doesn't seem to hear me. Or doesn't want to.'

'He's putting you under pressure and he needs to stop. How many times has he called here?' Flora was keen to know how far Buckley would go to get his way.

Rose took a while to answer. 'This last week,' she said at last, 'it's been two or three times. He's driven over from his Lewes office. And it was the same the week before. He brings me small presents, too.' She pointed to an orchid sitting in a pot to one side of the desk. 'And keeps asking me to go for coffee or for lunch. It's difficult to refuse and very awkward to deal with in front of customers.'

'It must be. Would you like me to speak to him? Tell him that you appreciate his interest, but you're finding it intrusive and would rather he keep away?'

'Could you?' The woman's face cleared. 'I'm not sure he'd listen to you any more than he has to me, but another voice might help.'

'As long as Michael replaces my bricks this afternoon, I'll be in Lewes tomorrow and once I've finished at Riverdale, I'll call at his office and have a quiet word.'

Rose managed a slight smile, her dimple beginning to surface. 'Thank you, and good luck!'

'I'd better be getting back for Michael,' Flora murmured. 'Now – where are those dratted accounts?' She bent down to fumble in the bottom drawer of the desk. 'Sometimes, I think they have a mind of their own.'

Michael Worthington was as good as his word and appeared just as Flora was making a lunchtime sandwich.

'This big enough?' He pointed to a ladder that to Flora looked as though it could reach the sky. 'Had to borrow my mate's van as well – my little motor's far too small to transport this monster.'

'Thank you, Michael. I'm grateful. There doesn't seem to be any damage inside the house – at least, not so far – but I wouldn't like to face another storm like this weekend's.'

'A corker, weren't it? But you're lucky – them bricks are intact and will just need mortaring in. I'll have a look at the roof tiles while I'm up there, check the ones nearest the chimney and check the roofing felt is OK. With that wind, there could be damage you can't see from down here.'

'Can I make you a sandwich before you start?'

'No thanks, my ducks. Had a fry-up for breakfast and I'll need to get on.'

Michael was repacking his ladder onto the borrowed van when Jack arrived back from a day at Cleve College.

'Afternoon, Mr Carrington. Your chimney shouldn't give you problems now – unless we get a hurricane next time. No promises then.'

'Thanks for coming so quickly.'

'Got to help the lass out,' Michael said. 'Knowed her from a nipper, and her aunt before her.'

'Thanks again.' Living in a small, rural community had its disadvantages, as Jack had discovered, but there were definitely bright spots.

'You're back!' Flora exclaimed. 'I thought you'd stay at the college tonight – I've just toasted a crumpet for myself.'

'I really couldn't stay in that flat on my own. And you can toast another crumpet.'

'I can, especially as you've saved me a very early start tomorrow and a tiring bus journey. I'm on the timetable to read with Rita Manville's class just after nine.'

She waved a cheerful goodbye to Michael through the window, Jack following her gaze. 'He's done well. The chimney looks as good as new.'

'He's a treasure. But how did your day go?'

Jack shrugged off his coat and followed her back into the kitchen. 'Not that wonderful. I met Florence Summersby.'

'And you don't like her?' Flora tossed another crumpet under the grill.

'It's difficult to say. I found her... a tad abrasive? She's a new broom, of course, and everything Dalloway initiated she wants gone. She's not at all keen on his idea of bringing people like me into the college. Qualified teachers are what she wants, she made that clear, so once my current contract has run its term, that will be that – unless I choose to train as a teacher.'

When Flora looked concerned, he pulled her into a tight hug, a blob of the butter she'd been spreading ending up on her chin.

'Don't worry. I've no intention of doing it. I've enjoyed my time at Cleve, more or less.' He fished a handkerchief from his pocket to wipe her chin clean. 'But I won't be hugely sorry to say goodbye. Keeping the writing going has proved a struggle and I know you've never felt settled at the college.'

Flora considered the truth of this, her head to one side. 'I'm really not that sure. I'm almost used now to having two different lives. I actually missed being in the town today – and I'm looking forward to going back tomorrow.'

Jack's suspicions were aroused. He couldn't remember a time when Flora had truly looked forward to her days in Lewes. 'What are you planning?' he asked, forcing her to look directly into his face.

A pair of hazel eyes looked guilelessly back at him. 'Apart from confronting Sullivan as I promised? Nothing much.'

16

When Flora walked into the staffroom the following day in search of her morning cup of tea, she scanned the gathering of teachers, looking for Bruce Sullivan. He was at the far end of the room, she saw, talking vigorously to a fresh-faced young teacher whom Flora had passed in the corridor but not officially met. The young man had joined the school at the beginning of this half term, and was still a probationer, she'd learned. Why was Sullivan so dogged in talking to him? Perhaps he was the young man's mentor. He appeared to have wedged his junior against the wood panelling and was clearly monopolising his attention.

Intrigued, Flora walked slowly over to the table that held the hot water urn and the tray of teacups, trying hard as she did to eavesdrop on the conversation. Small snatches came to her. The odd word, the odd phrase. 'My boy is sick,' Sullivan was saying.

His boy? Did Sullivan have a son? Flora knew very little of his domestic situation.

'... needs equipment ... expensive stuff.'

The young teacher murmured something that Flora couldn't catch. Commiserations, perhaps?

'I try... we try ... had to sell a few things here and there...'

What on earth was Sullivan talking about? She took her time pouring the tea and even more time selecting a couple of ginger biscuits from the open tin.

'Usually we get by OK ... but in an emergency ... up a gum tree. You know how it is.'

The young man nodded. It seemed he did know how it was.

'That damned machine ... would break down right now, wouldn't it? ... costs the earth to get an engineer in.'

Flora's stomach contracted into a fierce gripe. Was Sullivan hinting he needed money? Surely not. He was married to a wealthy woman, wasn't he, and this lad must be on the lowest rung of the salary scale.

'... if you could manage ... just a loan ... till payday.'

Hardly a hint! She'd heard enough. Sullivan was trying to borrow money! And borrow it from a new recruit who would be struggling for money himself and completely innocent of Sullivan's true situation. Flora felt sick. Is this what the man had done to Alex? Picked on someone he thought would be a soft touch and told a sob story that was wholly untrue? She had speculated on the possibility, but here was proof that it could have happened.

She huddled down into one of the scruffy chairs that populated the staffroom, abandoning all thought of the conversation she'd planned to have. Too shocked, in fact, to string a sentence together. Instead, she thought hard. What were the ramifications of this new piece of evidence? Could it shed new light on Alex's death? For Sullivan to be borrowing from a boy at the very beginning of his career, he must be in deep financial trouble – and his gambling had to be the cause – but where was the wealthy wife Hector had mentioned? Did the woman exist? And if she did, would she talk? It was time to spread their net, Flora decided – once she'd told Jack exactly what she'd heard.

Shocked by Sullivan's venality Flora may have been, but she wasn't too shocked to call on Kenneth Buckley. By three o'clock that afternoon she had recovered her spirits sufficiently to leave school and climb the steep hill that led to the town's high street. She had noticed the solicitor's office a while back on one of her forays around the town, tucked between a specialist cheese shop and an unusually flamboyant men's outfitters.

'Buckley and Moss, Solicitors and Commissioners for Oaths', the brass plate announced and, pushing open the heavy door, she walked into a spacious reception area. Several people were waiting for either Buckley or Moss and, as one, they looked up from the magazines they'd been flicking through to take note of the newcomer. Flora gave them a brief glance before making for the large and ornately carved desk that dominated the room and the young woman sitting behind it.

'Good afternoon.' The woman tweaked her curls behind her ears and looked over owl-like spectacles to give a businesslike smile. 'How may I help you?'

'I'm here to speak to Mr Buckley.'

'Have you an appointment?' the woman asked, her hand mechanically reaching for a leather-bound diary.

'No, I don't.'

The monosyllables appeared to send the receptionist into a fluster. 'Mr Buckley has appointments for the rest of this afternoon,' she fluttered. 'I'm afraid he won't be able to see you today. But I can fit you in on Friday if that suits,' she added, her smile a little less warm.

Flora's own smile broadened. 'I'm afraid it doesn't. I wish to see Mr Buckley this afternoon. I'll wait.'

The receptionist looked nonplussed and had begun to

stutter out another refusal when the door of the inner sanctum opened and to Flora's delight Kenneth Buckley strode out.

'Mr Buckley,' she bounced forward, 'just the man I've come to see.'

He blinked at her, then looked helplessly towards his receptionist for an explanation. Who was this woman advancing on him, a woman he only vaguely recognised? 'Miss, er...' he began.

'Flora Carrington. The All's Well in Abbeymead? You were there yesterday.'

'Ah yes.' His face lightened a little. 'Amazing building. Have you come to deliver a book?' His mood had become almost jovial.

'No. I've come to deliver an ultimatum.'

In the quiet atmosphere, the words rang crystal clear and an even greater hush spread around the room. Feet were stilled, coughing stopped, magazines left unruffled. Buckley's waiting clients sat straight in their chairs and Flora was conscious of every pair of eyes trained on her.

'I'm sorry,' Kenneth spluttered. 'I don't think I understand.'

'Then let me explain,' she said in her kindest voice. 'You are to leave Mrs Lawson alone. Stop calling at the bookshop. Stop bringing her presents. Stop pressurising her to act against her former husband. She is a vulnerable woman and you are a predatory man. So, stop – or you'll have me to deal with.'

'Well, really...' There was more spluttering from Buckley, now red-faced and furious. 'I think you've said enough, and I'll thank you to leave immediately.'

Flora felt his hand on her back and was none too gently pushed towards the door. The people she passed wore shocked expressions, but his receptionist, she saw, had a sly look on her face. Had she suffered from his attentions, too?

Exiting the office as gracefully as she could, she was in time to hear one of the waiting clients cancel his appointment and follow her out of the door.

That wretched man won't be bothering Rose again, she thought with satisfaction, striding down the hill to Cleve and the apartment. Would she tell Jack about the visit? Flora didn't think so. It was between her and Rose, she felt that strongly. Her assistant was sensitive about her divorce and found it difficult to talk freely of the painful event. And why wouldn't she when it had made her the subject of general gossip? There was no benefit in Jack knowing, unless, of course, love, or in Buckley's case, lust, was the reason that Alex had died. Flora would have to confess then.

She did, though, tell him of Sullivan's attempt to extort money from a young teacher.

'Are you sure that's what he was doing? Our suspects so far haven't come across as the most decent of people, but that would be reaching a new low.'

'I'm as sure as can be. At first, I couldn't make out what Sullivan was sounding off about. The conversation puzzled me, but when he said he needed money just until payday, it couldn't have been plainer. And the son who is sick? Does he even have a son?'

'Does it matter? Trying to fleece an innocent lad for whatever reason is beyond the pale.'

'It's possible that Hector might know something of Sullivan's family, though I wouldn't put money on it,' she said with a grimace. 'I could phone the Priory and ask him, but I'm reluctant to do it. Mention any possible misdemeanour that concerns the Knights and Hector becomes defensive. It's as if you're attacking him personally. Though he did call Buckley a louse – but then he is.'

'And so is Sullivan by the sound of it. Perhaps the existence of a rich wife is just a rumour and the couple are renting a two-up, two-down in the poorest part of town?'

'I'm pretty sure not. Not after the lunchtime meeting today. I went out of curiosity – well, there were sandwiches going – and it proved interesting. Mrs Sullivan was actually mentioned! She does exist and she must be wealthy.'

'Tell me.'

'For the last few years, the school has been fundraising for a new canteen and the builders are due this summer once school breaks up, but the fund is still several hundred pounds short. The meeting was called for urgent suggestions of how to bridge the gap. The maths teacher thought that Mrs Sullivan might be someone they could approach for an additional contribution.'

'Was her husband at the meeting?'

'Of course not,' Flora said scathingly. 'Bruce has no interest in the school, other than collecting a monthly salary. But... she's someone we should talk to, Jack.'

He frowned. 'At the moment I can't see how.'

'I can. I can find out where she lives from the school secretary and if it's a woman who knocks on her door – that will be me – she won't feel threatened.'

'There's the small matter of confidentiality, not that it's ever been a problem for you. But how likely is the secretary to hand over a private address?'

She jumped up from the table to clear their empty plates, brushing a finger down his cheek. 'There are ways of finding out! I'm afraid pudding is boring. Cheese and biscuits, but I'll buy something special for tomorrow.'

'A chunk of Cheddar and a splodge of Branston will be fine.' He delved into the tin-lined cabinet the college had supplied in lieu of a refrigerator and brought out the cheese. 'I'm not trying to create obstacles, but are there also ways of explaining why you're standing on the woman's doorstep – if you get there?'

'I'll come up with something, though any visit will have to

wait until next week,' she murmured, clattering the plates into the sink.

'I guess finding Mrs Sullivan is worth a try,' he conceded. 'If she's that wealthy, why is Sullivan in such money trouble? And how much does she know of her husband's activities? Is she aware of his borrowing – I know we can't be certain he borrowed from Alex, but we do know he was willing to cadge money from a vulnerable boy, so it looks likely. Gambling or drink, do you reckon?'

'Almost certainly gambling. Sullivan likes the horses – Hector mentioned that the three of them were regularly at Lewes racecourse together. If there's no sick son, and I'm pretty sure there isn't, that's where the money is going.'

'A teacher who gambles – I've wondered before if Sullivan could lose his job. If Alex loaned him money that wasn't returned, he *might* have threatened to report him.'

'It's possible, but again I don't like to think it. Hector Lansdale was a very close friend and what would that say about Hector? About a man we both like and trust?'

'Friends don't always turn out the way we expect – any more than sweethearts.'

'Well, this sweetheart has!'

'You're right. This one has,' he said, grabbing hold of her and waltzing her back to the table.

17

Cheese and biscuits were in Flora's head on Thursday afternoon when, freed from further classes for the day, she headed to the shops, determined to find a more interesting dessert for their first evening back in Abbeymead. Bereft of a properly functioning stove, she'd given up her earlier idea of cooking the fruit pie she'd fancied. After a few miserable efforts fighting the kitchen at Cleve College, she'd fallen out of love with anything approaching home cooking. If Jack's contract wasn't renewed, she would do a dance of delight around that wretched oven.

On her travels around Lewes, she'd discovered a small shop, next to the town's main grocery store, which appeared to specialise in cream cakes and tempting puddings. She was bending to peer through its window – was that a peach Melba? – when a voice behind her said teasingly, 'Disastrous for the figure, Flora.'

It was Diane Croft. 'But delicious all the same.'

Flora hadn't seen the girl since their evening at the Cross Keys although news had reached her via the conversation with Alice. Mrs Croft, Alice had said, was worried for her daughter, but on the surface and despite the rigours of Saturday's funeral, Diane appeared well. It was only when Flora looked more closely that she could see the pallor beneath the make-up and the hardly concealed dark rings around the girl's beautiful eyes.

'How are you?' she asked, genuinely wanting to know.

'Bearing up.' The stiff smile belied her words and after a short pause she confessed, 'Actually, not terribly well.'

'I'm sorry things aren't too good. Now the funeral is over...' Flora didn't finish, seeing the girl's eyes filmy with unshed tears. 'Your parents must be on the point of leaving for Scotland,' she said hastily.

Diane swallowed audibly. 'Next week. They leave on Tuesday. Most of the furniture is going this weekend. It will seem so strange...' She trailed off. 'But at least I've found a flat to rent. A nice one, too.'

'No second thoughts about going to Edinburgh?'

'I've had a few,' she admitted, 'but it wouldn't be sensible. I have a job here, I have friends, and now I've somewhere I can make a home for myself. If I left with Mum and Dad, I'd be running away. I can't do that.'

Flora forbore to say it was impossible to run away from your thoughts if they wouldn't let you and instead smiled and said what she hoped was the right thing. 'Life will look a little brighter soon, I'm sure.'

Diane nodded, but then put a hand to her hair and tugged at it quite viciously.

'The only thing is...' She stopped speaking.

'The only thing?' Flora prompted.

There was another hard tug on an errant curl. 'Look, why don't we share a pot of tea? I've the afternoon off from Play It Again and it looks as if you're free as well. *And* I'll be saving you from death by peach Melba!'

Flora responded to the attempted humour with a brief smile, happy to agree. It was plain Diane had something burdensome on her mind and just as plain that she needed to tell someone. Flora was keen to be that someone – she could always return for the dessert.

'What a good idea!' she responded. 'There's a pretty teashop a few streets away – do you know it?' Roberta Raffles' café was coming in useful, Flora reflected. At least the woman had done *something* for her.

'The one with the floral blinds?'

'That's the one.'

It was fortunate they were among the few customers taking tea that afternoon. It meant they could talk openly without risk of being overheard, but even so it took Diane time to confess what she needed to. They were on their second cup before she said quietly, 'I can't sleep at night.'

'That's not good.' Alice had mentioned nightmares, she remembered.

'I have such bad dreams. Even when I wake up, they don't go away, not completely, and as soon as I close my eyes, they're back again and more vividly than ever.'

'The bad dreams are about Alex?' she ventured.

Diane nodded.

'You're being very hard on yourself. I know the two of you quarrelled and you said things you wished you hadn't, but you can't unsay them, no matter how much you wish it. You can't reel back time, Diane. And I don't think Alex would want you to continue so upset. He loved you enough to ask you to marry him, didn't he?'

The girl stared at her. She wouldn't mention the ring, Flora decided. Let Diane think she'd heard of a proposal on the grapevine.

'We did talk about it,' her companion admitted, looking uncomfortable.

'Did you do more than talk?' They must have or why would

Alex have gone to the expense of buying a ring when he needed money so badly?

Diane looked down at the sanded floorboards. 'I kind of agreed.'

'You let him think you'd get engaged?'

'It was easier to go along with the idea,' she said abruptly. 'I thought if he had a definite "yes", then it would quieten things down. Ease the pressure on me. But it was the reverse. Once I'd agreed, Alex started pestering me to set a date. Every time we saw each other, it was when are we getting married? We should fix a day, book a church. And all the time, I had Kenny telling me I was too young, too beautiful, to marry the first man who asked me. It was hellish.'

'And how is Kenneth?' Flora asked nonchalantly, wondering if Diane had heard of her foray into his office.

'I don't know.' A frustrated sweep of her hand had her cup and saucer pushed to one side. 'I dumped him days ago.'

'A sensible move, I'd say. But the engagement and the quarrel you had – it's water under the bridge. You have to forget it.'

There was another long silence. 'It's not just that,' the girl said finally, speaking into her hands so that Flora could barely hear her. 'I think I may have been the one to push him.'

She couldn't stop her eyebrows shooting up in surprise. 'You're saying that you pushed Alex off that wall?'

'I think I might have. I don't know, Flora, I just don't know. It's all a muddle in my head. I was so angry with him, and there were all these people around. The other women in the keep, the King's men on the wall outside, de Montfort's troops surging forward. Alex and Hector and Bruce. Such a muddle.'

Flora reached out and took hold of one of her hands. 'This will be painful, Diane, but can you cast your mind back, focus on the moment that Alex fell?'

The girl nodded, her lips set tightly in a grim line.

'Are you seeing it in your head?'

She nodded again.

'How near to Alex were you at that moment? Standing next to him?'

'I think so. Yes, I was at the entrance to the keep. He had his back to me, fighting, but then he turned his head for an instant – he must have sensed someone behind him – and I screamed in his face. I'd already told him I was going to Scotland but he wouldn't believe me. But then I shouted it again... I said... I said I was going, and it was to get away from him.' The threatened tears were back.

Flora waited a few minutes. 'Were there other people nearby?'

'Yes.' Diane blew her nose loudly.

'Did a pair of hands seem to come out of nowhere and push Alex hard?'

'Yes,' she said, 'yes they did.'

'And were they your hands?'

'I don't know,' she wailed. 'I really don't know.'

'No wonder that poor girl is having nightmares,' Flora said, as she and Jack drove back to Abbeymead that evening. 'She thinks she may be a killer. And not just any old killer, but someone who ended the life of a man she was supposed to love.'

'Supposed is probably a good word. I think it's pretty clear what love there was existed entirely on Alex Vicary's side. It's feasible, I guess, that Diane *is* the killer – inadvertently, perhaps, but still murder. She was in a rage. She wanted to be free. She could have lashed out, hardly conscious of what she was doing.'

Flora retied the ribbon holding back her hair and looked blankly through the windscreen. 'I genuinely have no idea,' she said, 'and neither does Diane, but she's riven with guilt that she might have done something dreadful. I had to dissuade her from walking into Lewes police station right there and then to give herself up. She could be completely innocent.'

'So, why the nightmares?'

'It might be guilt. She's transferring the guilt she feels over not loving Alex enough into an action she never committed. Imagining that she's guilty could be the punishment she needs to inflict on herself.'

She felt Jack give her a sideways glance. 'No, I'm not setting up as a psychologist, I promise. But it does make sense.'

'It would make even more sense if she had done it, which is beginning to look possible.'

'If she'd been the only one on that wall, and the only one with a motive, I'd agree, but she wasn't. There were others, all with some kind of grudge against Alex. The fact that Diane feels so bad suggests it's remorse at work rather than truth.'

Jack pulled a face as the Austin turned off the main road towards the village. 'I'll look forward to Ridley's call telling me he's arrested a Diane Croft and has her safely tucked away in the cells.'

'It won't happen,' Flora prophesised. 'Even the inspector would work out that it was guilt talking. What *will* happen, though, is a brilliant dessert. No cheese and biscuits tonight.'

'Made by you?'

'Please! Made by' – she turned her head to look at the peach Melba nestling on the back seat – 'Heavenly Bites.'

She reached across to take hold of the decorative box. 'See?'

Jack took his eyes off the steering wheel for a moment. 'Oh! That looks – decidedly good. I vote we only eat dessert tonight.'

'We can't do that. Aunt Violet would never allow it. She always made me eat my first course, every bit of it, before I was allowed anything sweet. Maybe we could do simple tonight – stick with poached eggs?'

'In which case, I'll do the honours.'

Flora would have protested, but opening the cottage front door, she found a thick envelope sitting on the mat. It had a foreign stamp and she knew immediately what the envelope contained. Scooping it up, she danced with it into the kitchen.

'It's from Italy,' she said, tearing the missive open. 'From Venice... from the Cipriani.'

'I'll get the toast going. You enjoy.'

She spread the hotel brochure out across the table and for several minutes stared at it, dreamlike.

'It is the most beautiful hotel I've ever seen. And we're going there, Jack!'

In a sudden movement, she jumped up and squeezed him round the middle, causing the bread knife he was wielding to judder and cut unevenly.

'You can have that slice!' he said.

'I don't care. I'll eat any number of wonky slices. I bet the Cipriani doesn't serve poached eggs.'

'They wouldn't know how. At least, not with my level of expertise.'

'And look at the bedrooms!' She waved the brochure in front of him. We're going to be staying in one of those rooms. With a balcony! We'll look across at St Mark's every morning and every evening.'

'Not from that room.'

'Why not?' She felt just a little deflated.

'Because those rooms look across to San Giorgio Maggiore.'

'Why do you know everything? It is so infuriating.'

'It must be, but I quite like it. Don't worry.' He broke two eggs into the pan of boiling water, then turned to kiss her. 'There's a floating restaurant at the front of the hotel. It faces the city and when we eat there at night, you'll get to see St Mark's.'

Flora was slightly mollified.

'And illuminated, too.'

'I can't wait. In fact, I wish we were going right now.'

'We chose June for a reason.'

'Do you remember why?'

He shook his head. 'It must have seemed a good idea at the time.'

'We should be going now,' she repeated. 'Forget Alex Vicary, forget Hector, and just enjoy ourselves.'

'You wouldn't want to abandon Hector,' he pointed out.

'I suppose not,' she said sadly, then, looking down at the pan, 'I've never told you, but I like the eggs turned over.'

He shook his head. 'Definitely not the way a Carrington poaches.'

Flora pursed her lips.

'*I'm* making the supper,' he reminded her. '*You* can cut the peach Melba.'

'That was a surprisingly filling meal.' Flora lay back on her favourite sofa, enjoying the feeling of being home.

'It's all the cream and butter,' he said knowledgeably. 'Probably not the healthiest supper we've ever eaten.'

'Tomorrow, we're back to meat and two veg.'

Jack nodded, sifting through the few pieces of mail that had arrived for him while he was in Lewes.

'Arthur has written. A long letter – and helpful, too. I asked him for advice as to which synopsis I should go with. Neither of the options I'd sketched out seemed completely right, but Arthur has come back with an answer! Two foolscap pages of answer, by the look of it.'

Jack reached for his glasses, only to have the telephone shrill from the hall. 'Darn it! I want to read this.'

'I'd answer it only I can't get off the sofa.' Flora yawned. 'And the call is probably for you.'

It was. Alan Ridley's voice echoed down the line, sounding as though he was talking from the depths. The town hall basement could just about qualify, Jack supposed.

'Thought you'd be back by now, old chap,' the inspector began. 'I've some news for you, news you're going to like. We've arrested Larry Morton. The finance bods have come up with a tranche of evidence – some very deep irregularities popping up all over the place in our friend's accounts. The more they dug, the more they found. They're delighted, and so am I.'

'Have you locked Morton up? You sound as though you're calling from the cells.'

'I am.' The inspector managed a half laugh. 'But he's not with me. He's been released on court bail. Fraud isn't seen as a locking up offence, more's the pity. Not until he's found guilty, which he will be.'

'It's good news, nevertheless, and thanks for letting me know.' Jack prepared to put the phone down. Flora might not have been able to get off the sofa but he was almost asleep standing up. What had been in that dessert?

The inspector hadn't quite finished, however. 'I'd like to speak to you about this case. There's been some developments.'

Jack lost his sleepiness. 'What, exactly?'

'I'd rather not talk about it over the phone. Your postmistress – what's her name, Fowler, Fanthorpe?'

'Fuller. Dilys Fuller.'

'She'll have closed the post office by now but I wouldn't put it past her to have other ways of listening in. A diligent woman, I'd say, and I don't want this spread. Meet me at the pub? No pies, I promise. After supper tomorrow evening?'

Jack said a reluctant yes and walked back into the sitting room where Flora was already half-asleep. 'Budge up. Let's share.'

She shuffled along to the next cushion. 'What did the inspector want?'

'To meet. He has news, apparently, but in the meantime Larry Morton has been charged with... fraud, I think.'

'That sounds good.'

'And you sound dozy.'

'I am, but don't let me stop you reading. You've two pages of plot suggestions to go through.'

Abandoning his glasses, he put his arms around her and snuggled down into what, over the years, had become a truly squashy sofa.

'The letter can wait. This is more interesting.'

18

The three friends had agreed to eat supper at Kate's this evening so that she could be close at hand if Sarah was tetchy and refused to settle, Tony having arranged his own small party with friends from the Priory where he'd worked for several years before his marriage. Before he left, though, he'd done the women proud, spending the afternoon, when he wasn't serving customers, cooking their evening meal: a tomato bisque, a fish pie and a special treat of lemon syllabub. All Kate had to do, it seemed, was light the gas.

When Flora walked into the Farradays' small sitting room that evening, she was surprised to see Sally Jenner lolling in an armchair, a glass of her aunt's blackcurrant wine in her hand. Sally rarely came to the friends' regular Friday date and, when she did, it was most often if something truly gossip-worthy had happened in Abbeymead or, worse, if something was badly amiss in the village. Flora's spirits fell a little but, determined to stay cheerful, she decided there was no reason why Sally shouldn't enjoy an occasional meal away from the Priory.

'You're looking well,' the girl greeted her. 'And how's that lovely husband of yours?'

'Yes, how is Jack?' Kate asked, kissing her on the cheek, then ushering them both to the table where Alice had already taken her seat. 'We hardly see him these days, now he's working in Lewes.'

'He may not be working there much longer. Mmm, that smells delicious.' The tang of tomato bisque had reached her. 'There's to be a new principal at the college next term and you know what they say about new brooms...'

'If Jack leaves, it'll be a good thing.' Alice was unequivocal, picking up her spoon, ready for the soup Kate was ladling into four bowls. 'It's time you were both back in the village. You're missed, you know.'

It was a familiar refrain and Flora was keen to change the subject. 'And how's Charlie getting on? Now he doesn't deliver for the All's Well or garden for Jack, I hardly ever see him.'

Alice nodded. 'The lad's busy, that's for sure, working in two kitchens as he does.'

'Charlie has so much energy.' Sally let out a long sigh. 'I wish he could pass some on.'

'I have to hand it to the boy, he's a good worker. So far. Made some mistakes, mind – he forgot to salt the veg for the party we had last week and he can't get a risotto right for love nor money – but there, we all have to learn.'

'Once Auntie is completely happy,' Sally said, 'he'll be made permanent and Hector can start teaching him the fiddly stuff. I'm not sure he'll be able to carry on helping at the Nook, though.' Glancing across at her hostess, who'd jumped up to clear the soup bowls, she looked concerned.

'It might work out for the best,' Kate said in her gentle voice, walking to the door. 'Ivy's youngest is at school now and she's keen to increase her hours. She could take Charlie's. He's been a treasure, but we should be able to cope. And it will be good for him to work at the Priory full-time.'

'For Hector, too,' Alice added. 'He needs a project and that will be Charlie. Now who's for green beans?' Her serving spoon hovered in the air, as Kate reappeared from the kitchen with the fish pie and vegetables.

Flora, tucking into her pie, saw Sally and her aunt nod to each other. She hadn't seen Hector herself or spoken to him for days, but presumed that his life had returned to its usual rhythm, that he'd been able to put Alex's death to one side and concentrate on his work.

'Hector is still a problem,' Sally explained, trying to sound indifferent when clearly she wasn't. 'Some days he's fine and working as he always has. But on others...'

Alice gave a sad shake of her head.

'I hope, we hope, training Charlie will help,' Sally went on, 'but if Hector doesn't soon buck up, I'll have to think of employing someone else.'

'Isn't that a bit harsh?' Flora protested. 'He's had a lot to deal with – his best friend is dead and his best friend's mother is being hounded out of her house. He needs time to cope with all that.'

'Time is what we haven't got.' Sally's response was crisp. 'The Priory is attracting more and more customers and they expect a certain level of service. As it is, I'm finding it hard to keep the hotel properly staffed and I can't afford anyone who's not pulling their weight. Auntie tells me that she can't truly rely on Hector as her deputy any longer.'

Alice took a mouthful of pie. 'I've tried to make allowances, but there comes a point... it's not just that lad's death and his ma that's worryin' the boy. It's Rose Lawson, too. He seems to have taken on the woes of the village.'

Flora hadn't expected to hear Rose's name. She noticed Sally's frown and looked meaningfully across at her.

Sally interpreted the look correctly. 'It's not what you think, Flora. It's not jealousy on my part. Hector can see who he wants and, if Rose Lawson is his choice, so be it. But he's spending so much time fussing over her, or telephoning Alex's mother, or slumped in a black mood, that often we hardly get any work out of him.'

'Whatever's been worrying him about Rose shouldn't be a problem now,' Flora said with satisfaction. 'Kenneth Buckley has been bothering her badly, but he's been sent to the right-about. From now on, he'll be leaving her alone.'

'Let's hope so – I'll find out from Diane. She's sure to know. I still see her occasionally, even though I've dropped out of the Knights.'

'Have you?' her aunt asked. 'I didn't know.'

'It wasn't for me,' Sally said briefly. No, it wasn't, Flora thought. It was always Hector who had been the attraction. 'But I'm not the only one leaving the society. There's Ferdie Luxton, too. Ferdie, of all people!'

Flora looked up abruptly. 'Do you know why?'

'Maybe he's feeling old and finding the armour too heavy. To be honest, I've no idea.'

It was extraordinary. Luxton must be one of the founding members of the Knights and he was leaving! What had prompted that decision? Had their visit to the Masons Arms last week rattled the man, deciding him to keep a low profile for a while or even leave the area? But no, it couldn't be that. He was likely to have made the decision before she and Jack had even crossed the pub's threshold. It was an intriguing development, however.

'The Knights are giving him a send-off at the Masons Arms next week,' Sally was saying. 'I thought I could say my goodbyes at the same time.'

'I suppose Kenneth Buckley isn't leaving, too?'

Sally shook her head. 'No such luck. According to Diane, Buckley never gives up. I heard about your visit to his offices, by the way.'

'Really?' The lemon syllabub had arrived on the table and Flora eyed it with appreciation. 'News spreads, doesn't it!'

'It was Kenneth himself who spread it. Or rather, he told Diane and she told me. He came bleating to her that he'd never been so mortified in his life.'

'How very gratifying! He needs to stay mortified. But is he still hanging around Diane?'

'I think he sees her as an old flame now and someone he can complain to. But you need to be careful, Flora. Buckley may seem fairly harmless, but he can be a nasty character – I've seen it in the society – and you have well and truly damaged his pride.'

'How's he goin' to hurt Flora?' Alice demanded.

'He was talking about paying her back. All very vague, but Diane said he sounded as if he meant it. Sounded threatening. She told me to pass on the warning – she liked you and doesn't want to see you hurt.'

There was a sudden silence in the room, the syllabub temporarily forgotten.

'What does she think he'll do to Flora?' Kate's blue eyes were scared.

'He better not try anythin',' Alice said martially. 'Or he'll have us to deal with.'

The Cross Keys was already crowded when Jack pushed his way through the door and turned left into the saloon bar. For a moment, he saw only hazily, his eyes watering from the smoke-filled air, but, gradually, over the heads of those waiting at the bar, he made out the figure of the inspector. Ridley was weaving a cautious path through the tables, beer in one hand, crisps in the other, on his way to his favourite bench in the corner of the saloon.

Without waiting to order a drink himself, Jack followed. Back at the cottage, he'd left a first vital chapter of the new book half-completed and was desperate to return to his typewriter. If he were lucky, this would be a short meeting.

'No beer?' Alan Ridley asked, as soon as he caught sight of him. 'Not stopping for a drink?'

Immediately, Jack felt guilty. 'I think I've a cold coming and I can't face a beer,' he said, hoping the lie would pass muster.

Ridley shrugged. 'Suit yourself. I won't be here long, in any case. Got to get back to the station. I've left a load of work unfinished.'

Jack felt even guiltier. 'Thanks for coming to tell me – whatever it is you're going to tell me.' Did he sound sufficiently enthusiastic?

The inspector leaned back against the wooden settle. 'Like I said, I'd rather not trust the information over the telephone. I can't be sure it's true, for one thing.'

Jack was intrigued, ready to ask questions, but Ridley got in first.

'What do you know of Ferdie Luxton?' he asked. 'Apart from the fact that he's a member of the Knights of Mercia and was at the rehearsal the day Alex Vicary died?'

Jack assumed what he hoped was an innocent face. 'I've heard he was a publican, mine host at this very pub for many years. Landed in a spot of bother and moved to Lewes where he ran another pub, successfully, until he retired.'

'A spot of bother? You could call it that, I suppose.' Ridley took a large draught of his beer. 'He was hit with a very large fine for out-of-hours drinking. Took him ten years to pay it. But it was hosting illegal gambling that almost sent him to prison. Luckily for him, he had a good barrister who got him off with another large fine.'

'He seemed to have learned his lesson.' Idly, Jack's hand reached for a crisp from the inspector's open packet.

'As far as we know, but that kind of activity can have consequences, sometimes years later.'

Jack was mystified. 'What's going on, Alan?'

'Luxton seems to have become a target. Or thinks he has.
One of my constables was drinking in the Masons Arms – off
duty, you understand, in mufti – and Luxton drinks there, too.'

'Regularly, I believe.'

The inspector nodded. 'The constable was on the next table
to Luxton and two of his mates, and overheard some of their
conversation. Luxton sounded scared, my chap thought, telling
his friends he'd decided to leave the re-enactment society.'

'Leave? I thought he was one of the Knights' mainstays.'

'He's been in it a long time – I checked with the member-
ship secretary and he joined twenty-odd years ago. He was
telling his mates what a good time he'd had. It had been a real
interest, he said, something he'd loved being involved in, but
he'd no option now but to leave. It was too dangerous.'

The society dangerous? How could it be? Did it operate as a
mafia, disposing of members that in some way had stepped out
of line? It sounded ridiculous.

'My constable knew something of the incident at the castle,
and its fallout,' the inspector went on. 'He'd been one of the
men I'd sent to warn off the Mortons, so as you can imagine, his
ears switched to high alert. There was something going on in
the society, Luxton said, something he didn't like, and he was
getting out. One bloke had been killed already, and he didn't
bargain on being the next.'

'Have you any idea what he meant?'

'No sensible idea. It's possible he fears a threat from his past
– he's certainly had a chequered one. But how that ties up with
the Knights of Mercia, I haven't a clue. It's clear, though, that he
believes Vicary's death was no accident. When we first investigated, Norris drew up a plan of the battle. I could see from it
that Luxton was fighting for the opposing army, but must have

been very close to Vicary when the lad plunged from that top wall. Did he see something, I'm wondering? Hear something?'

'It's more than possible. He was fighting hand-to-hand with Alex when the boy fell. If there was anything amiss, Luxton would have seen it. Have you spoken to him?'

'Not yet. I wanted to find out what you knew before I got the show moving.'

'The show?'

'No more talk of an accident, old chap. From now on, I'm treating Vicary's death as unlawful.' So that was the reason Ridley had asked to meet this evening. It wouldn't be something he'd want to broadcast over the telephone.

'Luxton must genuinely believe he's in danger of ending up like Vicary,' the inspector went on. 'He couldn't have known who was listening to his conversation – it was quite spontaneous. He's running scared and there has to be a reason.'

Jack sensed a burden being lifted. A ripple of relief. It had felt as though he and Flora faced a stone wall of denial: Alex Vicary's death had been an accident, an accident, an accident. Now, at last, the chorus had changed.

'In that case, you might like to take a look at some of the people we've found interesting.'

'Always willing. Fire away!'

'First off, there's the Mortons.'

He was aware of a barely suppressed sigh, but hurried on. 'You've nabbed the uncle on fraud, Alan, and I know you've warned them off from making trouble for Mrs Vicary. But I think Hector Lansdale is right to claim that one or other of them – probably David – could be guilty of a much graver crime. He reckons it was David Morton who infiltrated the re-enactment and pushed Alex to his death.'

Ridley screwed up the crisp packet, aiming it at his empty glass. 'The Mortons are already in our sights, but I'm always willing to expand my thinking.'

Jack wasn't sure that was true but pushed the niggle to one side. 'If you've studied the plan of the battle that day, you'll see there were numerous people close to Alex when he fell: several women had come out of the keep and onto the wall, among them Diane Croft. She was Alex's girlfriend and earlier had quarrelled with him badly and continued to quarrel during the display.'

And Diane, he could have added but didn't, is fearful she might have done the deed.

'Ferdie Luxton you know about,' he continued, 'but a man called Bruce Sullivan was fighting just ahead of Alex. It's possible he may have wanted to harm the boy. And one member who almost certainly did is Kenneth Buckley. He was at the rehearsal though not a combatant, but could have easily climbed to the wall and mingled with the men fighting there.'

Jack wouldn't mention the staircase he'd discovered with Flora. If the inspector really intended to study the castle in detail, it would be a treat for him.

'Too many people, Jack,' Ridley complained. 'Far too many people and all of them, no doubt, with a motive. It seems young Alex Vicary made a fair number of enemies in his short life.'

'Yet he appears to have been a decent man.'

The inspector's expression was gloomy. 'I'll have to interview them,' he said, getting ready to leave. 'All of 'em.'

19

Jack walked away from the Cross Keys, his mind unsettled. Ridley had hinted that Luxton might fear repercussions from his past misdemeanours, but it had been the vaguest of suggestions. Was that likely after all these years? And, if someone from Luxton's past *had* materialised, what had it to do with Alex Vicary's death? Ferdie appeared adamant that it was belonging to the society that was dangerous, something sinister bubbling beneath its surface. Yet every member that he and Flora had talked to – Hector, Sally, Diane Croft – had spoken highly of the Knights. There'd been no hint of malice in any of the conversations.

Until now, Luxton had been their suspect. They'd speculated that Alex might have pressured him for money, using the landlord's dubious past as ammunition, and the man had decided to free himself in the most brutal fashion. What Luxton hadn't been was a potential victim. But the exchange overheard in the Masons Arms had turned things upside down. How had they got it so badly wrong?

Unless... it was Luxton covering his tracks? If Flora's guess were right – an extravagant guess even for her – and he *had* been blackmailed by Alex, Luxton was cute enough to know that sooner or later the fact would come to light, making him an immediate suspect. But a man expressing fear that he could be next in line to suffer an 'accident' would diffuse suspicion and muddy the waters.

Flora had already returned from her supper party when he walked through the front door and she rushed out of the kitchen to greet him.

'Guess who's leaving the Knights of Mercia?' she asked excitedly.

'Ferdie Luxton.' He gave her an apologetic smile.

'How did you know?' Her expression turned doleful.

'I had it from Ridley tonight. And you?'

'Sally. She came to the supper and *she's* leaving the Knights as well. The society is having a farewell do for Luxton next week and she intends to bow out then.'

'Quite an evening for us both,' he remarked, divesting himself of jacket and fedora.

'But why?' Flora demanded, dragging him into the sitting room. 'Why is Luxton leaving? No one seems to know. Does the inspector?'

Jack's grey eyes darkened slightly. 'Only that the man fears for his life and is convinced that if he stays in the society, he might follow Alex. One of Ridley's men overheard his conversation in the pub.'

'What! But that's crazy.'

'One of Alan's suggestions was that Luxton might have seen something the day Alex died and feels his only protection is to put distance between himself and his erstwhile companions.'

'That could be true,' she said thoughtfully. 'At least it tells us we were right to think one of the Knights could be our villain!'

'And the inspector, you'll be glad to hear, is with us in looking for a possible killer. The Luxton news has made him rethink – from now on, he's treating Alex's death as potential murder.'

'He took his time. But now he *is* rethinking, perhaps he'd like to treat Kenneth Buckley's harassment as the serious offence it is.'

'Buckley?'

'Oh, you won't know, but apparently I have to be very careful of Kenneth!' Flora sounded half-amused, half-indignant. 'I had that from Sally. I think she came to the meal tonight especially to warn me. He's not a very nice man, she told me – we knew that already – and now he's gunning for me.'

'Really?' This was yet another puzzle. 'Why would he be?'

Flora's expression changed, a wariness creeping into her face. 'I don't think I told you,' she said cautiously.

'Told me what?' A premonition gripped hold.

'I went to his offices and demanded that he leave Rose Lawson alone.' Jack said nothing, knowing there would be more. 'And... there were people there, waiting to see him. Clients, I suppose. He didn't like what I had to say.'

'How surprising! So, you've made an enemy of him. We could have done without that.'

'I'd rather have him as an enemy than a friend,' she said defiantly. 'And he's all bluff and bluster. The worst he'll do is tittle-tattle about me. He won't actually *do* anything.'

'Let's hope not. I've already made an enemy of the Mortons and we really don't need any more.' Kenneth Buckley had joined the list of people of whom they needed to be wary, and it wasn't something Jack welcomed.

He was uneasy. He wished now that he'd kept the news of Ferdie Luxton's fear of death to himself. Once they were back in Lewes, he couldn't trust Flora to keep away from the Masons Arms and start interrogating Luxton anew. At the moment, their investigation barely passed as such; it needed to be in far better shape before they charged further ahead. Perhaps when she'd paid the promised visit to Bruce Sullivan's wife, it would be. Or was that whistling in the wind?

The sun had only just begun to filter through a blanket of cloud when a loud hammering on the front door woke them abruptly.

'It's Sunday,' Jack moaned, pulling the counterpane over his ears.

'It's also the day you asked Charlie to call,' she murmured, scratching his back.

'Oh God. You're right. It's Charlie. I should recognise his fist on the door by now.'

In the last week or so, the rain had abated slightly and Jack had asked his one-time mentor for help in the garden. A few hours on Sunday morning had been the promise, he remembered. Neither he nor Flora ever found sufficient time for the numerous jobs that needed doing: seeds to sow, roses to fertilise, bedding to plant and the inevitable, inevitable weeding.

'So, are you going?' she asked. The hammering had resumed while he'd made no effort to move, he realised.

Swinging his legs out of bed, he felt around the floor for slippers, then groped his way down the stairs.

'I'm coming as fast as I can,' he muttered, fumbling for the keys. 'We'd like some door left, Charlie.'

'You said early.' His young friend stood on the threshold, wearing a piqued expression.

'I did? I must have been mad. You better come into the kitchen.'

Charlie hadn't waited for the invitation. He was already there.

'You won't have had breakfast, of course,' Jack said faintly.

'No time, Mr C. Toast would be fine, unless you're makin''

porridge. I like a bowl of porridge even in summer. Or cake. I can eat cake for breakfast. Whatever's goin'.'

'Toast,' Jack said definitely.

'A few slices'll do – and a cup of tea. Or two.'

Once they were seated at the table with butter, marmalade and a rack of hot toast, Jack took a long look at his guest, at his smart haircut and bright eyes. 'How do you like being a cook?' he asked, thinking the life must suit the boy.

'It's good,' Charlie managed to get out, his mouth crammed full. 'Specially now there's more I'm allowed to do.'

'It's definitely going to be the career for you?'

Charlie waved a slice of toast in the air. 'I reckon so. Mrs Jenner has been trainin' me, but I think she's goin' to ask Mr Lansdale to take over.'

'You'll be happy with that?'

Charlie nodded, taking a loud slurp of his tea. 'I like 'im. Most times.'

Jack was surprised. 'And when you don't?'

'He's got a real bee in his bonnet and it's givin' him trouble. Gets real angry sometimes. About his friend... you know, the one who died.'

'I do know, but I'm surprised to hear Mr Lansdale loses his temper at work.'

'I wouldn't say he loses his temper,' Charlie said judiciously. 'It's more a mutterin'. A kinda ragin' but not like everyone can hear. Says the police are useless. That he knows who killed his friend and if they won't do nuthin', then he will.'

It was David Morton that Hector blamed for Alex's death – for him, his fellow Knights were beyond approach. Jack sighed deeply to himself. Did this mean another of Hector's forays to Newhaven and more tangles with the police? Ridley wouldn't treat further mischief so leniently and Hector could find himself in real trouble. It was yet one more reason that he and Flora needed to find Alex's killer urgently.

'What do you think Mr Lansdale means to do?' he asked carefully.

'I dunno. I reckon he'll go for the bloke. Beat 'im up, mebbe.'

'And the bloke is?'

Charlie shook his head. 'He never says. Just mutters to hisself. I wish he didn't, but it's good for me cos I get to do extra stuff.'

'Hello, Charlie. What kind of extra stuff?' Flora had come into the kitchen looking, Jack thought, as fresh as any flower they were about to plant.

'Pastries for the old ladies. That's what I did last week. They said they were lovely.'

'Old ladies?'

'The Mothers' Union or somethin' like that.'

The average age of Union members must be around forty, Jack thought dismally. Even Flora blenched at the comment, he noticed.

'Next week,' the boy went on confidently, 'I'm goin' to learn shoo pastry. You spell it funny, but that's how you say it. It's *special*. Mrs Jenner says it needs a light hand.'

'And you have one?'

'I reckon so or she wouldn't have me learn.'

'Not such a light hand in the garden, I hope,' Jack said, clearing Charlie's plate and mug. 'So, if you're ready... we've a few hours of planting and weeding ahead.'

'That bloke who took your house, Mr C,' Charlie said suddenly. 'He arsked me to help.'

'In my garden? My old garden,' he corrected himself.

'Yeah, I went round there cos he telephoned Mum, but then I said I wouldn't have the time.'

'Was that true?'

'Nah, not really, but he was a queer bird. I didn't fancy the job.'

'What was queer about him?' He didn't need any more

puzzles, Jack thought, but it was his old home they were talking of.

'He was twitchy. Lookin' around all the time and lookin' over my shoulder, like he saw someone. It spooked me out. And he didn't even give me a glass of lemonade.'

'That's bad.'

'It was,' Charlie agreed wholeheartedly.

Three hours later, Charlie said a hasty goodbye to bike furiously down Greenway Lane, desperate not to miss his mother's roast dinner.

Having waved him off, Jack strolled into the kitchen and washed his hands at the Belfast sink.

'That was a useful morning,' he said to Flora's back, as she bent over the oven. 'Between us, we knocked off all the jobs on my list. And a few more that weren't.' He sniffed the air. 'Something smells good.'

She closed the oven door, her face flushed from its heat. 'Yorkshire pudding to go with the beef,' she announced. 'I'm spoiling you. What was Charlie saying as I came into the kitchen this morning? You seemed deep in conversation.'

'I wouldn't say it was deep, but it *was* interesting. In fact, more worrying than interesting. Hector is very angry – we knew that – but so angry that it's interfering with his work.'

Flora sat down at the table. 'It's what Sally has been saying. It's become so bad in the kitchen that she's thinking of replacing him.'

Jack was silent for a moment, then sat down heavily in the chair opposite. 'I'd no idea things were so difficult at the Priory. From Charlie's artless chatter, I gather that Hector is certain he knows who killed his friend and intends to go after him. It can only be David Morton that he means. And that's trouble.'

'He may just have been sounding off,' she said soothingly.

'Sounding off to a fifteen-year-old? I reckon if Hector is so angry he can't stop himself issuing threats in front of a young-ster, then he means it.'

'You think he'll go to Newhaven again?'

'I'm afraid so. For Hector, the Mortons are behind every-thing the Vicary family has suffered, including Alex's death.'

'Maybe we should warn Mrs Vicary.'

'What good would that do?' Jack got to his feet, reaching into the cupboard for a couple of dinner plates.

'If Susan Vicary knows what Hector is planning, she'll be ready for possible trouble.' Flora paused, while she rescued a saucepan of boiling water. 'She might even manage to dissuade him. And, in any case, we should go to see her, Jack. We've never checked whether Ridley's orders have had any effect, whether the presence of a local bobby has kept the Mortons from harassing her.'

'I feel guilty about that, but being in college for half the week skews things badly. Although...' He stopped, his hand on the cutlery drawer. 'It could prove an advantage. I can easily get to Newhaven between student appointments – it shouldn't take more than twenty minutes in the Austin – and with you plan-ning to call on Mrs Sullivan very soon, we might just turn up a new lead.'

'We might and, naturally, it's my visit that will shine,' she teased, her head once more bent over the oven, this time to baste the roasting potatoes.

'Wait and see! You could be very wrong.' He looked up from setting the table. 'Are we still destined for the green this afternoon?'

'It's the first Sunday in May. What else? You'll love the maypole dancing.'

'But of course I will.'

There was just the suggestion of a groan.

20

On Monday morning, as soon as he'd waved Flora goodbye, Jack settled himself to a day of writing, literally springing up the stairs to the room he'd made his study. He was eager to get down to work: Arthur's suggestions for how the book might develop lay on his desk and, having already written a first chapter, he was looking forward to an uninterrupted six hours of working his way through his agent's letter.

Flora, too, was looking forward to her day. There were new titles to catch up with: Rose had telephoned last night to apologise that she'd only just remembered the boxes of *Goldfinger* and *To Sir with Love* waiting to be unpacked. They had arrived late on Thursday and she'd stored them in the cellar in advance of the display she was sure Flora would want to create.

Cycling along Greenway Lane, Flora's mind was already busy. The All's Well enjoyed two large bow windows and, if she boxed clever, she could fit a substantial number of books into the space. Perhaps a window for each new title?

Throughout the day, a stream of visitors kept her busy. The Southdown bus company had recently begun a new service from Brighton that wound its way through Abbeymead and the surrounding villages to finish in Steyning. It brought extra trade to the bookshop, and extra trade, she was glad to see, to her fellow shopkeepers, but the constant ring of the All's Well's bell allowed her to finish only half a window of Ian Flemings, while the Braithwaite novel remained firmly in its packing case. She must leave her apologies to Rose who would have to finish the work tomorrow.

By the end of the day, Flora was tired but satisfied, happy to greet a patient Betty and wheel her from beneath her shelter in the cobbled courtyard. Cycling slowly along the short stretch of high street, she turned into Greenway Lane as she had done a thousand times before, her mind elsewhere. It had been a productive Monday and tomorrow she could leave for the college, confident that the All's Well was thriving. Life in Lewes, however, was unlikely to be such plain sailing and it was Hector Lansdale who was filling her thoughts.

He was a sweet-natured man, but he worried Flora. He was too stubborn, she thought, and he had it fixed in his mind that David Morton was his friend's killer. Morton might turn out to be, but no good would come to Hector from attacking the man, falling foul of the police, and very likely losing his job. After what Flora had heard on Friday evening, that was more than a possibility. She had to put her faith in Susan Vicary to talk some sense into their friend – tomorrow, perhaps, Jack would drive over to Newhaven and see Susan, or maybe—

Suddenly, she was sprawled across the road, hurting badly, with Betty lying injured beside her. For a while, Flora was too dazed to try to move, even to think, but the rumble of a tractor, louder by the second, woke her to imminent danger. Struggling, she attempted to get to her feet: death by tractor was not an attractive future.

It was fortunate it was travelling slowly, slow even for a farm vehicle, and its driver spotted Flora when she'd managed to raise herself only as far as her knees. Immediately, he cut the engine, jumping down from the cab and racing over to her. Very gently, he took hold of her arms and lifted her limp form from the tarmac, then before Flora could speak or even realise what he intended, he'd slung her over his shoulder and walked back to the tractor, depositing her on the buddy seat while Betty, her wheels still lazily turning, was heaved onto the back.

In minutes, and with great skill, he'd executed an amazing three-point turn at the junction with the high street – in the process holding up any traffic on its way to Brighton – before trundling back down the lane to reach her cottage. It was only when they stopped outside her garden gate that he spoke.

'There we are, my love. Husband home?'

Flora nodded, still unable to find her voice.

'Tha's good.' Jumping down once more, he strode up the garden path to knock loudly at the door.

Jack must have just finished writing for the day because he arrived down the stairs in record time. Standing on the threshold, his astonishment was clear: a strange man, a tractor, and—

'Flora!'

'Been a bit of an accident,' the driver said cheerfully. 'Your lass is OK. Just needs a cuppa, I guess. Not sure about the bike, though.'

'Never mind the bike!'

He ran down the path and wrenched open the cab door. Flora had recovered sufficiently to be helped down from the heights, her feet a little unsteady on the ground.

'You didn't say never mind the bike, did you?' she said in his ear.

He gave a weak grin. 'Betty didn't hear me, I promise. Can you make it to the door on your own while I look after her?'

Flora nodded, walking slowly through the gateway and passing the driver on the way back to his tractor. 'I haven't thanked you properly,' she said, 'but I'm truly grateful. Thank you for rescuing me.'

'Yes, thank you,' Jack echoed, carrying a mangled Betty towards her shed.

'All in a day's work,' the man said jokily. 'If you're goin' to fall off yer bike, make sure a tractor's close by!'

'How come you fell off the bike? And so badly?' Jack asked. He'd settled her on the sitting room sofa and brought a cup of hot sweet tea. 'Betty's handlebars are twisted and she'll need the chain fixing and the brakes checked, and you' – he peered down at her face – 'you have what's going to be a massive bruise on your cheek. And your fingers...' He pointed to the rapidly blackening hand emerging from her sleeve.

'Looking like the rest of me, I guess. I must have fallen flat on my face.'

'But how?' Jack was mystified. 'You're as solid as a rock on that bicycle.'

Flora was silent for a moment, trying to make sense of what had happened. One minute she'd been worrying over Hector and the next lying across the road, her body hurting from top to toe.

'There was a wire,' she said at last. As she'd lain on the tarmac, she'd felt something beneath her that shouldn't have been there. 'I didn't see it, but I must have ridden into it.'

'A wire? You mean across the lane?'

'I don't know. I think it must have been. I felt it lying beneath me. One end of it, at least. Perhaps it broke as I cycled into it?'

The lines on Jack's face were carved deep. 'Where exactly did this happen?'

'A few hundred yards down the lane, after I turned off the high street.'

For a short while, he sat staring at the opposite wall, his

hands locked in a tight clasp. Then, abruptly, he jumped up. 'Will you be all right on your own for a few minutes?'

'What are you going to do?' There was anxiety in Flora's voice.

'Don't worry. Nothing dramatic.'

'You're going to look for the wire?'

'I'm going to try.'

A second later, she heard the front door click shut.

Jack was true to his word, returning before Flora had finished the cup of tea he'd made for her.

Striding into the sitting room, he dangled a long piece of wire between his fingers. 'You were right and this is the culprit. Attached to a tree on the other side of the lane and, presumably, before you met it, to a tree on yours.'

Flora winced. 'Someone did that,' she said with difficulty. 'Someone actually did that?'

He waited.

'Was it a prank, do you think?'

'If it was, it could have been a deadly one.' He turned the wire over in his hands. 'It's copper, thin, unlikely to be noticed but quite able to cut a throat.' He knelt down by the sofa, reaching out for her. 'If you'd been shorter, it could have done just that.'

Flora sat still, holding on to his hand. 'Not a prank, then?'

'Would anyone be so stupid, even a child? And with the wire at the height it was, how could it be a child? *My* question is, how long had it been there?'

'A question we can't answer. And does it matter?'

'I think it does. This will be difficult to swallow, but if the wire was attached just before you cycled along the lane, it was clearly meant for you.'

She shook her head. 'It can't have been. How would anyone...' She stopped speaking.

'That's right. By watching you. Watching the bookshop, watching you pack up, turn the shop sign to closed, lock the door. In the time it took you to walk round to the courtyard and collect Betty, it would be possible – as long as the wire was already attached to one side of the lane – to string it across to the other.'

A fierce shudder passed through Flora's frame. 'I think I must have blacked out. For a moment, I'd no idea where I was, what had happened. It was the tractor that woke me. If it hadn't arrived ...'

'Who knows what might have happened? You were unconscious and vulnerable. Maybe it was enough for our villain to have you ride into that wire, but maybe he or she was still watching. And readying themselves to attack.'

'Kenneth Buckley's revenge, do you think?' She tried to smile but it hurt too much.

'Or the Mortons'? The nephew didn't get *me* so perhaps they've decided on you as easier prey.'

'I guess the Mortons are a more likely threat. It seems they've been able to act with impunity and, now that Larry Morton has been charged with fraud, they'll be doubly dangerous. They'll have put two and two together and blamed us for the interest the police are showing in them. David Morton attempted to drown you for simply calling on Mrs Vicary, so having their business destroyed must warrant much worse.'

'It could have been the Mortons staging an attack as revenge, or Buckley because his pride was badly damaged and maybe you've lost him clients. But when you think about it, whether it was either of them or someone else, it has little to do with Alex Vicary.' He jumped up to take her empty cup.

'And the someone else you mentioned? Buckley and the Mortons aren't our only suspects.'

'Diane Croft? Hardly. Although perhaps the warning Sally passed on was designed to deflect suspicion away from Diane and onto Buckley. Is she handy with a piece of wire?'

Flora ignored the comment. 'Never mind Diane. There's Ferdie Luxton and his questionable past which he knows that we know about. And Bruce Sullivan borrowing from a junior teacher – he must suspect I saw him. It could be a warning from either of them to keep quiet.'

'We've landed ourselves in the middle of something very nasty, Flora. You could have been killed this afternoon and I could have been killed in Newhaven. I think it's time we dipped out; the investigation has become too dangerous. Ridley intends to interview every one of these people and we should let him get on with his job.'

'Not yet,' she croaked, her face now so badly swollen it was difficult to speak. 'You should talk to Mrs Vicary, as you planned – at the very least, we have to save Hector from any further trouble – and I'll speak to Mrs Sullivan.'

'I doubt you'll be able to,' he said, smoothing her bruised cheek, now a violent shade of purple. 'Not without lisping!'

'I will,' she said stoutly. 'And without a lisp. The bruising will soon improve.'

'OK, but when we've done that, we go to Ridley with anything we've found – including this.'

He wound the length of wire into a small spiral and tucked it into his pocket.

21

Overnight, the swelling on Flora's cheek had diminished considerably and, after applying a layer of thick make-up, she decided to brave a day at Riverdale where she set about making discreet enquiries. Bruce Sullivan's marriage to a wealthy wife proved more than a rumour. Several of his fellow teachers had been invited to a summer party that Mrs Sullivan had thrown last year and talked of a large house, richly furnished, and a garden that needed at least two full-time workers to care for it. A breathless description from an overawed music teacher left Flora wondering why Bruce was still working. He couldn't need the salary, yet seemed to derive little pleasure from teaching, and his pupils appeared to feel likewise. Whenever Flora had taken his class for reading – infrequently, since Bruce, unlike every other teacher at Riverdale, had almost always refused her help – the children had seemed preternaturally quiet and only slowly emerged from their shells as the lesson progressed.

Sandra Sullivan, Flora learned, had inherited a fortune from a father who'd owned one of the biggest foundries in Lewes. It was early in the nineteenth century that a former Marchant – Sandra's maiden name – had established an ironworks on the north bank of the Ouse and from this humble beginning the business had developed to become one of the town's largest employers, their products ranging from kitchen stoves to magnificent bandstands. The foundry's decorative ironwork adorned many a Sussex seaside town.

Flora was able to appreciate what practically Mr Marchant's fortune had meant when, late on Tuesday afternoon, she walked up the hill from Cleve College to the leafy roads at the top of the town. The area was not unfamiliar to her. Roberta Raffles, someone she preferred not to remember, had lived close by, but Roberta's house had been small change in comparison to the veritable mansion Flora discovered at the very end of a long drive.

Walking towards the pillared entrance, she practised the speech she hoped might gain her entry to the house and persuade a woman whom she had never met to talk honestly to her. It wouldn't be easy; for Mrs Sullivan, Flora Carrington was a complete unknown. And she might not even get to see the woman, since the property was bound to be well-guarded – alarms, dogs, a forbidding servant or two.

There was no trace of a hound, however, or any undue security for that matter, when Sandra Sullivan stood on the threshold. The woman was a surprise, a plump, homely figure, casually dressed, her hair slightly tousled and wearing not a hint of make-up.

'Good afternoon, Mrs Sullivan,' she began. 'My name is Flora Carrington. I'm a tea—'

'I know who you are. You're at the school. Riverdale. A volunteer, I believe.'

'Yes,' Flora said uncertainly. Bruce must have spoken of her to his wife, but why?

'My husband's not here, I'm afraid – some social event at the Masons Arms. But please, come in.' Mrs Sullivan took a step back, beckoning her to follow. The welcome flustered Flora.

She hadn't expected it to be easy. Certainly not as easy as this, Sandra Sullivan treating her as though they'd met only last week.

'You have a beautiful house,' she murmured, stepping into an art deco–inspired hall, all mirrored walls and black-and-white-tiled floor. In contrast, a tall vase sitting to one side was ablaze with the scarlet of spring lilies.

'I do, don't I,' Sandra agreed. 'One of the few nice things about having money.'

Flora blinked. 'I wouldn't know,' she said faintly, 'though I'd think having money must be highly enjoyable!'

'Most people do and, of course, it's better than having nothing, but if you're known to be wealthy, it brings all kinds of problems. Can I get you some tea? You look as if you've walked a long way.'

'Only from Riverdale.'

'That's quite a way. And quite a hill. I'll put the kettle on. Make yourself comfortable.' She pushed open an oak-panelled door, revealing a large, square room, every inch as elegant as the hall.

Her hostess disappeared at speed and Flora looked around appreciatively. Walls were panelled in dark grey and met halfway by a sumptuous wallpaper, a sunburst pattern in matching grey and primrose. Chairs and sofa, their backs fluted, wore a matching yellow, and brass wall lamps had been chosen to echo their shape. The whole was an aesthete's dream – Sandra's dream, she was sure – for brutish Bruce could never have devised such beauty.

Flora had walked over to the huge window to view the garden that took two workers to maintain when Mrs Sullivan returned with a tray.

'Do you like my new curtains?' Sandra asked.

Flora glanced quickly at the cream-and-gold-jacquard patterned drapes. 'I was just admiring them,' she said. It was only a small lie. 'They're beautiful.' And they were. Sandra might appear personally mundane, but her house was testimony to an exquisite sense of style.

'I think they look good.' Her hostess sounded satisfied. 'Bruce doesn't like them, but there... he has no taste. Milk and sugar?'

'Please.' Flora shifted awkwardly in her seat. 'I should apologise for turning up on your doorstep unannounced.'

'Nonsense.' Sandra handed her a dainty porcelain cup and saucer. 'It's always good to see a new face. And a very pretty face at that. But what exactly can I do for you? I imagine you're here for a purpose.'

Her hostess was sharp, too, Flora thought. She would have to guard her tongue. 'I was hoping to talk to you about Alex Vicary.'

'Alex Vicary?' Sandra looked blank.

'I understand he was a friend of your husband's. I did try to talk to Mr Sullivan but...' she paused, trying to find the right phrase, 'he preferred not to.'

'That sounds like Bruce. He can be a bear at times, but I'm afraid you've had a wasted journey, my dear. I've no idea who the young man is.'

'Was,' Flora said quickly. 'He died at the rehearsal that the Knights of Mercia staged at the castle.'

'The Knights! Bruce is with them now, but what a strange society that is. To my mind, at least. I suppose people get fun from it, but it's always seemed a nonsense to me.' Sandra would have bonded well with Alice, Flora thought. 'Grown men, and I think they are mostly men, really shouldn't be play-acting. But this Alex? I do believe I read about it in the local paper. A frightful accident and I'm so sorry. You say that Bruce was a friend of his? He's never mentioned the name to me.'

'Mr Sullivan and Alex and Hector Lansdale – you might not know him either – were in the habit of meeting for a drink at the Masons Arms. Most Friday evenings, I think. And they sometimes went to the races together.'

Sandra's open face took on a pinched appearance. 'That explains it – why Bruce never mentioned the boy.' She put down her cup and saucer on a brass-framed side table and slowly smoothed out the creases in her cotton skirt.

'Bruce has a problem,' she said at last. 'With gambling, and it has become steadily worse. Did you know?'

Flora shook her head. A silent response. The frankness had stunned her.

'It started way back, of course. I knew several people who kept racehorses and quite often stayed with them in Suffolk. It's where I met Bruce – at a party they threw. He didn't know much about horse racing at the time, but he took to the sport straight away, which was fine. The gambling, however, wasn't. It's what I meant about the perils of having money. It can encourage excess and, with Lewes racecourse so close – Bruce moved down here just before our wedding – introducing him to that world was asking for trouble. Of course, at the time I had no inkling.'

Bruce couldn't be in debt, though, Flora thought. OK, the perils of wealth, she could understand, but there must still be money around him.

'Every penny my husband earns goes on betting,' Sandra said conversationally. 'I used to give him an allowance. For extras, impulse buys, silly things he might fancy, but when that was gobbled up by the bookies as well, I gave him an ultimatum instead. Unless he stopped, so would the allowance.'

'Did he listen?' Flora dared to ask.

'From your question, I'm guessing you don't know anyone who has an addiction.'

Flora shook her head again, her mind already working to fit the pieces together. If the situation was as bad as Sandra suggested, the guess she'd made that Bruce might have borrowed from Alex Vicary was probably right. And right that he'd been unable to repay the money. What would Alex have done or said if Bruce had said no to his request?

'Bruce didn't stop,' Mrs Sullivan continued. 'I don't know why I ever thought he might. What's an allowance, after all, if you have food, shelter, a comfortable home? After that, there was nothing else I could do but threaten divorce.'

'Divorce?' Flora stared, her eyes wide.

'Drastic, I know, but it seems to have worked.'

'That must be a relief.'

'It is for Bruce. He had a lot to lose. For me, I'm not so sure.'

The woman was devastatingly honest, more or less admitting that she wouldn't mind being free of her husband. Flora couldn't blame her.

Sandra poured more tea for them both. 'Between you and me, my dear, the threat was an empty one. I'd never divorce. What would that look like – a prominent member of the Women's Institute like myself, not to mention heading the flower arrangers at St Michael's? I'd never live it down in the company I keep! But Bruce didn't need to know that and he hasn't the imagination to think it out for himself.'

Flora murmured her thanks for a second cup, her mind still thrumming. If Alex had threatened to go to the county education department and report Bruce Sullivan's gambling, Bruce would lose his job, but he'd still have a comfortable home and his wife had enough money for them both. In those circumstances, it would be crazy to risk killing Alex to rid himself of debt.

But if Alex had known of Sandra's final ultimatum – an imminent divorce – and threatened to tell her that Bruce was still gambling? Having one's allowance stopped was one thing, saying goodbye to a job you didn't much like was another, but losing a rich wife, the provider of a comfortable home, the person who would be duty bound to step in if things got really bad for you, *that* could have made Bruce desperate.

'My father never liked him, you know.' Sandra interrupted her thoughts and pulled Flora back to the present. 'But I was young – well, quite young, a little older than Bruce, of course – but still foolhardy.'

'Your father owned a large ironworks in the town, I believe.'

'He did. It was in the family for four generations. Poor Dad, it broke his heart to sell – literally, I'm afraid – but really there was nothing else he could do. I would have been hopeless at running it.'

'You were an only child?'

'I was. I had a cousin, a little older than me. He was supposed to take over the business when Dad retired. Dad was getting ready to train him but then he died.'

'How sad. He must have been very young.'

'It was suicide. Simon was mired in debt and fell into the most awful depression. Debt from gambling on the horses,' she said without emotion. 'It's why Bruce has to stop.'

Mrs Sullivan's life wasn't quite the charmed existence that Flora had imagined. If Bruce were ever tempted to take Simon's desperate escape from debt, the WI would be even more disapproving, she reckoned.

Getting to her feet, she fitted her cup neatly on to the tray. 'I really must go, Mrs Sullivan. I've trespassed on your time far too long and for no good reason. You never met Alex, you didn't even know his name. I wouldn't have bothered you, except I'm trying to piece together what exactly happened the day he died – for his mother.'

Sandra got up, too, and walked with her into the hall. 'I'm sorry I haven't been able to help,' she said, opening the front door for her guest. 'That poor woman! I feel for her. We never had children. It was Bruce's decision – he never wanted a child.

Ironic, isn't it? Now, here he is surrounded by the little darlings every day!'

22

The clock at St Michael's was chiming six as Flora walked past the church on her way down the hill to the college. For a moment, she stopped and looked up at the giant hands slowly ticking the seconds away, then, on impulse, veered left to walk further into the town. It was the Masons Arms she was walking towards, she realised. Pure instinct. But she could say hello to Sally and Diane – hopefully no one would notice a gatecrasher – and take a look at who'd attended Ferdie's farewell party. Maybe even speak to Ferdie himself. Make an attempt perhaps to discover just what had made him so fearful that he was willing to relinquish a whole chunk of the life he'd loved.

How long could she stay? Jack had a late appointment, she knew, but he would soon be back at the apartment. She took a hasty glance at her watch as though time might have stopped since she'd passed St Michael's. Would he worry if she wasn't home? Or assume, rightly, that she'd slipped away on one of those missions he decried? She would need to be quick.

Gales of laughter emanated from the pub as she walked up to the saloon door. The gathering, it turned out, had begun in a smaller side room booked for the occasion but had now spilled over into the saloon itself. An already smoke-filled atmosphere clung to her clothes as she sidled through the door and looked around for her friends. There was no sign of either Sally or Diane but Ferdie Luxton, red-faced and smiling, was in the middle of a circle of equally jolly drinkers.

Flora caught his eye as he lifted his glass, a piece of luck, she thought, and immediately wove a nifty path around the small clusters of well-wishers to reach the guest of honour.

'Mr Luxton,' she began breezily, speaking over the heads of the men who had formed something of a protective ring around their companion. 'I was passing the pub on my way home' – it was only a half lie – 'and thought I'd pop in for a few minutes to wish you well.'

Ferdie didn't look too happy at being wished well, at least not by Flora. Their last encounter must still be vivid in his memory but, at the sound of her voice, the men had politely parted, allowing her to wiggle her way through and arrive at Luxton's shoulder.

'I'm so sorry you feel you have to leave the society,' she said in a low voice. 'I can imagine how hard that must be.'

'No, you can't,' he said gruffly. 'All you were interested in, if I recall rightly, was to rake up old hogwash, and accuse me of I don't know what.'

'That was a mistake,' she admitted, her head lowered, 'but I was misled.' Another lie, but would it help?

'You certainly were. Insulting, I call it.' Not much of a help then.

He took another swig of his beer and looked down at her. 'If you were really interested in finding out what happened to young Alex, it's not me you should be troubling.'

'I realise that now and I can only apologise.' She allowed herself a small pause. 'Someone has been "troubling" you, I think,' she suggested delicately.

'I've nothing to say.' The refusal was absolute.

She noticed Kenneth Buckley standing a few groups away. He'd stopped talking to his companion and was staring hard. There were other pairs of eyes, too, Flora realised. Eyes trained on her.

'Of course, I understand. You won't want to talk – I can see how distressing it must be. I just can't believe that someone might harm you...'

'They're not going to. Because I'm saying nothing about it.'

'"It" being what you saw that day at the rehearsal?'

The lines on his face had assumed a stone-like rigidity. 'Take my advice, Mrs Carrington, if you can take advice. Keep clear of this nonsense or it will be you who's troubled next.'

'How right you are! I already have been.'

He stared at her. 'Then you're more fool than you look,' he growled, before turning away.

'Flora!' It was Sally in fetching pale blue jersey. A newly acquired tea dress, Flora noted. 'Diane's here.' Her friend pointed towards the saloon entrance where Diane Croft was talking to the grey-bearded man Flora remembered from the rehearsal. 'We'd just popped in to the Ladies and missed you arriving. But I'd no idea you were coming.'

'I wasn't. Not really,' she said awkwardly. 'I was passing the Masons Arms and thought I'd drop in for a few minutes to see you.'

'And saw Ferdie instead.' The girl's eyebrows were raised. Really, she was getting as untrusting as Alice.

It was evident that Sally had heard nothing of the tumble from Betty – another sweep of panstick had kept the bruising covered – and really, it was better that she didn't. If it *had* been Kenneth Buckley who'd tied that wire between the trees, her friend would be sure to recite Diane's warning again, with a scold for Flora to be more careful in the future. Sally could well be turning into her aunt.

'I couldn't see you when I came in,' she excused herself,

'and I'd met Mr Luxton before and thought I'd have a chat with him. But I can't stay, I'm afraid. I've supper to cook.'

'You're leaving already? I suppose that's having a husband to look after. At least, I don't have that problem.'

'There's no problem and Jack can look after himself.' Flora felt a ripple of irritation. 'But I'll be seeing you soon in any case. We've a new Betty Crocker coming in next week. The book's taken a while to arrive but I know Alice is hoping for a copy.'

Giving Sally a light kiss on the cheek, she wove a path to the door, intensely conscious of eyes that were still watching.

Jack had already scrubbed potatoes for their evening meal when she walked through the door of the apartment.

'Sorry,' he said, looking up from the sink. 'It looks like another meal of jacket potatoes. I wasn't sure what else we had to eat.'

'There is nothing else. Maybe you can persuade the new principal to install a more modern stove.'

'Highly unlikely.' He dropped a kiss on her forehead. 'And where exactly have you been? Dare I ask?'

That was an easy one. She could recount her call at the Sullivan house, and her conviction that Bruce had questions to answer. But after she'd told him of an unusual visit and an even more unusual Sandra Sullivan, Jack refused to agree. He was adamant that, with a home such as she described, Sullivan would never have borrowed money.

'And if he didn't,' he said, piling the cheese she'd grated into a bowl, 'then the case against him falls to pieces. I mean, why would he borrow? He's sitting on a pile of money already!'

'His wife's money,' Flora reminded him, waving the cheese grater for emphasis. 'Bruce spent every bit of his salary at the bookies and, when the monthly allowance was no more, he would have had to borrow to fund his gambling. Sandra says he's an addict, that he can't stop.'

'There would be other ways he could get money – by selling what he owns, for instance. I imagine he has a fair number of valuables tucked away. And he must win sometimes. His winnings might not make up for what he loses, but they've probably helped keep him afloat.'

'Then why has he stopped gambling? Why not continue winning a few bets, losing a lot more, and selling stuff to make up the shortfall?'

'You're sure he has stopped?' He took their plates to the table. 'Don't forget you overheard him trying to extort money from that youngster.'

'I think it must have been to pay an old debt. Sandra Sullivan isn't stupid. On the contrary, she's a smart woman and if she's decided her husband has stopped, then he has.'

Jack sat down on one of the rickety kitchen chairs, resting his elbows on the table. 'What's your point, Flora? I don't understand why it matters.'

Flora matched her elbows with his. 'My point is that if Sullivan borrowed money from Alex and never paid it back – perhaps refused even to try, and he's quite capable of that – then when the Mortons began their persecution and Alex needed every penny to protect his mother, he would have a threat to hold over Bruce. Sandra had warned her husband that if he gambled again, she would divorce him.'

'Really? But would she have carried out her threat?'

Flora smiled slightly. 'She wouldn't. But Bruce didn't know that and I don't think he'd risk it. Think what would happen if his wife cast him adrift. He'd lose everything. His whole life would be ruined. He'd be desperate to stop Alex from going to his wife with the story, and if he didn't have the money to pay...'

Jack looked sceptical. 'What grounds would Sandra have for divorce?'

'Unreasonable behaviour. Bruce's addiction has put a huge strain on the marriage. Even cruelty, if Sandra proved it had affected her mentally and emotionally.'

When Jack's expression became even more sceptical, Flora was still certain. 'We should keep Bruce on our list. In my view, make him our new number one suspect.'

'Because you don't like him?' Jack mocked.

'I don't, though I did like his wife.'

'If you did, then gunning for her husband, hoping he'll be charged with murder, isn't exactly helpful.'

'Oh, I don't know about that.' She grinned. 'I'm not sure Sandra would agree!'

～

Flora had paid her visit to Mrs Sullivan, though with what result Jack was unsure, and he needed to make his own promised trip to Newhaven and the Vicarys' house before they left for Abbeymead once more. His chance came the following afternoon when a student, who had booked an appointment with him, developed a raging toothache and the West Country epic that would prove a bestseller – Ronald Goodman was convinced – had hastily to be put aside in favour of an emergency visit to the dentist.

Jack thought of ringing Mrs Vicary from the college to tell her he was on his way, but then decided a spot visit might be more helpful. If, despite police warnings, David Morton was still menacing her, it would be good to catch him in the act. Flora's disaster was vivid in Jack's mind; to risk harming someone so brutally, or worse, to set out to kill them in that fashion, was appalling. It spoke of a cold, vengeful mind at work, and that seemed to sum up Morton well. As for his uncle, Larry Morton appeared temporarily to have gone to ground, waiting, Jack presumed, for the fraud case to wind its tortuous way to court.

Susan Vicary, he knew, was employed in a grocer's shop and Wednesday was early closing in Newhaven. She should be at home, he calculated, a risk he was prepared to take. A risk that paid off when he found her at her front door, house keys in hand, and two large bags of shopping sitting at her feet. She looked weary.

'Mr Carrington!' she greeted him, trying for a smile. 'What brings you to Newhaven?'

'Here, let me take these.' He scooped up the bags and carried them into the kitchen, lining them up on the wooden table. 'Can I help you unpack?'

'No, thanks, love. I know where everything goes, and you'll be all at sea. But you can make us both a cuppa. I need a pick-me-up.'

'It's been a hard morning?'

'A hard week, but then every week is these days. I miss my lad.'

There was no adequate response he could make, and Jack set to work on the tea, ferreting out mugs and teapot from various cupboards and rescuing the last dribble of milk from the refrigerator.

'The milkie will have left a couple of gold tops,' she told him, unpacking the second bag. 'In the nook by the boot scraper.'

Once the last of the shopping had been packed away and mugs of tea sat steaming on the table, along with a plate of fairy cakes, Susan asked him again, 'What brings you here, Mr Carrington? Are you checking up on me?'

'In a manner of speaking. I thought it was time. I should have called before to ask whether you'd had any more trouble.'

'I haven't – it's been quiet, which is nice. A bit strange,

though, I'd got so used to things going wrong. But quiet is nice,' she repeated. 'Just lonely.'

There was little Jack could say that would in any way ease the woman's sadness, so instead he asked, 'Did you know that Larry Morton has been charged with fraud?'

'I did hear a rumour. It's true then? It probably explains why that horrible nephew of his hasn't been around.'

'Has Hector Lansdale been around, though?' This was a moment he could warn her of possible trouble, and Jack grabbed the opportunity.

She shook her head. 'I've not seen Hector for several weeks. He telephones, bless him, but he's a busy lad. The hotel is doing very well, he says, more'n more people staying there and eating at the restaurant.'

Jack cleared his throat. 'Flora and I are a little concerned, Mrs Vicary... We think that Hector might come here to... to threaten David Morton. Sort him out, I think his words were.'

'Sort him out?' She sat back in her chair, her expression serious, her worry lines deepening. 'He's not mentioned the Mortons whenever he's phoned, and why would he do something stupid like that?'

'We hope he doesn't, but we thought it best to warn you. Hector is unhappy with the coroner's verdict, you must know that. He seems convinced the Mortons are to blame for Alex's death.'

'I do know. The lad believes my Alex was pushed off that rampart.'

'But you don't?'

'Who would want to do that? Alex didn't have an enemy in the world. It's Hector, bless him, trying to make sense of his friend's death. I can understand why. I'm trying to as well.'

'Does making sense still involve moving house?'

Susan leant back against the wooden struts of the kitchen chair. 'I've had another thought about that,' she said placidly.

'The Mortons aren't bothering me any more and now that old villain is being investigated by the police, mebbe they won't in the future.'

'So, you'll stay?'

'I'd love to. It's my home,' she said simply. 'Here, have another cake.'

Jack chose carefully. 'A lemon icing this time, I think. They're very good.'

'Alex always said my baking could win a prize. But then I *was* his ma. If I stay,' she went on, 'I'll have to take a lodger to make ends meet. Since Alex died, things have been a bit difficult.' There was a pause. 'I've been clearing his room,' she said sadly. 'It's not been easy, but it's where any lodger will sleep.'

Jack studied her face and wondered if he had the right to intrude further. 'Perhaps,' he suggested, 'you'll find somewhere safe to store Alex's favourite things. His papers, too.'

It was the vaguest of mentions, but he hoped the idea of papers might lead Mrs Vicary to confide what she'd found, if anything, in her son's bedroom. The anything for which her recent burglar might have been searching.

'Alex didn't have that much, really, and what he had I've packed away in a suitcase. I'll get the postie to pop it into the roof space for me when he calls next.'

'Can I help—'

'That's nice of you, Mr Carrington, but the postie likes a cuppa on his rounds and we both enjoy a chat. But it's the savings book that has me in a puzzle.'

At last, maybe some tangible evidence. 'What kind of puzzle?' he asked gently.

'You see, I wouldn't want to use the money that's in it, that would feel bad, yet it's no good to Alex any more...'

'Does it amount to much?'

'Quite a sum. I was surprised. But then, if the boy was planning to marry, he'd want to save as much of his salary as he could. And there was the extra he earned being the society's armourer. Members would pay a fair price for a new shield or a helmet. One of my neighbours is a jeweller, and he's going to sell the engagement ring for me, like you suggested. But this savings account, it didn't feel right.'

Jack was itching to ask her for sight of the savings book, but it seemed too crass. He was rescued from embarrassment when she said, 'Alex saved a good amount but he took quite a bit of money out, too.' She frowned. 'I thought maybe it was to buy the ring but, though the ruby is beautiful, my neighbour tells me it wasn't as expensive as you'd think.'

'Did you notice the date of the withdrawal?'

'It was last year sometime. A big sum. But where the money went, I'm not sure. Alex didn't spend it, or I'd have known.'

'Could I take a look?' he asked, tentatively.

'I'd be glad if you did. Maybe you can make more sense of it than me. I've never had a head for figures. I'll nip upstairs and fetch it down.'

But when Susan handed him the bright blue savings book, Jack could see, even without his glasses, that there wasn't much to make sense of. Over the last three years, Alex had tucked away a substantial sum, more than Jack would expect. The young man had worked as a counter assistant in the tourist information office and Jack wouldn't have thought his wages large enough to warrant such a sum. Alex had evidently been on a mission – to marry Diane Croft, for which he'd need money. But, as Susan Vicary had said, one large withdrawal was registered in the book, made just before last Christmas. Jack ensured he memorised the sum.

'And you've really no idea where the money went?'

Susan looked uncomfortable. 'He did tell me once that a friend had asked him for help, but he said he'd be certain to get back any cash he'd lent. It was when things started to go wrong here and it looked like we'd need money to keep our home.'

'I'm assuming the debt was never repaid?'

'It might have been. I don't know.'

'Do you know who the friend was?' It was the crucial question.

She shook her head. 'Alex could be secretive like that.'

Flora's guess of borrowed money as a plausible motive for Alex's death had been right, Jack thought, and today they'd come a little further along the path to finding the truth. A little further but, he suspected, still a long way to go.

He went to hand back the savings book to his hostess and was surprised to feel a very slight bump in the cardboard cover. Flicking the book open, he turned to the final page.

'There's a small ridge at the back,' he said, holding the book up for Susan to see. 'Did you notice?'

She shook her head. 'I didn't. I just looked at my lad's savings – and cried.'

Jack laid a consoling hand on her arm, then peered down, tracing the outline of the page with his finger. 'I think this page has been stuck down. I don't think it was ever the final page. That's beneath. It seems to be covering something.'

'What?'

'I'd need to slit it open to find out. Would that be OK?'

Please, his inner voice was saying, let it be OK.

'I suppose,' she said doubtfully. 'Do you need a knife?'

'A razor blade would be better.'

'Right.' Her voice trembled a little but in a few minutes she was back with a blade.

Very carefully, Jack slit the page at the top, the bottom and one side, then peeled it back. Tucked into what had been a pocket made out of the two pages was a square of folded paper.

'Here's the something,' he said, unsure if it had been worth the excitement. Unfolding the square, he smoothed out a small scruffy sheet of paper.

'Well?' Mrs Vicary asked.

'It's an IOU,' he said slowly. 'An IOU for the sum that matches exactly the withdrawal from Alex's account.'

'That's it, then. That's the money he lent.'

The puzzle had begun to slot together. For Mrs Vicary, it had made a whole, but not for him. When Jack looked more closely, the name on the IOU was enough to destroy any smugness. It made him stare and his eyebrows rise spectacularly.

Not Bruce Sullivan, as Flora had predicted, but none other than Ferdie Luxton.

_____

23

Leaving Susan Vicary with a promise to keep in touch, Jack walked to the end of the road, his car parked around the corner. It was a quiet time of day in a quiet enclave. Most people were still at work or busy with young children home from school, and the bustle of the port close by went largely unheard.

As he turned the corner into the adjoining street, a sudden movement caught his attention – the fleeting sense of a figure slipping from behind one of the plane trees that lined the pavement. Keenly aware that he was on enemy territory, Jack was slow in approaching the Austin. The Mortons might be under police surveillance, but they were likely to be out for revenge.

His gaze travelled back along the street he'd walked, but there was no one in sight; front doors were shut and gardens empty except for the odd bike or toy tractor abandoned to the grass. Jack circled the vehicle, taking note of the doors, the windows, the tyres, and finally the boot. Nothing seemed to have been tampered with and, losing the tension that had built, he climbed into the car. Did he need to be quite so suspicious? After Flora's horrific experience, it was probably wise. The Mortons seemed able to operate largely unchecked, whenever or wherever they wished. And no doubt they did wish. Feeling some frustration, he switched on the ignition and headed for Abbeymead.

He had plenty to tell Flora, not least the bombshell that it was Luxton, not Bruce Sullivan, who had been borrowing from Alex. Did Ferdie have an addiction to gambling, too? Or maybe it was something simpler. It was possible, he supposed, that the man could regularly outspend his pension if he was drinking for hours each night in the Masons Arms. But to kill a man because you owe him for drinks – the tab must have been hefty, judging by the size of Alex's withdrawal – seemed to Jack the peak of brutishness, if not stupidity.

~

'We should go to the Masons Arms tonight,' was Flora's immediate response, clattering their empty plates into the sink, 'and find out what Luxton did with all that money.'

If her recent encounter with the man was anything to go by, he was unlikely to be co-operative, but the news that it was the ex-publican to whom Alex had lent money had come as a shock and she was desperate to take some action.

Jack glanced across at the Utility-designed clock with which the college had furnished the flat. 'Not a chance! It's past eight already and I'm full of beef stew.'

He rescued the boiling kettle and filled the teapot before he spoke. 'I think we should wait.'

'But why? You've discovered who really owed Alex money. My theory that it was Bruce Sullivan was completely wrong. We need to speak to Luxton and, if we don't go tonight, we won't be in Lewes again for another five days.'

'I'll be in Brighton on Saturday,' he announced to her surprise, 'and I've a feeling it could help.'

'Why Brighton?'

'When I got back to college this afternoon, I was asked to escort a group visiting the Pavilion.'

'But why you?'

'Vanessa Clarke was down to do the field trip – she's the art teacher who replaced Jocelyn – but she telephoned this morning to say she was sick. She thinks she has influenza.'

'I still don't see why you're her replacement. What have you to do with Brighton Pavilion?'

'Not a lot, except there will be a few writers in the group, students I already know. I reckon they'll love the atmosphere, the sheer madness of the place, and I expect their creativity to soar! The Pavilion holds an important archive, too, so for those writing historical novels, it should be fascinating.'

'I'm sure you'll have fun, but I can't see how it helps us move forward. Whereas questioning Ferdie just might.'

'And so might Saturday's trip. I'm planning to slip off at some point in the day – when I judge the students are sufficiently engrossed – and trot to the police station. Brighton Town Hall is close by and Ridley is likely to be there. I saw a billboard on my way home with news of a murder splashed across it. A body found yesterday in Preston Park, and the inspector is sure to be in his office the whole weekend. If I can talk to him face to face, I might persuade him to dig more deeply into Alex's finances. The savings book Susan found doesn't necessarily tell the whole story. The boy could have lent to other people, not just Ferdie and, before we talk to the chap again, it would be good to know. It's possible that Alex lent cash.'

'In that case, the loan or loans will be virtually impossible to trace.'

'For us, certainly, but I still think it's worth speaking to Alan. I can hand over the trip wire at the same time. That you were attacked in such a brutal fashion might spur him on.'

'Will it, though?' she said a trifle gloomily. 'Will he be interested, now he has another murder on his hands?'

'All I can do is try.'

Flora didn't feel much hope, but if Jack wanted to see the policeman before they invaded the Masons Arms once more, she felt bound to go along with it. He'd been the one to discover Luxton's debt. Hogwash, Ferdie had called the gossip about him. Not such hogwash, after all.

The delay, though, increased her restlessness. While the investigation was on the move, even if slowly, it added a smidgen of excitement to her days in the town, but increasingly she felt a yearning to be back in Abbeymead. She had tried hard to settle into this new life, knowing the move to Lewes had been good for Jack. Riverdale was a delightful school in which to spend time, and she had grown to love the children she'd helped these past few months. But it wasn't enough. Maybe, if she'd been a fully-fledged teacher, her feelings would be different but, as it was, she had a bookshop to run and she suspected she wasn't doing it terribly well.

The part of her life she spent in Abbeymead now seemed always to be at arm's length when, previously, it had been its centre. Rose Lawson was an excellent assistant, but the All's Well wasn't her business and she couldn't be expected to go the extra mile, though she often did: staying late to set up new displays, spending time tracing a difficult to obtain book, riding a heavily laden Betty for the Friday deliveries. They had ground to a halt once Charlie had begun work at the Priory, and she had Rose to thank for their reinstatement.

She sensed that Jack was restless, too, finding it more and more difficult to balance the demands of college work with his desire to write books that would sell. And since meeting the new principal, his restlessness seemed to have grown. His first impression, he'd said, had been of a hard-hitting business-woman, perfectly pleasant but with an entrenched opinion of how best to ensure the college remained financially stable, and that didn't appear to include employing journeymen such as himself. Flora had struggled not to feel pleased at this news, but for the moment she was trying hard to curb her fretfulness. Tomorrow they would be home again.

A loud knocking at the apartment door had Jack quickly finish cleaning his teeth and cast around for the house keys.

'Who on earth...?' Flora called from the bedroom. 'It's almost eleven.'

'Let's find out, shall we?'

A tired fumbling with the lock and Jack opened the door to the college's night porter, torch in hand, and standing glumly on the front path.

'Phone call for you, Mr Carrington,' he said.

'A phone call – at this time of night?'

'Exactly,' the man muttered. 'I'll tell the bloke you're coming.' He looked down at Jack's pyjamas. 'When you're dressed.'

That was something he wouldn't do, he decided, and instead reached for his old overcoat, fitting cold feet into a pair of outdoor shoes.

'What's happening?'

Flora had appeared in the tiny hall, pulling on slippers as she walked.

'I've no idea. A phone call. But why this time of night... I'll have to answer it, though. Go back to bed and keep warm. I won't be long.'

He was a bit longer than he'd expected. The tramp to the college building took some time, at night and in pitch dark – the porter had gone ahead and Jack had been unable to lay his hand on a torch – and the call when he finally got to the telephone was lengthy.

'Were you in bed?' Inspector Ridley asked, not sounding particularly interested.

'Pretty much.'

'Lucky man. We're still working here and will be for hours to come. By the look of it, we've murder number three on our hands.'

'You're ringing about another killing?'

'Wouldn't have bothered you otherwise – and why haven't you a phone in your flat? – but I know you're into this case good and proper and we need help. You don't mind?'

Jack, standing in an empty school foyer, his overcoat only half covering his pyjamas and with bare feet uncomfortable in brogues, murmured something inaudible.

'Ferdie Luxton,' Ridley began, 'found early this morning at the bottom of the Fairy Steps. Do you know them?'

Jack tried to picture the location and failed.

'They're the flight of stairs that lead down to the Pells Pond. The railway line runs close by.'

He had a better idea now. 'What was Luxton doing there?'

'Going home, I guess. He lives in a road just uphill from the Pond. He'd been to his farewell celebration at the Masons Arms. Those dratted Knights again!'

'Flora mentioned there was some kind of party. But wasn't it earlier in the day?'

'As far as my blokes can gather, the farewell went on for quite some time. Most of the partygoers had drifted off before closing but Luxton, according to the landlord, was still holding court until he pushed them out of the door.'

'By then, he was drunk?' Jack guessed.

'As a lord, I'd say.'

'And then fell down a flight of steps? So, why is it murder? If anything says accident, that must.'

'Except for a bloody great chunk out of the back of his head. A blunt object, the pathologist reckons. He'll be doing a detailed post-mortem today, but it looks pretty clear to me. Luxton was bashed over the head as he made his way down the steps and crashed to the bottom. His facial injuries fit. He'd have suffered them when he landed.'

Ferdie Luxton dead, Jack thought. That put paid to ever finding out what happened to the money Alex had lent him. And put paid to any theory that had Luxton guilty of pushing Alex from that wall. Unless, of course, he had and his murder was revenge for Alex's death.

'How can I help?' Jack asked, suddenly aware that he'd not spoken for minutes.

'For a start, you can hand over anything you and your lady have discovered about Luxton. I'm sure you've been digging around on the quiet; I know neither of you accepted Vicary's death was an accident. The situation I'm in is ridiculous – three murders on my hands in as many weeks. I've had to appoint a separate team to investigate the Preston Park killing, and there's simply not enough people to do a decent job.'

'I do have stuff I need to share,' Jack admitted. 'I was planning to come by in a day or two, if you're around.'

'Around? I'll be around until Christmas at this rate. Yes, bring whatever "stuff" you have. We need it.'

After a murmured goodnight to a disgruntled porter, Jack walked slowly back to the flat and found Flora hovering by the door, her expression uncertain.

'Well?'

'It was Ridley. Luxton is dead,' he said baldly.

Shrugging off his overcoat and shoes, he was glad to substitute a dressing gown and slippers. 'I need a cocoa. How about you?'

It was only then, turning to ask, that he noticed how white Flora had become.

'Is something wrong? You look... as though you've seen the ghost of Cleve! It's messed up the questions we had, but other-wise... a man is dead and maybe we should be thinking of him.' He was annoyed with himself. He'd sounded unusually prig-gish, but it seemed to have had little effect on Flora.

'I am thinking of him,' she said faintly and, walking into the kitchen, sank down on the first chair she came to. Her eyes had filled with tears.

'Flora, what's going on?' He was concerned now.

'I may have had him killed,' she said, and her voice trembled.

He must have looked bewildered because she tried to continue. 'I called at the Masons Arms yesterday after I left the Sullivans' house. Called in at Luxton's party. I didn't mention it.'

'You rarely do,' he said a trifle tartly. 'But how would calling in at his party have killed him?'

She looked blankly at the table top. 'I spoke to him, ques-tioned him. Obviously, I didn't know about the IOU then, but there were other things to ask. Why was he so fearful of being harmed that he was even at a farewell party? He wouldn't speak about it and warned me that I should stop looking for answers.'

'I still don't see—'

'We were watched. There were people in the room who were watching us as we talked. The killer was there, Jack, in the middle of that gathering. Clearly, now, not one of the Mortons, but one of the Knights. Whoever it was must have thought that Ferdie was talking out of turn, doing exactly what he'd been warned not to.'

And what *you'd* been warned not to, Jack thought, his heart tightening.

He came to sit beside her. 'It doesn't necessarily add up,' he said gently. 'The murderer could already have planned to kill Ferdie that night, without your intervention. He was well known as a drinker and it would be a reasonable guess that he'd get blotto on an evening held in his honour. Our villain could have waited for Ferdie to leave the pub – maybe he or she left earlier as a decoy – but then followed the man as he made his way home. The Fairy Steps would be an ideal location for an attack.'

Flora was silent, until she asked dully, 'Who found him?'

'Who often does? A dog walker early this morning.'

'And the inspector has only just called you?'

'He's frazzled. It's the third murder on his patch in not much more than a month. Added to which we're not the easiest people to get hold of when we're here – witness, the night porter – he was not a happy man.'

When Flora made no move to get up, he bent to put his arms around her, burying his face in her hair. 'You can't blame yourself, Flora.'

'But I do,' she said. 'I have the feeling that if I hadn't gone to the Masons Arms yesterday, hadn't spoken to Ferdie, he might still be alive.'

Jack had that feeling too, but it was not something he'd ever say. Instead, it was more comfort that was needed.

'Whatever the sequence of events, the man is dead. The best thing we can do for him now is find his killer. But first, it's sleep. Come on, we'll forget the cocoa, it's time for bed.'

Gently, he lifted her off the chair and, an arm around her shoulders, walked her into the bedroom.

24

Early on Saturday morning, the coach hired by Cleve College stopped at the bottom of the Steine to disgorge Jack and around twenty students. Today, Brighton Pavilion was looking particularly splendid, its gleaming minarets meeting an unusually blue sky, suggesting to the group perhaps that they'd arrived in India rather than the Sussex seaside.

Several of the students had visited before, but for the majority the palace was a revelation. Jostled together, they stood, amazed and dazzled, as they took in the extraordinary nature of the building. Jack was quick to wake them from their spell, ushering them through the entrance and into the Octagon Hall where an official guide was waiting. Clipboard in hand, she was ready to lead the group along the Long Gallery through the magnificent Banqueting Room to the restored kitchen and on to the King's apartments, and finally the even more magnificent Music Room. An hour spent in the Pavilion archives would follow, with tea and cakes, a special treat, provided in the Saloon.

It was as they left the rich scarlet of the Music Room, its silvered dragons and lotus-shaped chandeliers having effectively silenced student chatter, and were making their way down the stairs to the archive, that Jack thought it an opportune moment to slide quietly away and escape to the sunshine of a beautiful May day.

He strolled quickly along New Road and, since the town hall was only steps away, within minutes was walking down the stairs to the cellar that housed the police station. Reaching the bottom step, he almost cannoned into Alan Ridley. Surprised, the inspector took a step back, before an amused grin spread across his face.

'Am I seeing an apparition in my station or is this really Jack Carrington?'

'As promised, it's me all right. But you're on your way out.'

'Not for long, old chap. I need to breathe fresh air for a while. I thought a brisk walk along the seafront – fancy it?'

Jack did. A distant glimpse of sea at the bottom of East Street had sent him wishing for a walk by the beach.

'And an ice cream?' Ridley asked, as they crossed the main road to the seafront. 'You have to have an ice cream on a day like today.'

Jack laughed. 'A ninety-nine would go down well,' he agreed.

'Two ninety-nines,' the inspector ordered from the mobile van parked by the promenade.

'So... why come today? I expected you earlier.'

'I'm on a visit to the Pavilion – playing nanny to a group of students from the college.'

'Playing truant, too, by the look of it.' Ridley grinned. 'Shouldn't you be with them?'

'They'll be busy for the next hour or so, in the archives. Time enough to talk.'

'Here' – he handed Jack a giant cone – 'no eating the flake first.'

'Thanks. I have to ask, any progress on the Luxton case?'

'We've moved a little forward... but then again, we haven't.'

'And that actually means?'

'There was a note in Luxton's pocket. A "keep your mouth shut or else" kind of note.'

'Handwritten?'

The inspector shook his head. 'Individual letters cut, not from a newspaper, but from what looked to be some kind of flyer.'

'And that was a help?'

'We thought so. Amazingly, Norris recognised the typeface; it was one of those curly jobs, so a bit unusual. He'd picked up a leaflet himself a few days previously, advertising a sale of World War Two books. He's into the war.'

'He never took part then,' Jack said, his tone crisp.

'Norris? Too young. The sale was being run by a bookshop in Lewes. That's where he picked up the leaflet.'

Jack looked questioningly at him.

'A place called Play It Again. Do you know it?'

'I've heard of it,' he said cautiously.

It was the bookshop where Diane Croft had a job, a woman who was unsure whether or not she'd administered the fatal blow to Alex Vicary. Had someone confirmed her worst fears? Someone who had seen what she'd done – Ferdie Luxton, for instance – and she'd got busy with the scissors.

'Trouble is,' Ridley continued, 'so have a lot of people. Anyone could have picked up that leaflet.'

'Any fingerprints, though?'

'Plenty of Luxton's. He must have spent days cradling the note. But nothing else that's decipherable, just a load of smudges which tell us nothing.' The inspector stopped licking his cone, the ice cream beginning to slide down the side. 'I hope you've got something better for me.'

'I don't know if you'll think so.' Jack stood for a moment, looking over the green-painted railings at a sea that today was alive with light. 'Ferdie borrowed money from Alex Vicary – Susan Vicary has the IOU to prove it. Whether he paid it back or not, she has no idea, but the lad's savings book shows only a withdrawal.'

'I can't see how that helps.'

'No, neither can we. Not now. Until Luxton was killed, it seemed he might have had motive to get rid of Alex – if he couldn't repay the debt and the lad had proof of past wrongdoing. Now the man has been killed, the theory doesn't look so good.'

'Thanks,' the inspector said laconically.

'It might be helpful, though, to look into Alex Vicary's finances, particularly the bank account he used for everyday transactions. He plundered his savings account to lend what was a large sum of money to Luxton, but did he make any other withdrawals to help someone else? From his current account perhaps, for which he failed to get an IOU?'

'You're saying that it's money behind both these killings?'

'It seems a powerful motive. Alex lent money, that's a fact, and once the Mortons started their campaign against his family, he needed it back. Badly. If it hadn't been forthcoming, he may have resorted to threats to get it.'

'Threats which led to his death? But then why is Luxton dead if he was the one who'd decided to silence Vicary? It doesn't add up.'

'No, it doesn't. And it's possible that with Alex dead, the debt was no longer a worry for Ferdie.'

Ridley shook his head. 'You say Mrs Vicary has an IOU. Luxton would still need to worry, but it's a mess, that's for sure.'

'I've puzzled over it ever since I learned of Luxton's murder. All I've been able to come up with is that Alex might have lent money to another person, but the debt went unrecorded. Flora has a hunch that someone else in the Knights was borrowing money. If Luxton knew of such a transaction and, as you suggested, saw something at the rehearsal that he shouldn't, then...'

'A third player? It sounds unlikely.'

Both men continued to stare out to sea until the inspector asked, 'Is that it then, Jack?' He was clearly disappointed.

'There's a little more. The Mortons aren't obviously implicated in Vicary's death, but they're still wreaking havoc. That's despite the court case that's pending. Last Monday, Flora was on her way home from the bookshop and cycled into a wire that had been strung across Greenway Lane.

'She's OK,' Jack went on quickly, seeing his companion's face. 'She took a tumble and was badly bruised, but it could have been far worse if she'd hit the wire at a different angle.'

The inspector whistled between his teeth, seemingly picturing the scene for himself. 'And you think the Mortons were behind it?'

'They're the ones who have a grievance. With me, specifically. Ever since I met the nephew at the Vicarys' house and warned him off harassing Susan, he's been gunning for me and I'm wondering if now he's moved on to Flora. I never told you, but shortly after I left Mrs Vicary – it was a second visit – I was hit by a car driving at speed. I was on the road that runs beside the docks and it was only luck that saved me from a swim.'

'You should have reported it,' Ridley scolded.

'I couldn't prove it was Morton. I didn't even manage to get the number plate. Putting two and two together, though, I'm fairly sure it was him, but again I've no evidence. And there's always the chance it could have been someone else entirely who's out to get us both.'

The inspector groaned. 'Don't confuse me, Jack. I've too much on my plate already.' He finished his ice cream and wiped his fingers on a frowsy-looking handkerchief he'd pulled from his pocket. 'I'll speak to Newhaven again, make sure they're still patrolling regularly, and see if they can turn up anything new on the nephew. At least his uncle seems to be lying low, which is good news.' They turned and together retraced their steps along the promenade. 'And it shouldn't take long to check the lad's bank account. I'll let you know.'

'Thanks, Alan. And thanks for the ice cream.'

The inspector managed a rare smile. 'I don't know about you, but it's done me a treat. You can't beat a ninety-nine!'

On the way back to the college, the coach managed to pick up a puncture, and it was well into the evening before Jack walked into the cottage.

'I was getting worried,' Flora said, kissing him hello. 'You must be hungry.'

'Not particularly. Are you?'

'I was going to make a fish pie, but it's so late that now I'm thinking cheese on toast.'

He followed her into the kitchen, dumping his jacket on a chair. 'I'm thinking that sounds good.'

The fish pie unceremoniously shelved, the cheese on toast went down well, especially eaten from plates on their laps, sitting side by side on the sofa, before they settled to watch the evening's news summary.

Television had been an innovation. A few weeks ago, while browsing their favourite second-hand shop, they'd seen a set, its polished wood scratched and chipped, hiding beneath a pile of lampshades and, after the shop owner had guaranteed that despite its battered appearance it was in full working order, he had made a sale.

Neither of them had owned a television before and, after fighting Dilys for the privilege of buying a licence – the post-mistress had not lost her antipathy to 'new-fangled' devices – they had spent most evenings exploring the BBC's offerings. It turned out to be a bland diet and, except for the news, they'd largely given up watching.

Tonight, on the late evening summary, an article on the Cod Wars between Britain and Iceland over fishing rights in the North Atlantic passed them by, but the announcement that a new theatre, the Mermaid, was to open in Blackfriars at the end of the month had them planning a visit. It would be the first to be built in the City since the time of Shakespeare and one of the first to abandon the traditional layout. It was as they were calculating whether they could manage a trip to London before they left for their honeymoon that the inspector rang. The call had come much quicker than Jack expected.

'It didn't need too much effort,' Ridley said, when Jack thanked him. 'Apart from regular payments for rent and utility bills, Vicary's salary went largely untouched. He barely took anything out of his bank account. Mrs Vicary works, doesn't she, and they must have paid daily expenses from her earnings – food and suchlike. So, no mystery withdrawals for you to pursue.'

It was another disappointment, but not surprising. The payment to Ferdie Luxton had seemed the key to unlocking this mystery, but for the moment it was hard to see how it had contributed to Alex Vicary's death.

'There *was* a single entry that was slightly unusual,' the inspector said suddenly, as Jack went to put down the receiver. 'Nothing like an IOU, though. A cheque drawn in favour of the General Register Office.'

That blindsided Jack.

'Sounds like the lad was after a certificate of some kind,' Ridley went on. 'God knows why.'

Births, marriages or deaths, that was the reason you contacted the General Register Office. 'Alex was hoping to get married,' he said, 'though I'm not sure that's relevant.'

'Could be. Maybe he needed an additional birth certificate for some reason. Or he'd mislaid the original.'

'It's an odd payment, though,' was all Jack could think to say, 'but thanks for the information, Alan.'

'If it turns out to be more important than it seems, let me know!'

Jack put down the phone and wandered back into the sitting room. Was it important? Was the payment to the Register Office inconsequential, or a clue to something far more significant? He was half inclined to forget the inspector's comment, but Flora when he told her, thought otherwise. Her gaze became suddenly intent.

'It's a lead we should follow,' she asserted. 'And what else do we have?'

25

'I'm going up to the Priory,' Flora announced early the next morning. 'Hector might know why Alex contacted the General Register Office.'

'And he might not.' Jack paused, pouring cornflakes into a bowl. 'He doesn't seem to have been that close a confidant. He didn't even know Alex was planning to marry. He seemed convinced his friend's relationship with Diane Croft was casual, and that couldn't have been further from the truth.'

'Not for Diane, it wasn't,' she retorted. 'Hector could have been echoing her view, or saying what he hoped was the truth. And what else are we to do with the information the inspector has passed on?'

'I can ring the GRO tomorrow.'

'Is it likely they'll tell you what Alex ordered?'

'It might need a white lie,' he admitted.

Flora pulled a face. 'I think it's going to need more than a white lie. How much toast shall I do? A soft boiled egg?'

'Two slices, thanks. No egg. I write better on a half-empty stomach. The call is worth a try, though, isn't it?'

'Anything's worth a try, including talking to Hector. The sun is shining – at the moment – and the walk will do me good.'

Breakfast was a brief meal and, leaving Jack to wash the few dishes, Flora donned a lightweight jacket, hoping she'd guessed right and the sun would continue to shine. It was a beautiful morning for a walk and she was glad she'd left a newly repaired Betty in her shed, Greenway Lane living up to its name. Bright, fresh green everywhere, the kind that only comes in the early days of summer when the hedges are alive with birdsong and new growth.

Feeling deep pleasure in her world, Flora walked without a shudder past the spot where she'd been felled by a copper wire. Who had perpetrated that evil act? They still had no true idea. Jack seemed certain it had been David Morton, intent on revenge for the part they'd played in his father's arrest, but she was far less sure. What if someone else had been watching her that day? It was a question Flora had asked herself several times, and there'd been no answer. Someone watching and waiting for a moment to tighten the wire and cut her to shreds.

It wasn't something to dwell upon, especially on a day like today, and, quickly, she turned the corner into the high street, empty except for one or two early birds collecting their Sunday papers from the post office. Past the All's Well – Flora allowed herself an admiring glance at the *Goldfinger* display, a host of brightly jacketed books against Rose's cleverly fashioned background of gold foil – and on to Fern Hill and the Priory. Walking through the estate's tall gates, she thought the sweep of grounds and the golden stone of the mansion ahead had never looked better than in the softness of the May sunlight.

She hadn't been entirely sure that Hector would be on duty this morning but, since she'd no wish to knock on his door – along with several other members of staff, he had a room in the bowels of the hotel – she went directly to the kitchen.

Alice, wearing a newly starched pinafore, was bending over a pot large enough to be a cauldron.

She looked up, surprised. 'Hello, my love. What brings you here?' She tutted. 'Did that darn girl salt this or not?' She dipped a spoon into what Flora could now see was a thick vegetable soup. 'No, she didn't,' Alice decided. 'And where has she got to?'

'Is this your new help?'

'Help? I'd be lucky,' was Alice's pithy retort. 'We've a dining room that will be full to bursting for lunch and next to no staff. And there's Sally playing nurse to that girl upstairs.'

Flora concentrated on her mission. 'Hector?'

'It's his weekend off. Not that he's with us half the time when he is here, if you know what I mean. Anyways, my ducks, what can I do for you? It's Sunday morning – you should be with that fellow of yours reading the papers.'

'That fellow of mine is hunched over a typewriter. But you said Sally is with a girl?' There was little point in dwelling on Hector's absence and it appeared there was something more intriguing on the horizon.

'Diane. Diane What's-her-name.'

'Diane Croft?'

'That's her. Proper mess she's in. But go and see the lass for yourself, and while you do, tell Sally I could do with her help down here.'

'I will. Diane is somewhere in the hotel?'

'Course she is! Given the best suite! Upstairs, first floor and along the corridor. The end door.'

'Thanks, Alice.'

Flora thought it best to escape before she could be asked again why she'd walked up to the Priory this morning. In the event, her old friend was far too busy cooking lunch for thirty people to notice her slip out of the kitchen.

The Rose Suite on the first floor, so called because it had the best view of what in summer was a stunning rose garden, was simple to find. Flora gave a soft knock at the door and waited. Footsteps on the other side, then Sally's mop of blonde curls appeared in the doorway. Her eyebrows rose in surprise.

'Flora!' She opened the door wider. 'What brings you here?'

Again, it was better not to mention Hector. 'I fancied a walk,' she said brightly, 'and a chat with Alice but she seems run off her feet. She wondered,' Flora phrased the request as diplomatically as she could, 'whether you could spare her time in the kitchen. I don't think her new apprentice is proving too helpful.'

'Oh, goodness. It's Marilyn – she's not working out well. She's a nice enough girl, but slow. Very slow. Hector's on his weekend off – we only had a few lunch bookings when I agreed – and Charlie, bless the lad, managed to twist his ankle yesterday playing football. I'll go down straight away and see what I can do. But...' She looked back over her shoulder. 'I've Diane here,' she said quietly, half closing the door. 'And she's in a pretty bad way. Do you think you could sit with her for a while? She's been dosing on aspirin and I'm sure she'll nod off very soon.'

'I'd be happy to,' she said gladly, keen to get to the bottom of this new mystery. 'I've the morning free.'

'You're a pal. Thanks.'

Feeling a tad guilty at this undeserved praise, Flora tiptoed into the room, leaving Sally to make a hasty descent to the kitchen.

The girl was lying in bed, still in her overnight pyjamas but even buttoned to the neck and with sleeves down to her wrists, Flora could see the bruising.

'Hello, Diane,' she said, taking the chair by the bedside. 'Sally's popped down to the kitchen to help with lunch. Is it OK if I sit with you a while?'

Diane opened one swollen eye. 'It's lovely to see you, Flora,' she said thickly. 'Sorry I look so hideous.'

She was too pretty a girl ever to look hideous, Flora thought, but there was no doubt that her injuries were severe. Had she fallen off her bike, too, or, worse, been involved in a car crash?

'Whatever happened?' she asked, settling herself into the chair.

'I was attacked,' Diane murmured.

Flora's mouth dropped open. 'Where?' she asked quickly. 'And why?'

'Why, I'm not sure.' Diane was finding it difficult to talk. The whole of her lower cheek, Flora noticed, was as badly swollen as the left eye. 'But it was last night in Lewes.'

'Were you robbed?'

She shook her head. 'Nothing like that. I'd just left the Knights' meeting and this figure came running out of the narrow twitten near the White Hart and punched me in the face.'

'How awful!'

'I must have fallen down, I don't remember much, I think someone was kicking me, but then Kenny was there and helped me onto my feet.'

'Did you see anything of your assailant?'

She shook her head again. 'It was a man.' Well, yes, Flora thought. 'He seemed to be dressed in black. And he had a mask on his face.' Flora's mind was busy. The mask wasn't at all helpful, but Kenny?

'It was Kenneth Buckley who helped you up? He was in Lewes last night?'

'He was at the meeting, too. It was a small celebration for the show.' When Flora looked blank, she said, 'We staged the Battle of Lewes for real yesterday.'

'I'd forgotten,' she said slowly. 'Of course, it would be around the right date.'

'There was a debate in the society over whether we should go ahead – after Alex, you know, and now Ferdie Luxton – but everyone had put in so much work, Alex included, with the mass of armour he made, that most people voted to continue.'

'And the meeting?'

'It was just a get-together with food and some drink. The Masons Arms didn't seem right, not after Ferdie's farewell, so we booked the White Hart. I didn't want to go, but Sally said I should. I was hoping she'd come with me, but she had late deliveries to sort out and never made it.'

'Did you have a good time?'

'I tried... but no, not really.' She turned her head into the pillow. 'When I heard about Ferdie, it all came back again. The thing is, I can't get Alex out of my mind,' she burst out. 'Everything feels tainted. Everything feels wrong.'

Flora took a while to respond. 'You told me you were unsure what happened at the rehearsal. You said you feared it might have been you who pushed Alex.'

'I'm still not sure.' She brushed her hand against her eyes. 'I keep thinking about that day, trying to get a clearer picture. I am beginning to remember a little more. I can see some of the faces that were surrounding us both.'

'Do others in the society know how you feel?' An idea was coming to Flora.

'I made a small confession last night about wondering if I was the one who'd pushed Alex. I shouldn't have but I'd had a bit to drink,' she said, her smile lopsided.

'You told people you thought it might be you?'

'Only a couple of the girls I'm friendly with. They said it was nonsense. I couldn't have done it. And that when I remembered properly, I'd know that.'

'Did you happen to mention that you were beginning to remember more of the incident?' Who might have overheard Diane? she wondered. Who might have been worried that she would begin to remember? Remember too clearly, as perhaps Luxton had.

The girl stretched her bunched limbs, trying to get comfortable. 'My friends said I shouldn't worry, it would happen in time. It would come right. I did want it to, but now I don't. Not after I was attacked.'

'You think the attack was connected to your conversation with these girls?' Flora certainly did.

'I know it was. The man told me to keep my mouth shut.'

That was a piece of information Diane hadn't shared before, the message the same as delivered to Ferdie Luxton.

'Did you recognise his voice?' A stupid question. She would have said if she had. Although perhaps not. Something was keeping Diane Croft from being completely honest.

'I didn't. He had a mask on, like I said. And I reckon he was disguising his voice. It sounded odd, not natural.'

'It was almost certainly someone who was at the celebration with you. It would have to be.' She would be transparent, even if Diane were not. 'Did everyone in the society attend?'

Diane took some time to think about it. 'Not everyone, but most of the members.'

'And Kenneth Buckley, you say, was one of them.'

A shadow passed over Diane's face. 'He was there but he wasn't much fun,' she said. 'I heard him complaining to one of the chaps that women never know what they want. Then he started haranguing me about Alex. How he'd been so possessive. How Alex had deliberately made a mace for him that was faulty. Constructed it so the head would fly off and injure him. I think the new girl he's been after, the one who works with you, Flora, must have turned him down. He doesn't like being turned down,' she said perceptively. 'Alex was a useful scapegoat, a way to get rid of his bad temper.'

'And when you came round from being punched, he was standing beside you?'

Diane turned a startled look at her. 'You don't think it was him? I know he was angry but he wouldn't hurt me.'

'Are you sure? He *was* angry. He'd no doubt had quite a bit to drink. He hated Alex and you were Alex's girlfriend. When you started talking about the day Alex fell to his death, maybe he wanted to shut you up.'

'But that could mean...' She grasped the counterpane, twisting it between her hands, as the implication of Flora's words sank in.

'Was he still at the party when you left, do you remember?'

'No. He went a bit earlier. I saw him go.' She whispered the words, Flora barely able to hear them.

'He left earlier, but was still around to help you to your feet.'

Diane looked bewildered and, seeing her upset, Flora reached out a hand. 'For the moment, maybe, you should forget about last night, but if you do remember anything about the day Alex died, come and tell me – or tell Jack.'

The girl nodded and closed her eyes. For a while, they sat in silence, Flora brooding over what she'd learned and Diane gradually falling into a doze. When Sally came back into the room, she had a smile on her face.

'That's good,' she whispered, gesturing towards the sleeping Diane. Then beckoned Flora outside. 'I've peeled a ton of potatoes. Marilyn has been found and set to work. And Auntie is feeling a good deal happier. I've ordered tea if you'd like a cup, Flora.'

'Thanks but I should go. I've Sunday lunch to cook. I'm so sorry to see Diane so poorly. I imagine her parents haven't been told?'

'They left for Edinburgh last week and Diane doesn't want them worried. I'll look after her. Until she's well, she'll be staying here.'

Sally had become a mother hen, Flora thought, as she walked towards the Priory's gates, and Diane would be well cared for and safe from any further attack. But Kenneth Buckley. There was a thought! Buckley or someone else had overheard what Diane said and decided she needed not to remember what she'd seen on that tragic day. The attack Diane had suffered was brutal in the extreme, a warning that she should close her mind for good.

Approaching the gates, she noticed a shiny new Morris Minor pulling up outside and, climbing from the back seat, Hector Lansdale. He reached into the car and brought out a canvas holdall, then said a few words to the driver before waving him and his fellow passenger goodbye.

When Hector saw who was walking towards him, he stopped in surprise. 'Flora Carrington of all people,' he said. 'Did you come looking for me?'

'I did, as a matter of fact, but found someone else entirely.'

He looked quizzical, but she would let Sally do the explaining. 'Did you have a good weekend?'

His smile was genuine. 'It was the break I needed. I only wish it had been longer, but the friends I've been staying with offered me a lift back from Brighton and I couldn't refuse.'

'Hector, I came to ask you about Alex. Do you have a minute?'

'For Alex, any amount of minutes.'

'It's actually about something he wrote away for.'

'That doesn't sound like Alex. What was it?'

'A certificate from the General Register Office.'

Hector's face creased in puzzlement. 'What kind of certificate?'

'We don't know. We were wondering if you did.'

'Not a clue,' he said cheerily. 'They do birth certificates, don't they?'

'Marriage and death certificates, too. You can't think of any reason Alex would have been in touch with them?'

'It sounds a hum to me. Unless he was writing to them for someone else.'

'Who, for instance?'

'I dunno. At work, he dealt with some queer customers sometimes.'

'It was the Tourist Information Office, wasn't it? It's not likely to have been a tourist asking him to send for a certificate.'

'A lot of the locals used his office, he said – when they had nowhere else to go.'

That opened up a whole new range of possibilities, a local who might have involved Alex Vicary in something suspect. Someone they were already aware of or a new name to add to their list?

'There was one person he told me about,' Hector went on. 'She left quite an impression on him. I think he felt sorry for her.'

Flora was alert, hoping for a name. 'Someone local?'

'I don't believe so. A visitor. Alex said she didn't seem to know her way around. I think he tried to help – more than usual, that is.'

Which got them precisely nowhere, Flora thought moodily, as she made her way back to the cottage, a late roast still needing to be cooked.

26

Flora's return from the Priory with news of Diane Croft's ordeal had horrified Jack and prompted feelings of guilt. If they'd been successful in finding Alex's killer, the girl would never have been attacked, and he felt partly to blame for that; he'd not pulled his weight in this investigation, but left Flora to do most of the 'pokin' and pryin'', as Alice called it. She had been the one to talk to Hector, to Luxton, to Kenneth Buckley and Mrs Sullivan – the list was shamefully long – whereas he'd thought it sufficient to drift to Newhaven several times.

Maybe he'd been distracted by the thought of their honeymoon – it had been a long time coming but was now approaching fast – or maybe it was pressure over a book that was proving slow, very slow, to begin. And had he been misled by the Mortons' threat to Mrs Vicary? Too busy pursuing them when it looked as though, villains though they were, they'd had nothing to do with Alex's death.

Neither Larry nor his nephew belonged to the Knights of Mercia and wouldn't have been at the society's celebration last night. David Morton could have been lying in wait for Diane to emerge from the party, he supposed, but would he have known she was there and why suddenly decide to attack the girl? As far as they knew, he had no connection to Diane and no motive to harm her. It was likely, however, that someone at the party did, overhearing the girl say that she had begun to remember more of the moment Alex fell from the wall.

Flora's visit to the Priory had added a new dimension to the enquiry, not least from Hector Lansdale's suggestion that Alex often helped with questions normally beyond the scope of a tourist office, involving local people as well as visitors. It needed a long stretch of imagination, but it was possible the odd payment in Alex Vicary's account, highlighted by the inspector, was connected to his work.

Jack had offered to ring the General Register Office, more to feel that he was doing something than from any real conviction it would lead anywhere. But it was a call he'd make today, he decided, while Flora was at the bookshop. It wouldn't hurt him to take ten minutes away from the typewriter and might make him feel less guilty.

Halfway through the morning, he put the kettle on to boil before taking a seat in the hall chair, ready to make the call. In the back of his mind he'd been turning over how best to go about it and come to the reluctant conclusion that it had to involve deception, the white lie he'd mentioned to Flora. He would need to pretend he was Alex Vicary, telling whoever answered him that the certificate he'd ordered from the GRO hadn't arrived and could he have a replacement?

Quashing any ethical doubts, he lifted the receiver and was put through almost immediately.

'Vicary, you say?'

Jack heard a heavy thump at the other end of the line. A ledger being heaved onto a desk? Then a rustling of pages.

'Yes, here it is,' the woman confirmed. 'The certificate was despatched six weeks ago, Mr Vicary. You've never received it, you say? Most irregular. It must have gone missing in the post. I suppose we can send another.' She didn't sound too sure.

'I can pay for a replacement,' he was quick to offer.

'That won't be necessary,' she said crisply. 'But a new copy will take at least a week to get to you.'

'I understand and thank you. You've been most helpful. I'm staying with a friend at the moment and will be here for some weeks. Could you send it to this address?' Jack recited the cottage's address which was duly noted.

'Just to check,' he said, as the call was coming to a close, 'you are ordering the right certificate for me?'

There was a hint of indignation in the assistant's voice when she answered. 'The right certificate? We don't make that kind of mistake, Mr Vicary. A marriage certificate is what you ordered, I believe?'

'Yes, that's right,' he said, feeling totally fazed. Why on earth had Alex been asking for a marriage certificate? And whose marriage?

'Thank you so much,' he said hurriedly and rang off.

Wandering back into the kitchen, he made tea for himself without realising he'd done so. He was troubled, his mind every-where. A marriage certificate? What had Alex been playing at? Should he walk to the bookshop and tell Flora the result of his call? But she would be as confused as he and, in any case, could do nothing – she was chained to the shop until she closed at five – and Jack badly wanted to do *something*. There was no way he could go back to the book this morning.

He stood, mug in hand, looking out of the window. A whole week to wait! Damn! The original certificate had been mailed six weeks ago and, assuming it hadn't been lost in the post, it would have reached Alex in good order and he would... what would Alex have done? He'd gone to the trouble of obtaining a copy of someone's marriage certificate; it had to be part of an ongoing plan. The quest for money? Quite possibly. He would have kept it in a safe place, therefore, maybe with other of his papers.

Yet Susan Vicary had found nothing of importance, she'd said, when she'd cleared Alex's bedroom. But would the certificate have meant anything to her, even if she'd found it? She might well have discarded the item.

Walking swiftly back into the hall, Jack dialled the Vicarys' number. There was no answer and he felt such acute disappointment that instinct told him this had to lead somewhere. Susan was at work this morning, he remembered, and of course she wouldn't have answered, but she would be home within a few hours. He'd go to Newhaven! Straight after lunch. Meanwhile, he'd give the lawn only its second mow of the year. Anything to keep himself busy that didn't involve putting one sentence after another.

Susan Vicary was clearly surprised to find Jack on her doorstep again. 'Did you leave something behind?' she asked.

'I didn't and I'm sorry to bother you again, Mrs Vicary, and so soon. There's nothing I've forgotten, but I'm wondering if you have.'

She looked befuddled.

'When you cleared Alex's room recently, were there papers?' He saw the pain in her face and apologised. 'I wouldn't mention it, but I think there's a paper that could be important.'

Susan shook her head. 'I don't think so. It was just stuff about the Knights: minutes of society meetings, handbills for different events, and a big order for heavy foam. That would be for the new helmets Alex was making.'

'Nothing unusual then?' Jack felt his spirits take a dive and realised how much he'd be counting on the certificate being here.

'You can have a look for yourself if you like. I've finished clearing the room.'

He followed her up the stairs and saw the truth of the statement. There was an eerie emptiness to the bedroom, as though it were waiting to see who would walk through the door. It wouldn't be Alex, he thought sadly. A small row of books sat on the shelf above the desk and he pointed to them.

'You've left Alex's books.'

'Only a few. I sent most of them to the charity shop,' she confessed. 'Big history volumes that I would never read. But these are a bit lighter, something to pass the evening. I thought the lodger might be a reader.'

'You have someone coming?'

She nodded. 'My neighbour, the jeweller I told you about, has a new apprentice starting in his workshop next week and I've agreed to rent the room to him. He seems a nice enough lad.'

There was a deep sadness in her voice. A nice enough lad but not Alex, Jack thought. 'Could I...?'

'Help yourself, Mr Carrington. There's not much to see.'

There wasn't and it took only a few minutes to take each book down and flick through their pages. It was when he was riffling through the final book, a childhood copy of *Treasure Island*, that Jack found it. A certificate, new by the feel of it, and carefully folded to fit the pages of the paperback.

'Is that what you were looking for?'

He spread out the long sheet of paper on the desktop. 'It is.'

'But it's a marriage certificate,' she said, bending her head to read, her eyes narrowing. 'What would Alex want with that?'

Jack didn't answer. He was too astonished. The certificate recorded in bald detail the marriage of Bruce Sullivan to a Jennifer Rankin on the fifth day of January 1952.

'Well, I never!' he said.

. . .

'He's been married before! That's something he's kept quiet,' Flora exclaimed, when Jack told her of his discovery that evening.

'It's unlikely that Jennifer has died and, if he's been divorced, he's hardly going to shout it to the rooftops, is he? Divorce is frowned on. There's still a heavy stigma attached to it. Even in my father's louche circle, there were people shocked when my mother divorced him.'

'I wonder how long that first marriage lasted?' she mused. 'Do you think he abandoned poor Jennifer for a rich wife? Or maybe he was brutal to her and she was the one who left.'

'You have to make up a story! You can't resist,' he said, laughingly. 'Who did what to whom won't matter. What we should be asking is why Alex thought the marriage important enough to go to the bother of acquiring proof.'

'You shouldn't dismiss stories so readily.' A reproving finger tapped him on the chest. 'You write them, after all. The "why" behind their break-up could turn out to be crucial.'

'If it is, I don't see how we'll ever know.'

'I could ask Sandra. She's his second wife.'

'Would she know? It might be a taboo subject between them, something they've never talked about. Sullivan's marriage to Jennifer has to have been short-lived – 1952 is only seven years ago – so easy to brush under the table? In any case, do you really fancy asking the woman for details of her husband's previous marriage?'

'No,' Flora admitted. 'It would be easier and much more comfortable if you could find a mention of the divorce. I'm sure there *was* one. I've heard nothing at school to suggest that Bruce Sullivan was ever a widower and Alex must have had at least a suspicion or why send for a marriage certificate?'

'Me find a mention?'

'You're the one who's good at the legal stuff. If we discovered that Jennifer was granted a divorce because of cruelty, that's something Alex could have used against Bruce. Threaten to broadcast the man's history if he didn't pay up.'

'That's if Bruce ever borrowed money, which is something we're unlikely to prove. Particularly, if it was a cash payment. OK,' he said, seeing her face, 'I'll do some hunting, but it won't be easy. We don't know the legal firm Bruce used or even where he was living at the time.'

'Suffolk,' she said. 'Newmarket. Sandra told me that's how they met. She said how ironic it was that her racing friends introduced her to Bruce when she was staying with them, and now it was racing that was ruining their lives. And it's where he married Jennifer.' She pointed to the certificate lying open on the kitchen table. 'He must have moved down to Sussex when he married Sandra.'

'It will mean checking the local papers – the divorce should be recorded in the press somewhere. Granted, the lists of divorces will be short but going through every local paper in Suffolk won't be. And what if the grounds for divorce aren't mentioned or they turn out to be something vague like unreasonable behaviour, what do we do with that?'

'I'll think of something. Just try, Jack. You could always ask Ross Sadler for help. He enjoys this kind of enquiry.'

Jack grimaced. 'I'm not sure he'll thank me for this one.'

'We have a lot of details to help. The certificate gives Sullivan's date of birth, where he married, the parents' names.'

'Let's hope it is a help.' Jack let out a heavy breath. 'I don't like to pester Ross, but I suppose I'll have to. Unless I disappear to north London for a week.'

Ross, when he heard of the new research, was willing to pay a visit to the Colindale newspaper archive as long as his friend could wait until the weekend. In contrast to Jack, he didn't foresee much of a problem in locating the Sullivan divorce.

'There aren't that many local papers in Suffolk,' he said, 'and you've given me loads of information.'

The following day, however, things looked a little different. Jack was once more back in his office at Cleve, when the porter came running up the stairs to announce a phone call at the front desk. It was Ross.

'By chance, I had to go to Colindale this morning,' his friend announced breezily. 'Something I've been working on for the paper and, would you believe, I found what I needed straight away. So, I took a look for you – one way of wasting a morning, I guess. I went through the few local rags, all weekly, from 1952 to 1958. That was the end date?'

'Sullivan would have to have remarried by then.'

'Well, whether he did or not, he wasn't divorced.'

'What!'

'No sign of him in any of the papers. I've searched for his name, for his birth date, for the place he lived. Not a mention.'

'It might have been overlooked by the press.'

He could almost hear Ross's shrug of the shoulders. 'It's possible his divorce was missed from the list, but others were there. Very few in East Anglia, in fact, even fewer than for the rest of the country.'

There was a long silence. 'Have you got a bigamist on your hands?'

Jack was silent. No mention of a divorce. If Sullivan had married bigamously, that would have been a potent threat. It would certainly have warranted Alex sending for a marriage certificate. A way of getting money, whether Bruce borrowed from him or not. Pay up or I'll show this to your wife. For Sandra Sullivan, the bigamy would be more grievous than Bruce's addiction to gambling. The gossip she'd have to face. The shame and humiliation. She would almost certainly kick him out; the slur would be too great.

'Are you OK, Jack?'

'Sorry. Thinking.'

'By the look of it, you'll need to do a lot of that.'

'Thanks for the help, Ross.'

'Not much help, as it turns out.'

'I'm not so sure. It might very well be.'

And coming off the phone, for once the path ahead seemed clear. They needed to find the first wife. They needed to find Jennifer.

27

'We need to find Jennifer?' Flora wiped floury hands on her pinafore.

'She can tell us whether or not there really was a divorce.'

'Although Ross has already confirmed it.'

'As far as he could make out. But his search wasn't definitive. It couldn't be. There might be a reason it wasn't recorded by the press. Or the divorce might have been registered elsewhere. There are too many uncertainties.'

'Jennifer would certainly know if she'd been divorced, it's true,' Flora said drily. 'But how on earth are we to find her? Search Suffolk with a loud hailer?'

'The thing is...' He poked at the crust of the apple pie she'd just made, earning himself a slap on the hand. 'The thing is, how did Alex know Bruce Sullivan had been married previously? It wasn't a vague suspicion, was it? How did he know to send for that particular marriage certificate? I mean, he could have been sent one naming Sandra as the bride. He knew the date of the first marriage, but how?'

'Someone told him? One of the Knights perhaps.'

'That would have been indiscreet, if it wasn't widely known

among the Sullivans' social circle. Unless it was a close friend Bruce confided in who couldn't keep a secret.'

She shook her head. 'He's like a clam. I can't see him confiding in anyone.'

'Even at school?' he asked hopefully.

'Even less there than among the Knights, I'd say.'

'So how did Alex know? Could he have read about the divorce?' Jack asked the air. 'No,' he answered himself. 'That's impossible. Could he have actually met the woman? No, again.'

'Maybe, he could.' There was a spark in Flora's eyes. 'Remember what Hector said about people coming into the tourist office with all kinds of questions.'

'Jennifer just happened to be taking a trip round Sussex and called in to check on the local restaurants, whereupon she fell upon Alex's shoulder and confessed she was a divorced woman?'

Flora fixed him with a severe look. 'She could have come to Lewes for a particular reason – to see Bruce. Have you thought of that? In which case, she might well have mentioned a divorce.'

Jack frowned. 'But is it likely?'

'Not really,' she confessed, 'though it might be worth talking to the people Alex worked with. Just in case.'

The tourist information office occupied the ground floor of Lewes Town Hall, its wide, plate-glass windows overlooking a busy intersection of three different roads. On several occasions, Flora had walked past the office and seen how busy the place could become, particularly at this time of the year – May was a favourite for visitors to the South Downs – but was cheered to find that this morning they were the only customers, both assistants seeming to have time to chat to each other. It had been sheer good luck that Jack had a morning free of appointments and the first group that Flora was to hear reading wasn't timetabled until later this afternoon. The babies, as she thought of them, five- and six-year-olds; it was a class she always enjoyed.

The questions they needed to ask at the office would be difficult to pose. Attempting to trace a woman to whom they had no relation might seem odd and suggest perhaps a malign intention. Even if it didn't, was it likely that either of the two assistants would remember a woman called Jennifer who'd called here weeks ago, if indeed she had, let alone the information she'd been seeking? A definite strategy was needed and it fell to Flora to initiate the awkward conversation while Jack began a casual saunter around the room, appearing to admire the display of local artists' works that covered each of the walls.

At first, ignoring the chatting assistants, she made for a tall, wooden shelf unit that stood to one side of their desks, holding a collection of brochures and town maps. After a few desultory minutes of flicking through leaflets, she moved on to the selection of guide books, picking one up and pretending to read its back cover.

'Not too busy this morning,' she observed to the woman at the nearest desk.

'Nice and peaceful,' the elder of the two agreed with a slight smile. 'But it will change soon enough. Come lunchtime, we'll have a queue out of the door.'

Replacing the guide book in its allotted slot, Flora glanced towards the window as though looking for the line of visitors to begin massing. No queue yet, she thought, just a constant stream of cars and a solitary figure standing on the corner opposite. Standing quite still, she noticed. Her eyes narrowed as she tried to focus. And then the figure was no longer there.

Flora shook herself awake. 'Do your customers come from

far afield?' she asked the woman who'd spoken, hoping this might be a path to the questions she needed to ask.

'They can do. We've had Americans, Australians, plenty of French and once a Chinese gentleman who spoke no English. That was a difficult one, wasn't it, Paula?'

Paula looked up from the paper she was reading and nodded. 'We passed him on to Alex.' She gave a small sigh.

'Alex Vicary?' Flora felt her heart lift a little. Might this prove the way in?

'Yes.' Paula looked puzzled. 'Do you... did you know him?'

'We did.' She turned to include Jack, now hovering close. 'He was a good friend of a friend of ours. It's so sad what happened.'

'We certainly miss him,' the older woman put in. 'He was very good with people. Never got in a flap, even when we were rushed off our feet. Took his time with them, you know. When they couldn't say quite what they wanted, he'd make suggestions. And keep making them until one of his ideas chimed with them and they'd say it sounded just the job!'

Flora decided that this would be the moment to introduce Jennifer.

'Do you remember a woman who might have spoken to Alex for a long time? It was quite recent. This spring.' She hoped that wasn't too wild a guess. 'She'd travelled from Suffolk, I think, and was looking for someone in Lewes. A man called Bruce Sullivan.' Again, another wild guess.

The women looked at each other, both wearing fazed expressions. Flora was unsure whether it was the nature of her question that was puzzling them or, more hopefully, that they were trying to remember the woman.

'Suffolk... Sullivan... I don't remember anyone...'

'Yes, there was,' Paula jumped in. 'You remember, Carol. The woman who burst into tears the minute she walked through the door. It was a couple of months ago, the end of

March, I think. I remember it because she was so upset and so pale I thought she'd faint at any moment. Alex sat her down and made her tea. He was so good like that.'

'And she mentioned Suffolk?'

'I think so. I didn't hear that much of their conversation but I remember she said that she was staying in Brighton but was trying to trace someone who lived in Lewes.'

'Was Alex able to help her?'

'She went away with a smile, so probably.'

'I don't suppose you remember the hotel where she was staying?' Not that she'd be there now, Flora thought.

'Actually, I do. My ears pricked up when she mentioned it. At the time, I was looking for a hotel myself – I'm getting married this year – and wanted to book somewhere in Brighton for the reception. She said she'd checked in at the Metropole but that it was too expensive to stay long. I crossed that one off my list! If she came back to Sussex, she said, she'd have to find a cheaper one.'

'Were you able to recommend one?'

'We're always careful about giving recommendations,' Carol put in. 'It can be tricky if the hotel's changed since we heard about it last, but she was so upset – I do remember her now – that we broke our rule. It was the Mayfair we said, wasn't it, Paula?'

Paula nodded. 'The Mayfair's always been good value if people are a bit strapped for cash. And she looked like she was. Cheap coat and hat, and her shoes had seen better days. The Mayfair's only a small place but they look after their guests. They do a smashing English breakfast!'

'And the Mayfair is...?'

'In St James's Street,' they chorused.

'Near the county hospital,' the older woman added.

'Thank you. You've been amazingly helpful.'

When Flora smiled and turned to go, Paula's face resumed its puzzled expression. 'Did you want some brochures? A map?'

'Not this time, thanks. But we'll be back.'

'Will we?' Jack asked, once they were out of the door.

'One day, maybe, but right now we need to find the Mayfair Hotel.'

'And why are we doing that? Jennifer won't be there.'

They had begun to walk towards the town's car park where they had left the Austin, but, at these words, Flora stopped.

'How do we know that?' Her hazel eyes were alight with excitement. 'Jennifer evidently intended to come back to Sussex or why would she have asked for the name of a cheaper hotel?'

'That doesn't mean she's there now,' Jack repeated.

'It doesn't, but if she's been and gone, the hotel staff might have useful information. And if she hasn't yet visited, we could leave a message for her.' She looked at him hopefully. 'We have the time,' she said persuasively.

Jack looked at his watch. 'Barely. My first appointment is immediately after lunch.'

'If we drive fast...'

'We're talking of the Austin, remember!' He gave her a quick hug. 'OK, sleuth, we'll give it a go, but it will have to be a quick visit.'

If the Mayfair Hotel didn't exactly match the district it was named after, it did possess a certain charm. An end-of-terrace, three-storey, bow-windowed Regency townhouse, with whitewashed walls and a brightly striped canopy over the entrance. A pot of geraniums, not yet in flower, sat on either side of a shiny black front door.

The man who responded to their knock was every bit as

neat, wearing freshly laundered shirt and trousers and a beard that evidently received regular trimming.

He looked at them through a pair of wire spectacles. 'I'm afraid we're full.' A slight smile softened the disappointment.

'We're not actually after accommodation.' Jack had stepped forward. 'We have a... a friend,' he extemporised, 'who might be staying with you. We wondered if we could speak to her or, if she's been and gone, speak to you about her.'

It all sounded horribly vague and the man hesitated before asking them into the blue-and-white-tiled hall.

'A friend, you say?' He's not sure he believes Jack, Flora thought, but then she wouldn't either.

'Yes. She's from Suffolk.' That sounded better. 'A lady on her own.' Better still. 'By the name of Jennifer Sullivan.' Possibly the coup de grâce.

The man's forehead puckered. 'I don't think we've had a Mrs Sullivan staying with us...'

'But at the moment?' Flora hadn't been able to contain herself.

The man's puckering deepened and she felt Jack's warning touch on her hand.

'Let me check for you.'

Whisking himself behind the small desk that sat sideways across the narrow hall, he reached for a chunky, leather-bound volume and began running his finger down the list of registered guests. He had a glass of milk he'd been drinking, Flora saw, the half-empty bottle still on the desk. Somehow, it seemed appropriate.

When he looked up, he appeared uneasy. 'We do have a Jennifer staying with us, but the last name isn't Sullivan.'

Flora's spirits took a swoop downwards. 'Her surname?'

'I'm afraid I can't divulge that information. There are rules —' he began, when a terrifying crash overhead had him abandon the sentence, his wire spectacles almost dancing on his nose.

'My goodness,' he'd started to say when the sound of breaking glass filled their ears, thundering through the ceiling.

'Her room number,' Jack demanded. 'Quickly!'

'Number sixteen.' The man's voice was suddenly hoarse. 'What on earth?'

But neither of them stopped to discuss the problem, Jack spinning on his heels to run towards the carpeted flight of stairs to one side of the hall and, before Flora had caught her breath, leaping them two at a time. Without waiting for the owner to make a move, she followed, snatching the open bottle of milk from the desk for no other reason than a crazy idea that it might come in useful.

Number sixteen was on the third floor – it would have to be, she thought, panting heavily up one flight of stairs after another – finally reaching the top landing and an open door just as Jack rugby-tackled a man standing in the midst of widespread devastation.

With one swoop, he brought the man down, crunching through broken china and glass, the crash once more shaking the floorboards and causing the hotel owner who had followed in Flora's wake to flinch violently.

'We have to help Jack,' she urged him. 'He won't be able to subdue the man alone.' The hefty figure sprawled on the ground, with Jack atop, was fighting back furiously: a flurry of punching arms, kicking legs, a sweat-filled face.

Flora's mouth formed a silent 'o', her eyes riveted. That face! She knew that face. Bruce Sullivan! But of course it was.

'We have to help,' she shouted at her companion. 'Now!'

The spectacles quivered, but their owner stayed rooted to the ground.

Flora stared at him, a dawning contempt on her face. 'I'll have to then, on my own.'

True to expectation, Sullivan had thrown a fist at Jack's chin, the blow successful in loosening himself from his opponent's grip. He staggered to his feet and for a few seconds stood wavering amid the rubble. But there was something in his hand, Flora saw. A chain. A small round ball. A mace! And one no doubt made by Alex – the irony of it. Sullivan lifted his arm, swinging it in a wide circle, the wicked metal ball high in the air. Ready to bring it down on Jack's head as he lay prone.

Galvanised, Flora rushed forward, holding the milk bottle aloft. Unable to take proper aim, she threw its contents into what she hoped was Sullivan's eyes. It was, and gave Jack the few seconds he needed to roll clear from the flying mace. The ball and chain hit the floor with an almighty thud, scattering the remnants of porcelain and glass even further afield.

Flora, faced with an enraged Sullivan, cast frantically around for anything she could use as a weapon. The hotel owner, it seemed, had disappeared. To ring the police? She could only hope. Otherwise, a fat lot of use he'd been.

As Sullivan bent to retrieve the mace, her glance fell on a basket-weave chair pushed against the wall and, as a desperate last resort, grabbed hold of it and charged at Bruce as though she were a matador and he the bull. He swung round, snarling angrily as one of the chair legs caught him in the stomach and the other pummelled his right thigh.

It was enough distraction to allow Jack to stumble to his feet, though looking decidedly the worse for wear, an enormous bruise beginning to swell one cheek. It was only then that Flora noticed Jennifer. Her whole attention had been on Sullivan, on disabling him, on saving Jack from harm. Jennifer was crouched in the corner and what looked like the remnants of a scarf drooped from her neck. Had Sullivan tried to strangle her? If so, she had fought back – the broken lamps, the broken vases, were evidence of a fierce battle – and somehow, she had saved herself. But not quite. Sullivan was here in the room and relatively unharmed. All three of them needed to save themselves.

The woman was clearly unable to stand and, though Jack

had regained his feet, he was swaying badly. Sullivan had yanked the chair from Flora's hold and was thrusting it back at her, pushing her towards the wall, meaning, she could see, to crush her. To pierce her with the ends of the chair legs. And she didn't have the strength to stop him.

Jack started forward, but whatever he'd hoped to do was set aside when a pair of burly shoulders appeared in the doorway. Too solid for the hotel owner. A policeman who had lost his helmet in the rush up the stairs but from whose pocket dangled a pair of handcuffs. Jack exchanged a glance with him and, as one, they powered forward, grabbing Sullivan and sandwiching him between them. The man fought them off, his face mottled, his fists flailing, but when Jack bent to retrieve the mace in a threat to use it, Sullivan gave in. Grabbing hold of his wrists, the constable handcuffed him securely.

'Come on, my lad,' he said with satisfaction. 'We've a nice little cell waiting just for you,' and pushed him towards the stairs and down to the hotel foyer from where the sound of more police arriving drifted upwards. A posse of them, it turned out. The owner must have telephoned the station for help, she realised, but it was the lone policeman – dragged off his beat, no doubt – who had saved the day.

Jack was beside her now, cuddling her close. She reached up and stroked his cheek. 'Your poor bruised face.'

'It will mend, but Mrs Sullivan...'

Flora turned immediately and walked over to the woman still crouched close to the floor. Bending down, she said quietly, 'Jennifer? Can you stand if I help you?'

The woman nodded and, with one of Flora's hands beneath her elbow, stumbled to her feet. Before she could try to walk, however, a heavy thud on the staircase brought a face that both Flora and Jack knew well. Sergeant Norris appeared in the doorway.

'Mr Carrington? And Mrs Carrington! Why am I not

surprised?' he said. 'My lads are getting our joker back to the station, but we'll need statements from you all. Including you, miss,' he said to a wilting Jennifer.

'Not this minute surely,' Flora protested. 'You can see what state Mrs Sullivan is in.'

'Perhaps a drink first, don't you think, Sergeant?' The owner had reappeared, having seen his unwanted guests off the premises, and Flora's estimation of him rose several notches. 'We can do tea in the garden. Or something stronger, if necessary.'

'Tea will be more than enough,' Norris decided. 'But then, it's down to the station.'

'And biscuits if there are any,' Flora called after the departing owner.

28

'Can you tell us what happened today?' Jack asked, once they were settled at a table in what, surprisingly, was a delightful walled garden at the rear of the hotel: wide borders filled with early flowering anemones and a newly laid Yorkstone terrace glowing brightly in the sunlight.

Jack had recovered from his mauling, Flora saw with relief, but Jennifer was still exceptionally pale and her hands as she sipped her tea were shaking slightly.

'I'd arranged to meet Bruce,' she said. 'He promised to come to the hotel so we could talk properly.'

'He certainly came, but it was hardly to talk.'

'No.' Her face crumpled. 'I barely got a sentence out before he walked up to me and grabbed hold of the scarf I was wearing.'

Sullivan had brought a mace as a weapon, Flora thought, one small enough to sit in the pocket of a utility jacket, but decided at the last moment perhaps that strangling might be less messy.

'Before I realised what he meant to do,' Jennifer went on, 'he'd wound it round my neck and then started to pull. I begged him to stop, it was so painful, but my voice... I could hardly whisper and I couldn't hear... and he kept pulling until I couldn't swallow, my eyes... everything was blurred... but somehow I lashed out, kicked him as hard as I could, with these' – she pointed at the sharp heel of her shoe – 'and then...'

She broke off, clearly too upset to continue.

Flora let a few minutes pass before she asked, 'Did you arrange the meeting? How did Bruce know you were staying here?'

'I wrote to him,' she said simply, her voice wobbly. 'I wrote a lot – three times – asking him to meet me.'

'I imagine it was the third letter that he answered, but not the others?'

'That's right. I told him I was coming back to Brighton, that I'd be here for a few days and offered to meet him anywhere he chose. I knew he wouldn't want me to go to the school. It would have been too embarrassing for him.'

'You knew where he was working?'

'It's how I found him. Well, it was the education department who found him for me. Suffolk education. I went to them when the police said they couldn't help.'

'You wanted help to find Bruce?'

She nodded. 'I should explain.' Her voice was getting stronger. 'I've had tuberculosis and it's taken me a long while to get better. I was in a sanatorium for nearly three years and lost touch with Bruce.'

'When you say you lost touch,' Flora said carefully, 'how did that happen?' How could you lose touch with a husband? was her unspoken thought.

'He'd disappeared. When I came out of hospital, he wasn't there.'

'But when you were in the sanatorium all those years, you never saw him?'

'Visitors weren't allowed. Not in the section I was in. I

hoped that Bruce would write or telephone – you could take occasional calls – but I never heard from him and then when I was discharged and went back to our house, it wasn't mine any more.'

Flora wasn't the only one struggling to make sense of Jennifer's words. 'What do you mean, the house wasn't yours?' Jack asked.

'It had been sold while I was away. There were other people living there.'

'How extraordinary.' Absent-mindedly, Jack poured fresh cups of tea. 'But what about your furniture, your clothes, your books?'

'The new owners gave me a ticket Bruce had left with them. It was for a storage unit. I don't know what happened to the furniture but all my clothes, books, even my old make-up had been packed and left there.'

Appalled, Flora could think of nothing better to do than hand round the plate of biscuits and, encouragingly, Jennifer took one.

'How could he sell the house without your permission?' she asked, choosing a ginger nut for herself.

'It was his house. His name on the deeds. It looks as though he sold it a few months after I was admitted to hospital and then he must have left Suffolk. Just disappeared. The people who bought the house knew nothing of his plans. They'd no idea where he'd gone. He left no forwarding address.'

'In the circumstances, you did amazingly well in tracing him to Lewes.' Jack was impressed, Flora could see. And so was she.

'Did I?' Jennifer gave a sad smile. 'I'm not so sure.'

'Did you come to Sussex a few months ago?' Flora needed to know the whole story before she made her statement to the police.

'I did. How did you know? And how,' Jennifer said, realisation dawning, 'did you know my name and where I was staying?'

'We did some searching, too,' Flora said vaguely. 'We suspected Bruce might have hurt a friend of ours.' Still vague, but introducing Alex's death after this poor woman had stared her own in the face would be too cruel.

'I see,' Jennifer said uncertainly. Flora's response had left unanswered questions, but for the time being that might be best.

'Your previous trip?' she prompted.

'Oh yes.' Jennifer picked up the thread again. 'I stayed at the Metropole. So nice, but too expensive for me to go back. I've managed to get a job in Suffolk and I'm renting a flat, but most of my earnings go on just getting by.'

'And the Mayfair hotel? You had the name from the tourist information office?'

'I did. How did you know that?' Her face lightened.

'That was where our friend worked. Alex Vicary.'

'He was the young man who helped me? He was so kind. When I arrived, I was desperately upset. Overwhelmed, I suppose, with what had happened. I'd travelled miles looking for the man who should have cared for me. Instead, he'd walked out of my life and left me destitute. Alex was so gentle, made me tea, comforted me.'

'Bruce was your husband?' It was an obvious statement of fact.

'Bruce *is* my husband.'

'You were never divorced?'

'Never. Why?'

This was going to be the trickiest part of the conversation, but Jennifer needed to know. Was this the right time, though? Only an hour ago she had escaped being strangled by the man whom she rightly said should have been the person to care for her.

Jennifer, however, seemed uninterested in the right time. 'You might as well tell me the worst. After today, nothing can shock me.'

'Your husband married a second time,' Flora said baldly.

She gasped. 'But how could he do that? He couldn't have done.'

'Well, he did. He must have lied. Pretended he was free to marry.'

There was a long silence, before Jennifer spoke. 'And this other wife, the woman he left me for?'

'You mustn't think that,' Flora was quick to say. 'He didn't leave you for her. Not at all. It was after he came to Sussex that he met her. I'd say that Bruce is an opportunist and, when the chance came, he found himself a wealthy woman, a little older than himself, who was charmed by him into marriage.'

'Is she still charmed?'

'Somehow, I don't think so. Apart from bigamy, Bruce has developed an addiction to gambling, a habit that Sandra despises.'

'Tell me, Mrs Sullivan.' Jack clearly thought it time to leave Sandra to one side. 'When you came to Lewes before, it was to find the school where Bruce was teaching?'

'It was the tourist centre that gave me the information. After that young chap had made tea and calmed me down, he told me how to get to the school.'

'And did you?' Flora was intrigued.

Jennifer nodded. 'I hung around the school gates for ages and finally the afternoon bell went, and that's when I saw Bruce. I knew I was on the right track then. I knew where I could find him.'

'You didn't try to speak to him at the time?'

'I wanted to, but when he saw me and turned away, I chickened out. I decided I'd go back to Suffolk and write to him again. I hoped that this time he'd answer and maybe we could make an arrangement to meet and talk things over. I thought – how stupid I was – that perhaps he was ashamed of what he'd done. Abandoned me in the hospital, sold the house beneath my feet. But if we had a serious meeting we could perhaps come to terms with what had happened... and start again,' she finished wistfully.

Flora put her teacup down. There would be no starting again for Jennifer, at least not with Bruce. 'I think maybe we should make our way to the station now. It's getting late and Jack and I should make phone calls. We've apologies to make. We should both be at work.'

'It's probably best to get it over with,' Jennifer agreed.

'Try not to worry. We'll be with you.' Flora reached out for her hand and squeezed it hard.

29

It was a week later that Jack and Flora returned to Brighton, this time to sign the statements they had made on the day Bruce Sullivan was arrested. It was a beautiful summer's afternoon, what cloud there was too high to dim a sun that had shone since early morning.

'We could take a walk on the beach once the formalities are over,' Jack suggested, parking the Austin in Ship Street, a few roads from Bartholomews and the police station.

'The promenade, that's where we'll walk,' Flora said wisely. 'The beach is too pebbly and I'm wearing my best shoes.'

'Why the best shoes? What's the occasion?'

'This is' – she gestured to the wide blue dome above – 'and an afternoon together. What more could I want, once Inspector Ridley is done and dusted!'

'I doubt we'll see Alan,' he said, helping her out of the car. 'It will be his desk sergeant doing the honours.'

In that, Jack was wrong. They were halfway down the stairs to the basement that housed the police headquarters when he heard Ridley's voice. The inspector was saying goodbye to earlier visitors.

The visitors turned out to be Jennifer, here also to sign her statement, and of all people, Sandra Sullivan.

Flora's eyes were popping. She would find it difficult, he knew, to contain her curiosity.

'Mrs Sullivan and Mrs Sullivan,' she greeted them, somewhat tactlessly, in Jack's opinion.

'Don't call either of us that,' Sandra said. 'We've lost the name for ever.'

'Well... it's really good that you've met,' she said more quietly, turning to Jack for confirmation. The situation was strange enough, he thought, to subdue even Flora.

'Met and made friends, eh, Jennifer? Two women, one predicament.'

'Except that it's no longer a predicament.' Jennifer sounded surprisingly cheerful.

She was looking a great deal better than when he'd last seen her. But then they'd hardly met in ideal circumstances.

'Jennifer is staying with me,' Sandra explained, 'until she feels well enough to go back to work. After that, we have plans.'

'Sandra has,' Jennifer put in. 'She has been immensely kind.'

Her companion gave a *pff* at the thought. 'What else could I be after that... that...' They waited for the word, but then Sandra must have thought better of it. 'We're thinking of buying a house together, maybe next year – in Suffolk,' she said blithely. 'I've been looking for somewhere I could use for holidays, a kind of escape, and it would help me if Jennifer could live there full time. Suffolk is a beautiful county and it would be fun to explore.'

'That's... quite an idea,' Jack managed. Amazingly, both women seemed to have come through their ordeal, not untouched, he was sure, but with their spirits undaunted.

'It's been lovely to see you both,' Sandra said brightly, 'but we must be off – we have a cream tea at the Grand lined up. A little reward for having been forced to relive the ghastly events of the past few weeks.'

'Years,' Jennifer reminded her.

'You're right. Years. I should have got rid of him long ago, and now the police are doing it for me.'

Jack was tempted to say that it was certainly a different way to bid a final farewell but he bit back the urge and, after waving them goodbye, ushered Flora up to the sergeant's desk.

'That was a surprise,' she whispered to him.

'A good one?'

'Absolutely. I couldn't have foreseen it but it's a brilliant outcome – for both of them.'

'Though not for Mr Sullivan.' The inspector, who had temporarily returned to his office, was back and waving them to follow him along the passage.

'How is Mr Sullivan?' Jack asked, as Ridley cleared chairs for them, the familiar mounds of paperwork dumped on the tiled floor of his office.

'As well as can be expected. Isn't that what they say? Preparing himself for what's likely to be a grim future and a short one. Now, I've your statements here.'

He pulled several sheets of paper from the top drawer of his desk. 'They make an easy read and shouldn't take long to check. How you cottoned on to Jennifer Sullivan, I'll never know, but thank God you did or her husband would be facing a triple murder charge.'

'What about Mrs Vicary?' Flora asked anxiously. 'Has she been told the news? We haven't contacted her yet in case she was still thinking her son's death was an accident.'

'She knows it was murder. A female police officer visited her the day after Sullivan's arrest, so you can be easy. The poor woman was shocked, very shocked, but WPC Dudley reported back that she left Mrs Vicary in a calm enough state. In fact, she felt the more she said about Sullivan and what he'd done, the calmer Mrs Vicary became. It was as though she'd suspected all along that something worse had happened to her boy and now her suspicions were being confirmed.'

'And her house? Susan Vicary will stay in her home?'

'Almost certainly. The Mortons won't be bothering her. The uncle is awaiting trial – you know that – and young David has been left in no doubt that we know exactly what he's been up to, even though we can't charge him. If he takes one step out of line, we'll have him.'

'Alan, when you say you know what he's been up to, does that include the attacks we suffered?'

'He was definitely the one who drove the car at you, Jack,' the inspector verified. 'One of my chaps in Newhaven went to talk to the dockers who came to your rescue. They described enough of the number plate for me to be almost a hundred per cent sure that it was Morton who tried to ram you into the sea. And as for Mrs Carrington's fall from her bicycle, we have an eyewitness who can place Morton in Abbeymead at that time, but nothing much else. Not enough to nab him but, with his uncle in jail, he'll be too busy to think of causing more trouble.'

Remembering the shadowy figure he'd felt watching him on his last visit to Newhaven, Jack hoped so. The need to protect Flora was uppermost in his mind. He looked across at her. She had remained silent on the Mortons, but now said slowly, 'It wasn't Bruce Sullivan behind the attacks then?'

'I don't think he had you in his sights for a long time. It was Alex who'd threatened him with a marriage certificate and it was the certificate he tried to find when he broke into the Vicary house the day of the funeral.'

'That *was* him. Evidently he didn't find it.'

'His search couldn't have been sufficiently thorough. He must have come away assuming that either Alex had been bluffing or the certificate had gone missing for some reason.

When nothing happened and no further threats appeared, he'd have thought himself safe. Except for Jennifer popping up.'

'He could have come to an arrangement,' Jack said. 'He didn't have to kill her.'

'Bought her off, you mean? Possibly. But when he saw you both in the tourist office that day, alarm bells rang. He's talked enough this week for us to put together a fairly full picture. Seeing you there had him panic. Had the marriage certificate surfaced after all? Had it been found by someone – Hector Lansdale, perhaps – who could have passed it on to others? People like you who, now he thought about it, had been poking around in places they shouldn't. You'd developed an interest in the Knights of Mercia and he'd seen you both at one time or another at the Masons Arms. Might the certificate be in your possession even now, and that's why you were asking questions in a place that spelt danger for him?'

'It's always possible we were there to pick up brochures,' Jack remarked lightly.

'Sullivan panicked.' The inspector was succinct. 'He admits as much, though he denies any intention of hurting his wife. Maintains she went wild, throwing a vase, glasses, a jug, and he was simply trying to protect himself. Won't wash, of course, not with the medical evidence we have. But that office was a red flag. It was through them that Jennifer tracked him down and through them that she'd found the hotel where she was currently staying. So... if you *were* on his track and somehow you'd found out about Jennifer, you might be thinking of paying her a visit.'

Flora looped a stray wave behind her ears. She was pensive. 'That morning in the tourist office, I saw someone staring at us from the pavement opposite. If that was Sullivan, he must have rushed to Brighton immediately.'

Alan Ridley nodded. 'He'd probably been toying with the idea of getting rid of Jennifer, but seeing you asking questions, maybe ones that could incriminate him, was evidently the decider. He wouldn't go to the Mayfair to talk, but to kill.'

'You've charged him with Jennifer's attempted murder and it's impossible for him to plead innocent – we were witnesses – but has he confessed to killing Alex?'

'He's getting there. A few more sessions, a few hundred more questions, and he'll realise it's easier on him if he comes clean. He did mutter something about Vicary threatening him if he didn't repay money he owed.'

'Alex lent him money then, but without getting an IOU?' Jack was surprised.

The inspector tidied his moustache with one finger. 'This is where it becomes complicated. It was Luxton who borrowed money from Alex, as you know, but it wasn't for himself. It was for Sullivan.'

'Why on earth would he do that?' Jack asked.

'Because Sullivan threatened him,' Flora said immediately. 'Threatened to reveal that he'd lied to the brewery over his criminal conviction when he took over the Masons Arms.'

Ridley looked slightly annoyed. 'That was a guess, I take it.'

'It was what we thought Alex might have done if Luxton had been the killer,' Flora said smoothly. 'Do you know how Sullivan came by the information?'

The inspector shrugged. 'You two knew about it. Rumours travel. It was just the thing Sullivan needed. He was aware that Luxton lived off a brewery pension – they were fellow drinkers at the same pub and no doubt it came up in conversation – and if the pension was withdrawn, the chap would be destitute. He gambled on the threat being enough to induce Luxton to go to Alex in his stead. Sullivan seems to have borrowed where he could and must have reckoned Luxton would be more successful than him in tapping Alex for a loan. The man is a gambler through and through. He might have occasionally won, though not often, and when he won he didn't necessarily want to pay back money that he owed.'

'So... when Alex asked Luxton for his money back, he obviously couldn't pay.' Jack shifted in his seat, trying to think his way through the thicket of lies that had left two men dead.

'I think young Alex must have had a soft spot for Luxton, that's why he lent the money in the first place. Did you want some tea, by the way?' the inspector asked suddenly. 'I can get the sergeant to rustle up a couple of mugs.'

With one accord, they were swift to refuse the offer. The tea at Brighton police station had only a passing acquaintance with the original plant.

'Of course,' Ridley went on, 'we've no idea what actually happened between the two, but I reckon Luxton must have spun some kind of hard luck story – and Alex plundered his savings account.'

'But when Luxton couldn't repay, he must have told Alex that the money had never been for him after all, but for Bruce Sullivan,' Flora suggested. 'Was that why Ferdie was killed, because he told Alex the truth?'

Ridley shook his head. 'Luxton was a danger. He knew too much, and it may have been at the back of Sullivan's mind that, at some point, he might have to get rid of him – he sent Luxton that note warning him to keep his mouth shut – but it was only when Luxton decided *not* to keep his mouth shut that he became a definite target. The same for Miss Croft. She'd begun to remember what she'd seen at the rehearsal and was unwise enough to say it aloud. She had to be warned off, too.'

'Brutally.'

'Extremely so, but then Sullivan is a brute. Miss Croft would probably have heeded the warning but we're fairly sure that Luxton was about to tell the police what he knew about the loan which, in turn, would have prompted all kinds of questions as to what, if anything, it had to do with Alex Vicary's death.'

'And you're saying that Ferdie told Sullivan he was about to come clean?' Jack was incredulous.

'He might have warned him, I suppose, though it's doubtful. But Sullivan got wind of it somehow. Luxton was a drinker and not too discreet when he'd had a few. We've been searching his home for the last week, and what a chaotic mess he lived in, but a few days ago one of my men found a letter. Addressed to me.' The inspector seemed particularly chirpy at the fact. 'Luxton never finished the letter, but my guess would be that he was about to tell all. Sullivan had to act before he did.'

Jack felt Flora's gaze on him. Had it been the unfinished letter that had set Luxton's murder in motion or the conversation she'd had with the man at his farewell party? As they'd talked, there had been pairs of eyes on them, she'd said, and one of those pairs must have belonged to Sullivan. Was it then that he'd decided to follow Luxton into the night and help him down the Fairy Steps?

'Alex almost certainly demanded his money back,' Ridley continued, 'but Sullivan wasn't repaying. It must have incensed young Vicary. It's unlikely he would have ever lent the money to Sullivan – a man he knew was addicted to gambling. The loan had been obtained falsely and now Sullivan was refusing to repay money that Alex needed, or thought he needed, to fight off the Mortons.'

'That must have been the point at which Alex threatened to tell Sandra that Sullivan was still gambling. She'd given him an ultimatum, she told me: stop or she'd divorce him.'

The inspector shook his head. 'I don't think so, Mrs Carrington. I don't think Vicary ever knew about the ultimatum. He seems to have expected a threat to report Sullivan's gambling to the education authorities would be sufficient. Sullivan boasted about it when we questioned him. Laughed his head off. He would never have been sacked, he said. He'd promise to get treatment for his addiction and, even if he were dismissed, he'd still have a home and money.'

'But then Jennifer turns up at the tourist information centre...' Jack said thoughtfully.

'She was the real threat. Sullivan would have lost everything if his marriage to Jennifer came to light. Once Vicary realised that Bruce had another wife tucked away, a legal wife, then telling Sandra the truth would have made sure Sullivan was booted out of the marital home without a penny. That was a threat the man couldn't laugh away.'

'It was as we thought.' Flora sounded satisfied. 'The proof Alex had of Sullivan's bigamy and the threat to use it was enough to push that awful man to murder.'

'But having disposed of one danger, Sullivan was immediately faced with another. What are the chances?' The inspector grimaced. 'Jennifer was out of the sanatorium and trying to find him. She'd tracked him to Sussex, but no one else, Sullivan must have believed, knew she was here. No one had seen her loitering at the school gates on her first visit. No one had recognised her at the Metropole. No one else, in fact, knew she even existed, except Alex Vicary and he was no longer in the world. There would be no obvious link between Sullivan and a woman found dead in a small hotel in Brighton. She hadn't used her real name to register and has confirmed to us that she had nothing with her that gave a clue to her identity.'

'Why was she so keen to travel incognito?'

'It's a nasty irony. She did it, she says, to protect him. An unknown wife suddenly turning up might have caused him harm and staying anonymous meant there was no obvious connection between them.'

'That *is* ironic. If Jennifer had died, her death would likely have remained a mystery.'

'I reckon so, Jack. She played into his hands.'

'I've not thought of this before, but...' Flora paused. 'When we called at the hotel, the owner didn't mention to us that Jennifer already had a visitor. He must have known she had a man with her.'

'He didn't, in fact. Quite distraught when we spoke to him about it. Apparently, there was a disturbance in the street that morning, waste bins being turned over, and he'd gone out to look what was happening.'

'And Sullivan slipped in while his back was turned,' Jack surmised.

'He must have. Simple stuff, but effective. How he planned to escape after murdering Jennifer, I've no idea. Climbing from a third-floor window was hardly an option.'

'There was bound to be a time when the desk wasn't staffed.'

The inspector nodded. 'I guess so, although I reckon by then he wasn't thinking at all rationally. He had to get rid of a woman who was threatening the life he'd built. Like I said, it took quite a time for him to realise you were on his trail, and seeing you in the tourist centre that morning must have been a shock – the realisation that maybe you'd been tracking him all this time and still were. Up until then, Jack had been a vague figure, virtually unknown to him, and Mrs Carrington just a volunteer at the school where he taught.'

'A despised volunteer,' Flora couldn't resist saying.

'I don't imagine he thinks that now.' The inspector beamed. 'Now, where are those signed statements?'

30

A few days later, Rose walked through the All's Well's door, but instead of approaching the desk where Flora was ticking off invoices, she stood shyly to one side, her hands smoothing imaginary creases from her dress.

'Rose, hello!' Hearing the shop bell clang, Flora had looked up. 'How nice to see you.' She tapped the pile of dockets she'd been working through. 'I would love to have your help with this paperwork, only that wouldn't be fair on your day off.'

'I'm always happy to help,' the girl murmured, though she stayed lingering by the door.

Something was wrong, Flora thought, and just when life in Abbeymead had regained its calm rhythm and the only question left was who should feature on the guest list for Sarah Elizabeth Farraday's christening party.

'There's a problem?' she asked, hoping against hope that there wasn't.

'Not a problem,' Rose said in a voice that didn't sound like her own. 'Not precisely. But something you might not like.' She paused, then burst out, 'I'm engaged!'

'Engaged? Congratulations! But why on earth wouldn't I like it? It's marvellous news.'

Rose took a tentative step forward. 'It's Hector I'm engaged to.'

'Oh.'

'Exactly.'

There was a long silence until Flora pulled herself together and said determinedly, 'You still have my congratulations, Rose.'

'And Sally?'

'It will hurt, I've no doubt, but it's your life and it's Hector's. If you make each other happy...'

'We do,' she said eagerly, 'but Hector is really worried. About the situation with Sally. He feels bad that earlier he may have given her the wrong impression. He's saying that he'll give up his job at the Priory and find work elsewhere.'

Whatever wrong impression Sally might have gained, this seemed to Flora an extreme reaction.

'I'm sure Sally won't want that. She'd be losing a first-class sous chef. And Alice will be horrified. It would mean that she's lost two assistant cooks in the last year or so.'

And both to marriage, she thought. That wouldn't make it any more palatable. Alice wasn't one to rate romance highly, except where *she* was concerned, Flora thought wryly. Her old friend hadn't missed an opportunity to urge her into marriage.

'Do you think you could talk to Hector?' Rose's dress was getting another fierce brushing. 'Dissuade him from doing anything premature. Sally is a good friend of yours and you've known Alice for ever. You could maybe smooth things over?'

Inwardly, Flora allowed herself a long sigh. 'I'll do what I can,' she promised.

It wouldn't only be Sally and Alice that needed smoothing, she reflected glumly. The news that a divorced woman was planning to remarry was gossip the village would seize upon, and there were bound to be unkind comments from the more narrow-minded. A divorced woman should stay quiet, they'd say, retreat to the shadows, and certainly not find another man with whom to walk up the aisle.

The baptism was held the following Saturday afternoon at St Saviour's, Flora and Alice standing as godmothers and Jack as baby Sarah's one godfather. It was a small gathering: Sally and several of her staff whom Flora recognised; Tony's parents who had travelled from Hampshire and were staying at the Priory for the weekend; and Hector and Rose who seemed to have been invited on Sally's instructions.

'She wanted them here,' Kate whispered to Flora, as they walked together along the aisle, Kate carrying the bundle of white lace that was her baby. 'I didn't like to say no, but I hope it won't mean trouble. This should be Sarah's day.'

Flora looked back at the church entrance. 'Sally's not here yet. But it will be fine.' She gave Kate's arm an affectionate squeeze. 'I'll make sure I attach myself to Hector when we leave the church. That way, he won't stay in Rose's pocket all afternoon.'

Sally arrived just as Reverend Hopkirk raised his hands to begin. She looked ruffled and tired but, murmuring an apology, took her place behind the group around the altar. The ceremony was brief, a mere half an hour, during which Sarah behaved impeccably, uttering not a sound as Reverend Hopkirk recited prayers, a psalm, and verses from the Bible. It was only when he began the blessing by holy water that Sarah had something to say. And she said it very definitely, her high-pitched yells echoing around the near-empty church.

Mr Hopkirk smiled tolerantly. Infants bawling at the altar were hardly something new. A last scoop of water on the baby's forehead and Sarah had been baptised and the ceremony was over.

'You'll come to our small party, I hope, Reverend,' Kate said, once the baby's cries had decreased sufficiently for her mother to be heard. 'And you, Miss Dunmore?' The vicar's house-keeper looked hopeful, but Reverend Hopkirk excused them both, saying to Amy, 'We mustn't forget we have tea for the choir at five, Miss Dunmore.'

'Oh yes, of course,' she said, flustered. 'But such a shame. I would love to have come. Your baby is beautiful, Mrs Farraday.'

Kate beamed. 'Thank you. And thank you, Vicar, for coping with... with...'

'All part of the service, my dear. And enjoy your tea. You should have an enjoyable walk to the Priory this afternoon.' He gestured to the brightness streaming through the wall of stained-glass windows.

Flora made sure she walked out of the church alongside Hector. By now, the sun was at its height and he'd slung the casual jacket he'd worn over his shoulder. Rose, she noticed, had chosen a modest cotton polka dot with a matching navy hat. Both had dressed, it seemed, to fade into the background.

'I hear I have to congratulate you,' Flora began.

Hector's expression was that of a guilty man. 'That's nice of you, Flora – I hope you know that I didn't plan to hurt anyone. The thing is I love Rose. Truly. And want to be with her more than anything.'

'Well, you must,' she said placidly. 'What a fabulous day for the christening. Sarah won't remember it, of course, but Kate and Tony will, and they looked so happy in church.'

He nodded a trifle absently as they turned into Fern Hill to begin the uphill walk to the hotel.

'It's been a bit of a roller coaster,' he admitted. 'Loving Rose and losing Alex. I know Sullivan is in custody, but it still hurts when I think of my friend. He was a thoroughly decent man and his was such a needless death.'

Flora gave him a gentle pat on his arm. 'Think of Rose instead. She's your future and I'm sure Alex would be happy for you.'

He scuffed a foot awkwardly along the roadway, kicking a stray stone into the grass bank. 'I've never thanked you and Jack for all you did to bring that b— that man to justice. I should have, but somehow it was so difficult to believe he could have done such a thing. A Knight of Mercia guilty of murder!'

'Even Knights can harbour guilty secrets,' she said meaningfully.

There was a short silence. 'I should have come clean with Sally much earlier,' he admitted. 'It was fun going out together but—'

'Best to say no more. And I'm hoping very much that you won't feel you have to leave Abbeymead. Sally will get over her disappointment – she's here today, isn't she, sharing the event with you both? As for Alice, you'll have proved her right. Don't mix business with pleasure is what she keeps telling her niece. Now she can point to you as proof.'

'That's not much comfort when you work with a woman who barely speaks to you.'

'Alice will come round,' she said confidently, 'and you can't leave the village, Hector. For my sake.'

'Why is that?' They'd reached the ornamental entrance to the Priory and, swinging a gate open, he stood back for Flora to walk through.

'It's simple,' she said, once they were on the driveway and walking towards the house. 'If you leave, so does Rose, and where am I to get another such brilliant assistant?'

'Rose is brilliant, isn't she?' His face seemed transformed by the thought. 'And I certainly owe you. I guess with your trip to Italy next month, you'll need Rose to take over the All's Well.'

'Some of us are going to be lucky, aren't we, getting away mid-summer?' Alice had bustled up to join them, having deliberately, Flora reckoned, increased her pace to walk with them. Her old friend was breathing suspiciously quickly. 'I've told Sally she needs a break, she's working herself stupid, and we can cope for a couple of weeks without her. It will be Hector and me that aren't so lucky. We're stuck here until autumn. Nearly every bedroom in this place' – she nodded towards the golden stone of the beautiful old building that lay ahead – 'is booked solid.'

'That can only be good news,' Flora said hopefully. Perhaps life at the Priory would work out after all and she and Jack could leave for Venice with peaceful hearts. 'But you'll have to take that autumn holiday, Alice. Weren't you thinking of travelling down to Cornwall to stay with Jessie?' A daring question and Flora waited for an indignant rejoinder.

'I'm thinking I might,' her old friend said, startling Flora with the news. 'If you come back from Venice in one piece, it's something I might do. Though judging by recent events, that doesn't look too likely. The pair of you can't keep out of trouble.'

Jack, who had been walking a few steps behind, must have overheard and, in response, took a giant step forward to seize Flora by the waist and lift her off her feet. 'She'll return not only in one piece,' he said, spinning her around, 'but thoroughly rested and talking fluent Italian!'

'Put me down, Jack! This minute! Sarah is watching and thinking her godfather has gone crazy.'

'On the contrary. She's thinking what a beautiful godmother she has,' Jack announced grandly. 'In fact, two beautiful godmothers.'

A small smile started on Alice's face. 'He has the words, doesn't he?' she asked of nobody in particular. 'Enough of your flattery, Master Jack. Make sure you bring me back some useful recipes. I fancy cookin' that cheese dish, the one by that Eliza-beth David, it's made with aubergine.'

'*Melanzane parmigiana?*'

'If you say so.'

'But will there be time for recipes?' Tony asked mischievously. 'It's your honeymoon, after all.'

Jack looked down at Flora, grey eyes meeting hazel. 'It is,' he said, lacing his fingers in hers. 'And it can't come soon enough.'

And Flora, tickling the palm of his hand, thought so, too.

A LETTER FROM MERRYN

Dear Reader

I want to say a huge thank you for choosing to read *Murder in an English Castle*. If you enjoyed the book and want to keep up to date with all my latest releases, just sign up at the following link. Your email address will never be shared, and you can unsubscribe at any time.

www.bookouture.com/merryn-allingham

Lewes is a very old town, Anglo-Saxon in origin, but the castle is Norman-built, designed to keep the natives in permanent submission. Even now, on a dark day, its ruins can appear eerie and threatening. It seems inevitable that a re-enactment of the Battle of Lewes of 1264, an event that for a short time overturned the monarchy, would lead to tragedy and just as inevitable that Jack and Flora would become involved. I hope you've enjoyed the mystery they uncover; if so, you can follow their fortunes in the next Flora Steele or discover their earlier adventures, beginning with *The Bookshop Murder*.

If you enjoyed *Murder in an English Castle*, I would love a short review. Getting feedback from readers is amazing and it helps new readers to discover one of my books for the first time.

And do get in touch on social media or my website – I love to chat.

Thank you for reading,

Merryn x

www.merrynallingham.com

 facebook.com/MerrynWrites
x.com/merrynwrites

PUBLISHING TEAM

Turning a manuscript into a book requires the efforts of many people. The publishing team at Bookouture would like to acknowledge everyone who contributed to this publication.

Audio
Alba Proko
Melissa Tran
Sinead O'Connor

Commercial
Lauren Morrissette
Hannah Richmond
Imogen Allport

Cover design
The Brewster Project

Data and analysis
Mark Alder
Mohamed Bussuri

Editorial
Ruth Jones
Sinead O'Connor